BOOKS BY

Lori L. Lake
=====================

The Milk of Human Kindness:
Lesbian Authors Write about Mothers & Daughters

Stepping Out: Short Stories

Different Dress

Gun Shy

Under the Gun

Have Gun We'll Travel

Ricochet in Time

Romance for Life

Snow Moon Rising

Shimmer & Other Stories

Praise for Lori L. Lake's Work

"It is no wonder that Lori Lake's books are best sellers. Her characters are deep-bodied, multidimensional, and convincing. Her plots unfold like pedals on a flower, coming to full bloom at just the right moment." ~Foreword Magazine

"Considered one of the best authors of modern lesbian fiction, her work – part action, part drama, and part romance – gleefully defies categorization." ~Lavender Magazine

"Lori Lake is one of the best novelists working in the field of lesbian fiction today." ~Midwest Book Review

About Lori's Other Books

The Gun Series
"I find the 'Gun Shy' novels' languid pace and rich detail to be leisurely, rather than slow, and a fun, absorbing read overall. For those who enjoy police or mystery novels, this series is definitely one to add to the collection." ~AfterEllen.com

Snow Moon Rising
"*Snow Moon Rising* is an experience not to be missed. It offers readers an unforgettable heroine in Mischka who transcends the most depraved and despicable adversities humankind can inflict upon one another while never losing her own innate sense of decency, love, and loyalty. Both Mischka and Lake have accomplished something remarkable, and they have done it with grace." ~The L Word

Different Dress
"[T]he pleasure, like on some road trips, is in the journey, not the destination, and Lake's tale takes its leisurely good time as this love affair runs into detours and unexpected roadblocks. This lesbian romance is full of entrancing details that make the day-to-day tour come alive as the dazzle of show business and the joy of making music serve as backdrops to the lovers' deepening relationship." ~Booklist

The Milk of Human Kindness: Lesbian Authors Write About Mothers and Daughters

"One of the great things about this collection is that it doesn't only focus on daughters. The stories that take into account the mother's point of view are particularly insightful. Some of these writers are especially adept at showing a mother's confusion about her daughter's lifestyle or fear of the pain this path will bring the child." ~The Lambda Book Report

Shimmer & Other Stories

Lake has created distinctive and memorable characters in settings that will linger with readers long after the stories come to their satisfying and hopeful conclusions. Here are five compelling tales of outsiders: women ex-offenders, lesbians, cancer survivors alone with their altered bodies. All bump up against the harsh real world and find salvation in surprising ways, from the supernatural to a former nemesis turned guardian angel." ~Lee Lynch, award-winning author of *Beggar of Love, Sweet Creek, Rafferty Street,* and many other novels

Stepping Out

"Some writers write stories and have fun. In this collection, Lake fell in love with her characters. She cared for and nurtured them, making this not so much a collection of stories as an anthology of characters." ~The Lambda Book Report

Ricochet In Time

"When Dani and her lover Meg are victims of a hate crime at the beginning of the story, it is anybody's guess how the plot will develop. Will the killer get away with it? Will Dani be able to pull herself together enough to pursue justice for her slain partner? Or will she run away as she has from trouble in the past? The interesting point, here, is that this particular plot element becomes the background for a much more interesting story. Meet Ruth and Estelline, Grace, Bryce, Cleve, and a whole host of distinct characters, all of whom interact in various important ways with Dani as she fights her way back to full health from her physical injuries and emotional pain. You'll have to read the book to see if the perpetrator of the hate crime is brought to justice. The outcome is far more surprising than you can guess. ~Ronald L. Donaghe, author of *The Blind Season* and a professional book reviewer for Foreword Magazine.

Like Lovers Do

Lori L. Lake

Yellow Rose Books

Port Arthur, Texas

ISBN 978-1-935053-66-8

First Printing 2011

9 8 7 6 5 4 3 2 1

Cover design by Donna Pawlowski
Art Direction by Lori L. Lake

Published by:

Regal Crest Enterprises, LLC
4700 Hwy 365, Ste A
PMB 210
Port Arthur, Texas 77642

Find us on the World Wide Web at
http://www.regalcrest.biz

Printed in the United States of America

Acknowledgments

It's been so long since I've had the opportunity to write acknowledgments that I almost feel I've forgotten how. I'll try my best to remember everyone who helped me with this new novel. My first thanks go to Patty Schramm for never giving up on my writing (even when I did for a while), and for encouraging me to get back to the page. Her persistence (some would call it haranguing) and never-ending friendship is a blessing for which I'll always be grateful.

Jessie Chandler never stopped believing in me either. After damn near saving my life during the darkest period I can ever remember, she made me laugh and have hope again. If there's a Pen and Ink Heaven, she's going to be installed as a Saint.

My enduring gratitude goes to Patricia, creativity coach extraordinaire, who taught me that anxiety equals energy, and writing is the cure for it. Thank you for the encouragement and tough love.

To Nann Dunne and Verda Foster who both accepted this project on short notice and did a bang-up job with the editing, thank you. My publisher, Cathy LeNoir, has been a constant believer in my work for well over ten years, and I'll never be able to thank her enough. Donna Pawlowski's cover is exactly what I wanted! I'm so lucky to have such great support and assistance at RCE.

The BABA group has been a constant source of encouragement ever since we all discovered we were bad ass butches with attitude. You all kept me going, and I'll be forever grateful.

The most compelling and happiest memories I recall during the writing of this novel came when I picked up my nieces Christina, Andrea, and Samantha at the end of each day. Their liveliness and curiosity – and their penchant for asking bizarre questions at just the right time – made the writing all that much easier. I love you three little people like a fat girl loves cake.

And lastly, I didn't know Sandy when I wrote this novel, but it seemed rather fitting that we should meet shortly after I completed the first draft, when I realized I had recovered the hope of finding love again. I want to walk with you, and talk with you, and dive into that ocean of love, like lovers do. Thank you for sharing the dream.

Lori L. Lake
May, 2011

For Sandy
With Love

Chapter One

KENNIE MCCLAIN WATCHED out the window of the Allen Arms, pondering that in one short week she'd turn forty. Was it any coincidence that while drying her hair earlier she'd found a tuft of gray at her temple in her near-black hair? Time was passing, and she felt out of control, unable to find a balance for her life. She turned away from the window.

Usually she waited at the guard desk for her replacement to arrive, but today she was restless. She paced the lobby, adjusted the cuffs of her uniform, and kept coming back to peer out at the sunny spring day. Simms had been late three days in a row, always with plausible excuses, but she was tired of it. He wasn't the only one who had things to do, people to see, places to go. Actually, as she thought about it, she merely had things to do. The repainting in 4C was taking a lot longer than she'd expected.

The shiny-clean glass entry door opened, and Simms hustled in. He wore the same dark gray suit pants and jacket she did, with a lighter gray shirt and black tie. At five-ten, she was almost as tall as he was, but his shoulders were much broader. While her uniform looked lived-in after an eight-hour shift, his was neatly pressed without a single wrinkle. She wondered how anyone could ride in a car and not crease his trousers. Must have something to do with how his wife ironed for him.

"Sorry, sorry," he said, his face red and worried. "It's my wife. She's felt so ill the whole damn day. The baby's kicking. She couldn't sleep. I just couldn't leave her until she settled down."

"That's all right," Kennie said. "I understand." She watched him take a seat behind the elaborate wooden desk and stood at the mahogany counter in front of it. "But one of these days I'm going to call on you to come in early to make it up to me."

Simms exhaled, as though he'd been holding his breath in frightened anticipation. "Absolutely. I'll definitely make it up to you. Don't tell management, okay? I can't afford to get canned." His face brightened. "I still can't believe it—I'm going to be a father!"

Kennie smiled at his enthusiasm, but also because she wondered how much longer she could keep up the charade. Two years earlier, she'd bought the Allen Arms, an old but sturdy turn-of-the-century building in northeast Portland's Laurelhurst District. The seven-story fixer-upper had needed considerable repair and upkeep, but it had originally been well-built using marble in the entryway, quality light fixtures, wood trim, and oak floors in the apartments. The construction was solid.

Unlike many of the area apartments that lacked adequate parking, her building sat by itself on an entire city block, half of which was a parking lot with enough spaces for all the tenants' cars. She'd gotten the property at a fire sale rate after the housing market crashed, and she hadn't stopped working on it since. The investment was paying off nicely now, and until recently, she'd been happy for the distraction from the pitiful state of her personal life.

The elevator dinged, and the elderly man from 2A shuffled out followed by his wife. She slowly pushed a walker and stepped carefully. The green tennis balls attached to the front legs of the walker were so worn they made a squeaking noise across the white marble floor.

Simms said, "Hey there, Mr. Faulkner."

"Good afternoon, young man. How's that wife of yours?"

"Excellent. Not too long and she'll have the baby."

Kennie stepped aside so Mr. Faulkner could pause in front of the desk, a gnarled fist resting on the wood surface.

Mrs. Faulkner smiled at Kennie. "And how are you, dear?"

"Just fine. Thank you for asking."

"How's the refurbishing coming along in 1A?" When Kennie hesitated, Mrs. Faulkner said, "I have some friends who would love to move into this building. Neat, quiet, wonderful people."

"I'm sure the management team will eventually get to that one, Mrs. Faulkner. For now, they've got me working on 4C."

"Let me know when one of them is available then, all right?"

Before Kennie could answer, the front door opened and Lily Gordon stepped in. She carried a shopping bag with the name of the local art store emblazoned on it.

Mrs. Faulkner fairly lit up to see her. "Why, Lily, how lovely you look today. How's the painting going?"

"I'm making good progress." Lily held up a shopping bag. "Ran out of supplies, though." She smiled, and the lobby seemed a brighter place. Lily's blonde hair was pulled back in a loose braid, and she wore a white blouse and tan slacks that showed off her lean body. Kennie swallowed and tried to offer a smile. Her heart beat too hard in her chest, and she wondered if the others could hear it.

Lily was graceful and as beautiful as a movie star—like a young Grace Kelly—but there were dark smudges under her eyes. She'd lost weight in the months since the departure of the police lieutenant who'd formerly lived in the penthouse with her. The lieutenant, a tall, imposing woman, had swept through the lobby every morning and given Kennie the stink-eye. Obviously a mere security guard didn't meet her law-enforcement standards. Kennie didn't miss her, but she thought Lily still did.

Kennie wondered how anyone could hurt, much less leave, such a kind-hearted woman. Lily was creative, a painter with a studio in the penthouse, and she was generous to all. Her art brought in great gobs of money, and she was constantly donating funds to foundations or offering her work for charity auctions. She'd taken on a number of college student protégés and contributed to various "Art in the Schools" programs.

"...don't you think?" Mrs. Faulkner said, turning and patting Kennie's arm.

Blood rushed to Kennie's face. "I—I'm sorry?"

"Woolgathering?" Mrs. Faulkner asked, a grin on her face.

Kennie could only nod. When she hazarded a glance, Lily was pressing her lips together in an effort not to smile. Kennie blushed even further and had no time to pull herself together before Mr. Faulkner stepped away from the desk and said, "Let's go, woman. We've got steaks and baked potatoes waiting for us."

Lily said her goodbyes and headed for the grand stairway. Kennie knew she shouldn't watch, but those long legs were irresistible. When Lily reached the landing and turned to go up the second flight of stairs, she met Kennie's gaze. For a heartbeat, Kennie's world seemed to stop—no sound, no smells, nothing but the sensation of being pinned in place.

Then Lily rose out of sight, and the world came whooshing back in. Kennie let out a shaky breath.

Simms tapped her shoulder. "Jesus, Kennie," he said in a low voice, "get ahold of yourself. You're like a dog in heat."

She looked at him in fury. If ever she wanted to fire a man, it was now.

He put both hands up, palms out, and rolled back in the desk chair. "Whoa, whoa, I didn't mean it the way it came out. I'm just saying, you know, you could be a little less obvious. She's gorgeous. You've got great taste. But hey, we're glorified doormen. You'll just get your heart broken."

"Simms, you're what? Twenty-five?"

"Yeah, so what?"

"How'd you get so enlightened?"

"I don't know what you mean."

"Never mind." She moved away from the counter, stalked down the hall to the right of the elevators, and unlocked a door.

"I've got a gay sister," he called after her.

"It figures."

She closed the door and leaned back against it. What had come over her? Simms was right. She was like a dog in heat. Her whole body still tingled from the encounter with Lily. Had Mrs. Faulkner noticed? She hoped not. How embarrassing. But wow, who could resist?

Even more disconcerting was that Lily seemed to be flirting with her. She was, wasn't she? Kennie had been out of circulation long enough that she'd previously doubted her perceptions, but lately she wasn't so sure. Every day for the last week, Lily had stopped to chat with her. She went out of her way to lay a hand on Kennie's arm or to ask her advice about clothes she'd purchased and brought into the lobby in shopping bags. The day before, Lily had brought her down a piece of French silk chocolate pie out of the blue. Kennie remembered mentioning weeks ago that she liked French silk pie. Was it a coincidence that Lily just happened to buy some?

Kennie stripped off her jacket, hung it on a hook behind the door, and loosened the old-fashioned tie she liked to wear. Simms's clip-on tie was constantly askew; hers was never a problem.

The twenty-by-twenty room was bright from the light of three huge windows. They rose from waist-level all the way to the ceiling. She'd paid a pretty penny for louver blinds to cover them and prevent prying eyes from gazing in. Below the windows, she'd placed a dining table and chairs where she could sit in the mornings and drink tea — or liquor in the evenings if she felt like it. To her left near the entry sat a couch and a wingback chair. To the right, an alcove contained a full-size bed built into the wall, with drawers underneath and overhead. Kennie had slept in it when she first moved to the Allen Arms and thought it claustrophobic. To the left and near the windows was a fully outfitted galley kitchen. Three closed doors took up the remainder of the wall. One opened to a huge walk-in closet. The middle one led to the bathroom. The last was the only door with a lock on it. She took her keys off her belt, opened it, and passed through.

The Allen Arms advertised 20 apartments, but counting the efficiency Kennie had just stepped out of, there were really 21. She had installed a door between the efficiency where she "lived" and apartment 1A, which was where she really spent all her free time. Through the building's back door she'd been able to unload all her boxes and furniture and have other items delivered, and the tenants hadn't noticed at all. Every day she wondered how long that would last. Everyone thought she lived in that small one-room place, and in the rare times when they needed something in the night, they rang there. The buzzer was also piped into her real apartment for the hours between one and seven a.m. when no one was on duty in the lobby.

Above her, floors two through five held four apartments on each level. The sixth floor was composed of two luxury suites, and the penthouse on seven took up the entire floor. The building didn't have much turnover, but as people moved out, she made repairs, repainted, and installed new appliances, carpet, or tile. She upgraded the laundry room and moved the storage units down to the basement so the huge room behind the first floor elevators could be used as a party room. In less than two years, she'd made great progress with the Allen Arms, and if she wanted to, she suspected she could sell it for a tidy profit. That had been her original intention, but now...now she couldn't stop thinking about a certain someone in 7A.

IN THE NIGHT the buzzer woke Kennie. She hustled from the comfort of her warm bed into the efficiency apartment. The cold floor chilled her bare feet, and her flannel pajamas didn't do much to keep her warm. She reached for the doorknob then realized how things would look. Quickly, she went to the bed, peeled back the covers, and rumpled the pillow.

When she opened up, she was struck silent by the woman standing there. Lily Gordon, her hair loose and messy, held a paintbrush stained red. She was dressed in a baggy white t-shirt and white painter's pants, all of which were splotched with reds, greens, oranges, and yellows. Even her cheek sported a smudge of something maroon colored.

"I'm sorry to wake you," Lily said. "The power went out in my studio, and I'm on a roll. I can't stop now." She sounded out of breath, slightly desperate.

"What time is it?"

"I don't know. Sorry. Maybe four a.m.?"

"I'll be right up. Give me a few minutes to throw on some clothes." Kennie closed the door and stood toying with her flannel collar. Oh, boy, she thought. Her heart wouldn't stop racing.

When she'd purchased the building, Kennie's inspector had toured every apartment, but because she hadn't wanted to advertise her ownership, there were half a dozen occupied units she'd never seen more of than the front hallway. 7A was one of them.

Carrying a Maglite and dressed in jeans, a sweatshirt, and running shoes, she took the elevator up. It opened into a plush foyer with a dark blue carpet, rich wood trim, and crown molding. A crystal chandelier cast prisms of light against muted gold wallpaper. A Tiffany lamp sat upon a shiny cherry table next to an old-fashioned fainting couch, patterned in gold and red and blue.

Every time she came up to vacuum or wash the windows on either side of the foyer, Kennie wondered if Lily would open her door or maybe come up the elevator. She always laughed about that. If Lily ever actually appeared, Kennie was pretty sure she'd have occasion to use the fainting couch. The vision of collapsing onto the dinky Victorian piece of furniture made her feel nervous as hell.

The apartment door was open, and she poked her head in the darkened entryway and shouted, "Hello!"

"Back here," Lily called out.

Kennie walked across the parquet floor to the hallway, crossed an Oriental rug, and made her way to the right. Every step she took sent her into darker realms. She clicked on the flashlight and stepped through double doors. Pale light shimmered in through tall windows at either end of a giant room that ran the entire width of the building and was half again as deep.

A white apparition came toward her, slowly materializing with each step. "This has never happened before. Can you do something?"

"Are the lights out in the entire apartment?"

"I don't know."

"May I check?"

"Knock yourself out."

Kennie retraced her footsteps and went down a hallway until she came to a doorway that led into the kitchen. She groped around and found the push-button light switch. Let there be light, she thought, and there was. Another switch farther down the hallway also worked.

Back in the darkened room, she said, I think it's just this circuit. Do you know where the breaker box is?"

"Sorry, I have no idea."

"I'll track it down."

Starting behind one side of the double doors, Kennie systematically swept the light along the wall. When she came to the first window, she found Lily standing close to a canvas on an easel, trying desperately to take advantage of the miniscule amount of light coming in from the streetlights.

"If you didn't need it," Lily said, "I'd snatch that light away from you right now."

Kennie paused and illuminated the canvas. Powerful ocean waves covered the middle, but instead of the customary blue and green hues, the water was also accented with reds and silvers which gave it an angry, bloody appearance. "You're painting this?" As soon as the words spilled out of her mouth, she felt like a complete dunce. Of course Lily was painting it. If the smell of oil paint and turpentine didn't give that away, the palette in one hand

and paintbrush balanced in the other did.

"I've been working on it all night. Watch your step there for cords. I've got some spotlights plugged in."

Kennie moved past, continuing to search for any evidence of a breaker box. She got all the way around the room before she found an old-fashioned fuse box behind the other double door. How typical, she thought. Seems like I always start on the wrong side of things. She cracked it open and shone the light about, looking for a burned-out fuse. When she found the smoky-looking one, she looked for replacements in the bottom of the box, but no luck.

"Lily, I'll be back shortly with the fix." She dashed out, rode the elevator down to the basement shop, unlocked it, and grabbed a handful of fuses. It seemed to take forever to make it back to 7A. She had no idea what time it was, but when she returned, the first traces of the dawn were leaking in through the window. Lily had shifted her canvas to take advantage of the meager change in light.

The first fuse did nothing. Glad she'd brought four along, Kennie screwed in another and said, "Voilá." High overhead, two lines of chandeliers illuminated. Across the room, three sets of spotlights burst on.

"Hurrah!" Lily said. No sooner was that out of her mouth than the place plunged into darkness again.

"Uh-oh," Kennie said. Half blind, even with the flashlight, she carefully crossed the room and pulled the plugs for all the spotlights. She returned to the fuse box and replaced the fuse. This time, when the lights came on, they stayed on. "Your extra lamps are overloading the electrical line."

"Oh. Odd." Lily set her palette and brush on a side table covered with tubes of paint and clear bottles full of different colored liquids. "I've never had any trouble before, but I did just recently replace this third one."

Kennie bent over it. "That's a very nice halogen light, but it pulls a lot of juice. The other two are much lower wattage."

Lily tucked her blonde hair behind her ears. "It worked great. Kept me warm, too. Damn thing exudes heat."

"I bet. I imagine this room can be pretty drafty."

Kennie looked around the space, which was big enough to hold a dance. The ceiling was at least sixteen feet tall, and the parquet floor, though worn, looked to be the originally installed flooring. A counter she had walked past searching for the fuse box was a wet bar, and the chairs stacked high in one corner could seat at least a hundred people. In earlier days, the room was probably used as a ballroom. After more than a century, she could imagine ghosts inhabiting it, still dancing in old-time clothes.

Lily Gordon had turned it into her painting studio. In addition to the canvas she currently worked on, there were over a dozen canvases on easels in a line down the middle of the room. Below each easel, plastic overlaid with heavy-duty tarps protected the floor. Lily had obviously made sure she wouldn't stain the parquet.

"Please," Lily said, "don't look at those. They're either unfinished or wretchedly bad."

From what Kennie could see, every painting was amazing, but she obeyed Lily's request and looked away. "I'll leave you to it then. I know you want to get back to work. Please don't plug in the halogen lamp for now. I'll have management send up an electrician in the next couple of days. We'll get rid of this old electrical system and set you up a couple of circuits so this never happens again."

"Thank you." Lily's voice was faint. She'd turned back to her painting and stood, hands on hips, examining it as though it were the only item of interest left in the whole wide world.

Chapter Two

THREE DAYS BEFORE her birthday, Kennie wakened from a night of troubled dreams. Janeen again.

She made a pot of strong coffee, sat at her kitchen table, and looked out at the light rain falling. Would she ever get over Janeen? Would these long, draggy nights ever pass?

Janeen, a highly-sought-after web designer and IT expert, never let anything get in the way of her ambition, whether it was professional, personal, or romantic. She'd set her sights on Kennie, and she used all her extensive feminine wiles to get her. They both fell hard, and from the moment they committed to one another, neither ever looked at another woman.

Kennie was constantly amazed at all that Janeen could handle. She soldiered through any IT disaster, any family problem, and any issue that got in her way.

When she fell ill, however, she ignored the symptoms until she was near collapse. Being a bit rundown was something Janeen regularly mocked in others, so when she felt exhausted for several weeks in a row, she continued to say, "Buck up — this'll pass," and, "The show must go on." Even the persistent indigestion she experienced was one more thing to conquer. She wasn't going to let an upset stomach derail her projects, not when there were plenty of Tums to be had.

When the pain started doubling her over, Kennie convinced her to see a doctor. As bad luck would have it, he misdiagnosed her symptoms. Acid reflux meds did nothing to stop the spread of cancer from her ovaries through her bloodstream and lymph nodes. By the time Janeen got the final diagnosis, the afternoon before Valentine's Day, it was too late. By Easter she was dead.

Kennie had never really understood the cliché about events making one's head spin, but that's how she'd felt for weeks on end after Janeen began failing so fast. Even when Kennie's parents died, the pain didn't hurt the way Janeen's final days did. And then her death was so unreal. Though in Kennie's day-to-day life she'd eventually come to accept Janeen's death, the shock still visited her dreams.

Kennie faced the weeks after losing her lover in a fog of fear and tears. For a long time, she'd been so angry at Janeen. Why hadn't she taken care of herself? Why did she have to be so headstrong? After Kennie's bereavement time ran out at her job as a computer installer, she could barely force herself to go to work each day. But then the insurance policies — one through work, another from Janeen's college days, and a half-a-million-dollar plan Janeen had taken out on a lark and never mentioned to Kennie — combined to dump $725,000 in her lap. She only told people about the twenty-five-grand policy, most of which went to closing out Janeen's business debts and paying off bills from the funeral. Kennie never told anyone about the other policies or the half-mil that the sale of Janeen's business brought in. She kept all the money a secret, especially from her money-grubbing older sister Suzanne and Suzanne's ne'er-do-well twin brother, Sterling.

Kennie's twin siblings were fifteen years older than she was, and she'd never felt close to either of them. They treated her like an interloper, and despite all the efforts she made throughout her childhood, Kennie was never able to properly bond with either of them. After the deaths of her mother and father, Suzanne and Sterling had scooped up much more than their share of the meager inheritance, so Kennie stopped trying.

Once she'd come through some of the grief about Janeen and stopped being completely immobilized, Kennie quit her job, packed up, and moved from New York to Portland, which had always been a favorite place she and Janeen had visited. Over their thirteen years together, they'd skied Mount Hood, stayed on the Pacific Ocean at Cannon Beach near Haystack Rock, and rented a houseboat and traveled down the crystal clear waters of Lake Billy Chinook. Though Kennie was born and bred in upstate New York, Oregon felt oddly like home.

Nearly three years had passed since Janeen was ripped from her life, and now, facing age forty, Kennie considered herself well past her shelf-date. She spent her days watching out for the residents at the Allen Arms and her nights watching TV or rehabbing the apartments as residents moved out.

Was this to be the extent of her life?

THE DAY BEFORE Kennie's birthday, Mr. Faulkner shambled into the lobby with his wife bobbing along in his wake.

Kennie rose from behind the desk where she'd been doing the morning crossword puzzle and greeted them both warmly.

"Whoopsidoodle," Mrs. Faulkner said. "We got some of your mail by accident." Her husband held tight to a bright pink envelope. "Norm, give it to her."

"Kendra McClain, huh? I wondered what Kennie was a nickname for." He held the envelope up to the light and said, "If I don't miss my guess, this is a birthday card."

"Shame on you, Norman." His wife snatched the card and handed it to Kennie. "He's lost all the manners his good mother gave him, may she rest in peace."

"Well, is it?" he asked.

Kennie frowned. "What?"

"Your birthday."

"Tomorrow," she said.

He turned to his wife. "See how easy that was? She's not all worked up about birthdays like you think other women are. What does she care? She's still a whippersnapper." He turned back to Kennie. "You thirty? Thirty-five?"

Mrs. Faulkner clamped a surprisingly strong claw around her husband's forearm. Kennie got a glimpse of blood-red fingernails and a gigantic diamond solitaire before she wrenched him half around. "Norman Martin Faulkner. Shame on you. You never ask a woman her age."

He made a pshaw noise as he backpedaled. "Calm down, Evelyn. Happy Birthday early, Kennie. You've been doing a great job here, and we appreciate you."

His wife pulled him away from the counter and continued to upbraid him as she squeaked her walker toward the elevator.

Kennie slit open the envelope and read the card sent by her Aunt Clara, who lived in Watertown, New York. She was the one relative Kennie kept in touch with, and the fact that she never forgot her birthday brought a lump to her throat.

She opened the door to her efficiency unit, left it ajar, and put a kettle on to boil. Her back to the door, she looked out the window at the clouds scudding across the sky. She hoped the rain had passed. She felt the need to take a nice long run after her shift ended.

A tap interrupted her thoughts, and she turned to find Lily Gordon in the doorway. She looked much more composed than she had the night she'd blown the fuse. Her hair was swept up and knotted in the back, and she wore a lightweight rain jacket over a polo shirt and blue jeans. Nary a drop of paint was smeared anywhere on her shapely figure.

"Sorry to bother you, but I wanted to thank you for fixing my lights the other night. And I can't believe how fast the electrician upgraded everything. Thank you for arranging that. Will the owners be charging me a fee?"

"Oh, no. I, we—I mean they take care of that. The building's being gradually updated. You won't be billed."

The teakettle took that moment to whistle, and Kennie hastened to pull it off the burner. When she looked back at the doorway, Lily was smiling hopefully, so Kennie gathered courage and took a deep breath. "Cup of tea?"

"I'd love it." Lily stepped across the threshold, dropped a satchel inside the doorway, and sat in one of the chairs next to the window.

"What kind of tea do you like?"

"Anything except lemon. No milk either."

Kennie set out teaspoons, cups, and saucers. "Sugar? Honey?"

"Sure, honey." Lily grinned at Kennie's befuddlement. "Sorry about that. Couldn't resist. Toss the sugar bowl on the table. I don't need any honey."

No doubt about it, Kennie realized. The woman was definitely flirting. She delivered the sugar, set the kettle on a hot pad, and lowered herself into a chair.

"So," Lily said, "I hear it's your birthday."

"How the heck—"

"The Faulkners were having quite the entertaining row in the elevator." She selected a tea bag and poured hot water into their cups. "I turned right around and came back down to wish you well."

"It's not actually until tomorrow."

"That gives everyone time to track down a gift for you."

Kennie laughed aloud.

"Don't laugh. It sounded to me like Mrs. Faulkner was insisting that her little hubby take her out to purchase something to make up for being rude to you."

"That isn't necessary. He didn't bother me."

"What else have they got to do?" She stirred two generous spoons of sugar into her cup.

"Would you like a snack to go with the tea?"

"No, I just had a huge lunch. Thanks." She paused, meeting Kennie's eyes. "You're single, right?" When Kennie nodded, Lily said, "In the olden days, my grandma—and probably Mrs. Faulkner—would say that I'm being awfully forward. But you're single and available?"

Kennie gulped and couldn't speak. Her heart dropped from its normal location in her chest to someplace closer to her groin. Was this beautiful woman sitting at her table propositioning her? Her thoughts flashed to her apartment and the dishes in the sink, the unmade bed, the magazines all over the living room table. She felt a touch of panic.

Lily reached across the table and patted her forearm. "Don't look so nervous. I'm just wondering if you might want to go out for dinner tomorrow night, that is, if you don't already have birthday plans with someone else."

With a shaky hand, Kennie raised the teacup, took a sip, and at last found her voice. "I don't have plans, and I'd very much like to go out with you." She felt an enormous sense of relief that her words came out clear and unjumbled.

"Excellent. Do you have a favorite restaurant?"

Kennie shook her head.

"Anywhere you've been wanting to try?"

"I haven't been out much. Why don't we go to your favorite place?"

Lily grinned like a Cheshire cat. "Shall we exchange phone numbers then? Just in case you change your mind?"

"I'll give you my cell number, but don't worry, I won't change my mind."

Chapter Three

ON THE AFTERNOON of her fortieth birthday, Kennie paced in the lobby, feeling one attack of nerves after another. She hadn't seen or heard from Lily. Every occupant who came down the stairs, every ding of the elevator, every tiny noise from the settling of the building sent her heart into overdrive. No amount of exercise the evening before had calmed her down, and she'd awakened several times during the night, wondering whether she might have dreamed the dinner invitation.

When Simms arrived, early for once, he encouraged her to go off duty and leave the desk to him, so she did. She closed the door to the efficiency, rushed into 1A, and did something she'd never done before: she laid out every stitch of her nice clothing on the bed and agonized over what to wear. She matched shirts with pants, swapped them, laid jackets next to the combinations, tossed a few items on the floor, and grimaced.

The phone rang. She fished it out of her jacket pocket. Lily greeted her warmly, wished her a happy birthday, and said, "I have an unusual request."

"Oh?"

"You may think I'm crazy, but, well...I am crazy. You'll figure that out soon enough. What I'm hoping you might agree to do is wear your uniform to dinner."

"My uniform?"

"Yes. You look handsome in it, and I'd be honored if you'd wear it for me."

"What are you wearing?"

"I'll be in blue pants, a flowered blouse, and some sort of jacket—haven't decided which one yet. The place we're going is very private, so will you do this for me?"

Kennie thought about how much that would simplify things and couldn't think of any reason not to agree. "Where shall we meet?"

"Come up to my place at seven, why don't you?"

"I'll be there."

The next couple of hours were sheer madness for Kennie. She paced, she worried, and after a while, she shucked her clothes and took a long hot shower. When she got out, she donned an entirely new set of undergarments and a clean uniform shirt, jacket, and pair of pants. Shortly before seven, she was ready.

Standing at the entrance to 7A, she looked sheepishly at the fainting couch, almost wishing it were closer to the doorway. Before she could knock, a man in classic black formal wear opened the door.

"Ms. McClain, good evening. Ms. Gordon is waiting for you in the dining room."

Feeling slightly unnerved, Kennie followed him around the corner to the left and was ushered into a formal dining room. The table could probably seat sixteen comfortably, but only two places were set, one at the head, where her hostess sat and the other to Lily's left.

Lily rose and guided her to the table, one hand on her shoulder. "I hope you aren't upset, but when you said you wouldn't mind going to my favorite place, I took you seriously. This is my favorite."

Kennie recovered quickly to say, "I love the flowers." An enormous pot of purple, white, and red chrysanthemums sat in the middle of the table, garnished with other brightly colored flowers Kennie couldn't identify.

"I hoped you would. Come sit while the caterer brings us the first course. I arranged for a couple kinds of soup, a main course of chicken, and the salad course is a variety of cooked vegetables. Do you like cheese? And wine?"

Kennie settled in the comfortable Queen Anne style chair. "Yes, and I could use a shot of that wine anytime you have it available."

"Don't be nervous now. It's your birthday."

Despite Lily urging her not to be on edge, it took a glass of wine and a lot of conversation before Kennie settled down, but once she did, two hours blew by without her having any sense of time passing at all. She followed Lily's lead and ate lightly, not wanting to overwhelm her stomach with the savory chicken, the new potatoes, or the vegetables and cheeses. Everything was prepared perfectly and served piping hot or properly chilled. In between bites, she shared information about her life, and Lily told her about her painting and her travels to France, Greece, and Italy.

Kennie was surprised to hear she'd lived in the Allen Arms for almost a decade, and Lily seemed surprised that Kennie had moved from upstate New York. "You have a bit of a different sound to your vowels than Oregonians, but you definitely don't have the New York accent."

"It's a whole different world when you grow up so close to Canada you could throw a stone and hit a border crossing guard."

"I've lived my entire life here on the West Coast. Portland, Seattle, Fresno, and San Francisco."

"San Francisco was Janeen's favorite city." The statement slipped out before Kennie could clamp her mouth shut. "Didn't mean to bring that up."

"Janeen must have been someone who mattered."

Kennie nodded.

"Girlfriend?"

"Thirteen years."

"Where is she now?"

"She died. Cancer."

"I'm sorry."

As if it were the most natural thing in the world, Lily took Kennie's hand, drew it to her, and kissed it. She entwined their fingers and rested their hands on the table.

The tears that had threatened for a brief moment burned off in the heat that suffused Kennie's body from head to toe. She couldn't stop trembling then. A part of her wanted to get up and run to the safety of her efficiency apartment. At the same time, she wanted to rise from the chair, engulf Lily in her arms, and sweep her off to 1A. The connection with her hostess was so powerful that she couldn't meet her gaze. Kennie couldn't take her eyes off their hands, and she didn't want Lily to stop stroking the top of her hand with her thumb.

After a long moment, Lily said, "Excuse me for just a sec. I'll be right back." Kennie let go of her hand and felt a visceral loss. She sat back in her chair, shaken, feeling such a myriad of emotions that she couldn't quite take a deep breath. What was happening between them? Was this really happening?

The murmur of male voices wafted in, interspersed with Lily's voice, and a door closed somewhere.

Lily reentered the room, saying, "The caterers are gone now," and then her hands were on Kennie's shoulders. She spoke into Kennie's ear. "I hope you don't mind, but my gift to you is in another room. Do you have time for me to give it to you?"

"Yes." Kennie put her cloth napkin on the table and rose. No way did she want this night to end. She'd follow Lily into every room in the penthouse if that's what she wanted. She turned to find herself so close to Lily she could almost kiss her. For the first time, Kennie realized how much taller she was. Lily carried herself as though she were much bigger, but if Kennie wanted to kiss her, she'd have to lower her head several inches to meet her lips. Lily tipped her face up, and as if in a dream, Kennie leaned down.

The kiss was nothing short of smoldering. Kennie was amazed she'd been brave enough to attempt it and was stunned by Lily's passion. She brought her hands up to touch Lily's face then slid her fingers down her neck until her palms came to rest on her collarbones and her fingers danced lightly on the tops of her shoulders. Lily reached inside Kennie's jacket. When she tightened her arms around Kennie's middle, Kennie had to pull her mouth away to draw a ragged breath. They were so close, fitted so perfectly together, that breaking from the kiss felt like a loss she couldn't bear. She leaned in to capture her mouth again, but Lily pressed a finger to Kennie's lips.

"Your present. Come with me."

The last thing she cared about was a gift, but she followed Lily, trying not to clutch her hand too hard. They passed the ballroom and the doorway that led out to a roof terrace. She caught a quick glimpse of the moon, then they were past. As they moved down the hall, the smell of oil paint and turpentine gradually receded, supplanted by the fresh, minty scent of eucalyptus.

The room they entered was dark at first. Lily led her across an open space carpeted with a cushy rug. As Kennie's eyes adjusted to the dimness, she saw a cozy queen-sized bed. The coverlet was splashed with reds and oranges. For a moment, she wondered if perhaps Lily had painted it, but the spread was indeed cloth, and its hues echoed the vibrant ochres, plums, and golds in the painting over the headboard.

Lily lit a candle and settled at the foot of the bed. "Come here," she whispered.

Kennie took in the room once more. Though small, it was magnificent. Splashes of color adorned the walls, and as she stepped into the V of Lily's legs, she had the distinct impression they themselves were in a painting.

Lily's arms encircled her hips, and with a sigh, she relaxed her forehead against Kennie's abdomen. Kennie stroked her hair and tried not to breathe like a racehorse after a derby.

Lily looked up at her, blue eyes full of silent pleading, and Kennie felt worry slash through her. Could she do this? She hadn't made love to anyone for a very long time. How badly would she mess up?

She leaned down to kiss Lily anyway, soft at first, full of hope and tenderness. Lily responded with a moan. She clutched at Kennie's shirt and deepened the kiss. Lily's tongue, her lips, her hands...suddenly Kennie didn't know how to breathe anymore. She broke away, nearly panting.

Lily smiled, her expression knowing and satisfied. She reached for Kennie's belt and unbuckled it. Mutely, Kennie obeyed her commands to remove pants and shoes until she stood naked from the waist down.

"Will you undress me?" Lily asked.

"Oh, yeah." Kennie still couldn't believe this was happening, but if it was a dream, it was the most thrilling one she'd had in years. In her excitement, the buttons on the flowery silk blouse seemed unusually small and unwieldy and the silk slipped in her hands.

Lily giggled as Kennie fumbled and finally opened up the blouse, then she unhooked her own bra in front and pulled the cups away.

"Now isn't that wonderfully convenient," Kennie said. "Can I touch you?"

"Please."

Lily's breasts were warm and full, the nipples a deep brown. Kennie pushed her back gently until she rested against the coverlet, her feet still on the floor. Kennie's mouth found a breast, and under her tongue she felt the nipple contract. She felt for the other breast and cupped it.

"Oh, yes, that's good. Yes, yes..." Lily choked out her pleasure, words not always making sense, and Kennie felt a surge of power shoot through her chest, down her torso, and into her groin. With shock she realized she had nothing to fear. She'd forgotten nothing, lost nothing. She stood and slipped out of her jacket, leaving Lily on the bed looking up at her in wonder.

"I'm going to love undressing you, Lily."

"Will you leave your shirt on for a while?"

"Have you got a thing for women in uniforms?"

"Maybe." She sat up. "Let me get some things we might need."

Kennie gripped her shoulders and stole another kiss. The silk blouse fluttered against her hands. She stripped it away along with the bra and let them drop at the foot of the bed. Lily's skin was hot and felt like velvet under her palms. She rubbed her back, stroked the soft skin, and brought her palms up to cradle Lily's face. "You're incredible." Kennie slid her hands down under the waistband of Lily's pants.

"Wait." Lily pressed against Kennie's chest to hold her back. She stepped around the side of the bed. With a sweep of her arm, she tossed the coverlet and sheets aside, then bent to open a drawer in the bedside table. "Come here."

The drawer contained a jumble of harnesses, towels, vibrators, and little bottles of lube and lotions. "Wow," Kennie said, "that's a lot of toys."

"Will you wear this for me?" Lily asked. She held out a complicated-looking set of straps.

Kennie felt breathless. "I'll do pretty much anything you want."

"How noble of you."

"I aim to please."

Lily laughed, the sound deep and throaty. She came away from the drawer holding a black harness and multicolored dildo. Once again, Kennie's legs went weak.

Lily said, "Do you want to put this on, or shall I —"

"You. Definitely you." Kennie had had enough trouble getting blouse buttons undone. She had no idea how she'd manage an unfamiliar harness. But then Lily's hands were on her hips, teasingly touching her thighs and butt. Kennie flushed with a mixture of embarrassment and pleasure. With sure fingers, Lily adjusted everything perfectly, then said, "Lie down."

"Yes, ma'am."

Kennie slid into the bed. The sheets felt slinky and cool against her legs. She settled on her side, her head in her hand and one elbow sunk deep into a pillow. Shivering with anticipation, she watched Lily kick off shoes and step out of the rest of her clothes. Her body looked golden in the dim light. Full hipped, large breasted, and with a waist Kennie envied, she was a goddess. Lily met her gaze and reached up to release her hair. The golden tresses tumbled down around her shoulders.

Lily crawled across the bed like a lioness ready to devour her. She took hold of Kennie's tie and pulled her toward the center of the bed.

"Whatever you want," Kennie said breathlessly. "Whatever you command." She settled on her back, the harness straps snug against her. She glanced down at the strange toy emerging from the flaps of her shirt, but before she could fully consider it, Lily straddled Kennie's waist and blocked her vision. Kennie looked into smiling eyes. Lily tucked her hair behind her ears and reached down to explore Kennie's face, her brow, her jaw. Kennie felt a gush of her own wetness and wondered how Lily merely touching her face could be such a huge turn-on.

Lily opened one button of the uniform shirt and slipped her hand in. "You've got a t-shirt underneath."

"I can take it off."

"That's okay. I'll work around it for now." She pulled up the bottom of the undershirt, and Kennie let out a groan as Lily's hands slid along her stomach. She closed her eyes and shivered as warm fingers found their way over her hip bones, abdomen, and ribs, and then settled upon her breasts, stroking and fondling.

"That feels so good. Lily. Oh, God, I want you. I want to please you."

"Shhh...soon enough. Lie still."

Kennie palmed both of Lily's breasts and she arched slightly, eyes closed, moaning with delight.

"So good," Lily said. "You've got great hands."

Kennie pulled her knees up until her thighs were against Lily's back. The harness and dildo tightened against her skin, but not uncomfortably. "Just lean back and relax."

"Lucky I do yoga."

Kennie smiled.

Mouth open, knees bent under her, Lily rested against Kennie and gave her free rein. Her skin was warm and moist, and the little bit of padding on her belly was soft. Kennie stroked her sides, and Lily's abdominal muscles tensed. "Does that tickle?"

"A little."

She turned her attention to the tops of Lily's thighs and ran her hands down and back up until her thumbs were close to the patch of hair. Pressing gently, she found the wetness within. Lily let out a whimper, her breathing sped up, and for a moment she rocked against Kennie's hands.

"No," Lily whispered. "Not yet." She came up out of her relaxed position and shifted forward so that her forearms were on either side of Kennie's head. Her breasts hung tantalizingly close. Kennie gathered them in her hands and alternately tongued the nipples until she and Lily were both wheezing for air.

"You taste good," Kennie said. "You're so soft."

"You're making me feel wonderful."

"I want you to feel me in every way. I want to be inside you and touching and kissing you."

"Me, too."

She put her arms around Lily, and pulled her close. They lay for a moment, and Kennie felt a wave of possessiveness she hadn't expected. "I want you. In every way."

"I'm yours."

Kennie levered herself to the side and guided Lily beneath her. She shifted onto her knees, suddenly aware of harness straps snug against her skin. She looked down at the shaft and shivered with an unexpected wave of nervousness.

Lily spread her legs wide and met her eyes. She took hold of the tie dangling around Kennie's neck to pull her closer.

Kennie, said, "I don't want to hurt you."

Lily laughed, a warm sound that soothed Kennie. "You won't. Come inside me." She let go of the tie and strained upward to find Kennie's lips.

Kennie couldn't hold herself up any longer. She sank down, her breasts heavy against Lily's, and lost herself in Lily's mouth. Her body burned and shook and pulsed. She pushed herself away, grasped the shaft, and guided it into Lily's wetness. Halfway in, she stopped, shocked at her brazenness. "Are you okay?"

"Don't stop, Kennie. Please." Lily's breath came fast in little gasps. She grabbed Kennie's shirt and jerked her forward. Kennie eased in as deep as she could go and paused, holding herself above Lily with strong arms.

Lily let out a sigh. "That's good. So good. Oh, stay right there for a moment." She took a deep breath, then opened her eyes. "Let's take your shirt off. I need to feel your skin against me."

Kennie watched in silent amazement as Lily unbuttoned the shirt, her fingers flying competently. She cooperated in shrugging it off one arm at a time, but when it came time to take off the undershirt, she balked. "I need both arms to get it off. I'll crush you."

"No you won't. Just do it."

"Don't blame me if I knock the wind out of you."

With a smile, Lily said, "You already have."

Kennie relaxed gradually against the smaller woman, and when she saw that Lily seemed entirely comfortable, she pulled the shirt over her head.

"Ah..." Lily sighed. Her hands found Kennie's breasts and stroked. "This is just what I want."

Kennie arched, pushed the shaft in, and raised herself up so that Lily's questing mouth could find her nipple. A shot of pure pleasure blasted through her, straight to her clit and out to the tips of her fingers, to the ends of her toes. She throbbed with fire. Her whole body was a mass of quivering nerves. She needed to move, to feel her muscles flex and contract.

Lily released her breast and tucked her face into the soft skin at Kennie's neck. "Go," she whispered. "Make me feel you."

Like a wild horse suddenly unpenned, Kennie fell upon Lily with a passion she thought she'd never feel again. The harness straps tightened as she reared back and relaxed as she plunged in. The base of the toy jammed against her clit, giving her an exquisite pressure she hadn't expected. She rode Lily with an animalistic pleasure unlike anything she'd ever felt before. Lily goaded her on, at first murmuring quietly, gradually groaning her delight, and then shouting, "Yes, yes!" into Kennie's ear.

At one point, the sensations buffeting Kennie's body became so intense that a sudden orgasm rolled through the center of her and outward, and yet instead of sapping her strength, she was filled with energy. A white light pierced her vision, even though her eyes were closed, and she felt herself lifted to another level. She drove hard into Lily, holding her hips steady. "You're incredible, Lily. I could do this...all night long. You...make me feel...immortal."

Lily's response was guttural. She moved in concert with Kennie as though they'd practiced together for years. With each thrust, Kennie concentrated on the pressure against her own clit.

When Lily made a keening, strangled sound, Kennie opened her eyes and watched Lily coming. Lily's body went rigid, and she demanded "More, more..."

With every stroke, Lily cried out, over and over, in an orgasm lasting so long Kennie couldn't quite believe it. With a final whimper, Lily's grip went slack and her muscles relaxed. Eyes closed, her breathing continued to come fast and hard. Kennie held steady. She eased back a tiny bit then surged forward. She rocked gently, and Lily cried out again. With a wicked grin, Kennie kept moving.

In a few strokes, Lily responded like a wildcat. She grabbed Kennie's arms and thrashed against her, growling with every plunge. Kennie matched her movements in thrust after thrust until she wondered how anyone could last that long. Once again, Lily suddenly went still. She let out a long groan. "Don't stop...there...there...oh..." With one last yowl, she pulled Kennie's hips toward her and gripped her as she whimpered and panted. Her eyes fluttered open, and she looked deep into Kennie's eyes. The moment was so intense, Kennie felt naked to the soul, but she couldn't look away.

Lily loosened her hold, and Kennie settled against her, still buried deep. Very gently, Kennie rolled and disengaged from her. They lay side by side. Kennie put her arms around Lily and nestled her face in the crook of her neck.

"How did you know?" Lily asked, still breathless.

"Know what?"

"That I wasn't finished."

"I don't know. I just sensed you weren't done. Call it woman's intuition."

"You really know how to wear a girl out."

Kennie grinned. "Rest then. Sleep if you need to."

"You think I've run out of gas?"

"If I were you, I would have."

With a feline purr, Lily reached around Kennie, unbuckled the harness, and removed it.

"You're pretty good at that," Kennie said.

"Practice makes perfect. You've obviously spent some time in something similar."

Kennie felt her face flaming, but she resolved to tell the truth. "Actually, I've never done that in my life." When Lily didn't respond, she said, "I've always wanted to, but it never was an option in previous, uh...well, I mean..." She trailed off, shaking her head helplessly.

Lily's lips found hers. The kiss was sweet, and when she pulled away, she said, "All I have to say is you're a very quick study."

She smiled, and in the candlelight, Kennie was struck once more with how beautiful she was. Never in a million years had she ever expected to have an experience like she'd just had, and she felt somehow grateful, as though she had done something very good in a past life and was now being rewarded.

Lily kissed her again. "I'm also happy to report that I'm like the energizer bunny, ready to bang that drum as soon as you're ready."

Kennie whispered, "I was so excited, I came, you know, during..."

"I think you'll have to trust me when I tell you that you're not done." Lily's hands caressed their way down Kennie's body, stopping in all sorts of sensitive places, and Kennie soon realized Lily was right. Her body responded with heat and a shuddering she couldn't control. Lily's fingers found her clit, and Kennie groaned with pleasure.

Lily whispered, "Just let me have my way with you. You'll like it, I promise."

"I believe you." Kennie closed her eyes, shifted onto her back, and opened her legs.

Lily straddled one of her thighs and hovered above her, her fingers stroking Kennie's clit, driving her wild. Kennie opened her eyes long enough to see Lily's smile. She reached up and tangled her hand in Lily's hair, then sat up enough to kiss her. With a groan, she sank back down. When she felt Lily's fingers abandon her, she almost called out, but all words were driven from her mouth when she felt the tip of the toy against her. She was so wet that, with a little pressure from Lily, the shaft filled her.

"Whoa, that feels—odd. I've never—wow."

"You've never used a toy before?"

"There's a first time for everything."

Lily shifted above her, still straddling her leg, but now one knee was jammed tightly in between Kennie's legs, pressuring against her. "I think you'll like this. Just relax."

And she did like it. Once more Lily's fingers found her swollen clit. The waves of sensation quickly changed from pleasurable to intense, and Kennie went from moaning and twitching gently to giant gasps for breath. One moment she was rocking gently against Lily, then the next she was thrashing like a wild thing. Lily rode her like the bucking bronco she was, never letting up, never allowing her fingers to stray from the one place in Kennie's body that became the focal point of so much energy she felt she'd explode.

She cried out for Lily not to stop, begging, panting, pleading. Every time she thought she'd reached the limits of her ability to bear orgasm after orgasm, she was assailed with a new and even more powerful wall of sensation that took her up to another level of joy. When the final overwhelming climax crashed upon her, blast after blast of sheer intensity coursed through her. Every part of her body pulsed. An amazing sexual electricity surged through every vein, every muscle, every limb.

It took a long time to catch her breath. The sensations gradually ebbed, leaving her feeling sated but gleeful. She opened her eyes to find Lily watching her with interest. "Unbelievable."

"I thought you might like that."

"I'll have to leave myself in the good hands of the energizer bunny more often."

"I hope you will."

Lily removed the toy, and Kennie felt one last throb before she relaxed into a pleasant fatigue.

Lily kissed her way up to her neck. "Happy birthday, Kennie."

"I can't think of a better gift you could have given me. Thank you."

"I should be thanking you. What an amazing lover you turned out to be."

"Not bad for a security guard, huh?" The words fell out of her mouth, and Kennie was suddenly struck with a feeling of inadequacy. Lily was a nationally famous painter, a gorgeous, wealthy woman. She could have any woman—any man—she wanted. In contrast, what was so great about Kennie? How could she even hope to have a relationship with a woman like this? She wanted to ask if this was a one-time thing, some sort of temporary diversion before someone else, someone like the lieutenant, came back into her life, but she couldn't make her tongue work.

"Kennie," Lily said, "before I became a painter, do you know what I was?"

Merely beautiful and accomplished? Kennie thought. That alone was daunting. "No."

"Let's see if I can remember in order: waitress, hotel clerk, waitress, telemarketer, art store clerk, waitress, hostess, and let's see, waitress again. It took me a long time to get to where I am now. I'm forty-four years old. I spent the first thirty-plus years of my life just barely making ends meet." When Kennie was silent, she went on. "I'm no prize. I keep odd hours, and I get fixated on my painting. I have plenty of ups and downs."

"Sounds like you're normal then. We all have ups and downs."

"Exactly. What I'm getting at is if you'll have me, I want to explore a relationship with you. You're different from other women I've gotten involved with. You're like...grounded somehow. There's something real about you. I don't care if you're a security guard or a waitress. I don't care what you do, I care what you are. I care how you make me feel."

Kennie didn't know what to say. She grabbed the sheet to cover them, then wrapped Lily in her arms, a lump in her throat. She kissed both of Lily's eyelids and pressed the side of her face against her hair, reveling in the softness of the golden locks.

Lily said, "You could move up to the penthouse sometime, when you feel like it, if you feel like it, I mean. Your little apartment is cute, but it's awfully small."

Kennie swallowed and took a deep breath. "About that. I...I...well, I don't actually live there."

"You don't? But you're always here. Why would you keep another apartment someplace else?"

"I live in 1A."

"1A? Here?"

"Yup."

"I don't understand."

"Guess I'm going to have to 'fess up. It's like this. I own the building."

"What?"

"I own the Allen Arms."

Lily pulled away. "Since when?"

"Ever since I moved in." The gap between them felt almost painful. Kennie reached out gently and touched Lily's breast with the flat of her palm. "Does that change anything?"

"Yes, it changes everything."

Alarmed, Kennie took a deep breath but she didn't stop caressing Lily's breast.

"Everything." Breathlessly, Lily said, "I think that means you can afford better uniforms."

Kennie focused on the blossoming areola.

"Much nicer uniforms," Lily gasped out, "with piping and gold buttons." Her breath caught. "And epaulets."

Kennie laughed. "Definitely epaulets because you —"

"Yes." Lily covered Kennie's body with her own, her hands warm and exploring. "Because I love a woman in uniform."

Kennie laughed. "Are you sleepy yet?"

"Nuh-uh. Not a bit. And I have some new massage oil I've been wanting to try. And some lube that heats up all on its own. I may have a few other delights to share."

"Bring it on," Kennie said, laughing.

Chapter Four

ON THE DAY after her fortieth birthday, Kennie awoke when the clock radio beside the bed clicked on. "Here Comes the Rain Again" was playing with Annie Lennox's voice sexy and full of longing as she begged her baby to dive into her ocean and to talk to her like lovers do. The melody sounded magical.

Kennie reached beside her, thinking she'd find Lily, but the sheets were cold. She rose from the bed, stretched, and yawned. Her legs and lower back were deliciously fatigued. Every muscle felt as though she'd given it a workout. With a sheepish grin, she admitted she had.

She threw on her long-sleeved shirt and went in search of Lily, buttoning a few of the buttons on the way. She found her in the first place she looked: barefoot, barelegged, in the ballroom. Lily wore a long white t-shirt and held a palette in one hand and a paintbrush in the other. Her blonde hair was tied back, but some locks had fallen forward and partially obscured her face. She moved like a dancer, going up on the tips of her toes, rolling back on her heels, swaying a little, then darting forward with a steady hand to stroke paint on the canvas. Her motions weren't overtly sexual, but they were sensual just the same.

Thinking of that steady hand caused a hollow place in Kennie's middle to twinge, and heat spread to her groin. She shivered, and the motion must have caught Lily's eye because she looked toward the door and smiled.

"Good morning," Lily said.

Kennie crossed the parquet floor, and Lily set her paintbrush on the lip of the easel. She stepped out from behind the painting and held her palette away so that Kennie could take her in her arms.

"Careful, I don't want to get paint on your shirt."

"I don't care." She kissed Lily gently, then more deeply as Lily responded.

Lily was the first to break away. "I'm a wretched hostess. I haven't prepared any breakfast or even coffee to offer you."

Kennie nuzzled her neck and breathed in a flowery scent. Lily smelled good enough to eat. "How long have you been up?" She looked into the deep blue eyes, saw up close the fine lines in her face that gave her character, and decided Lily was the most gorgeous and enticing woman she'd ever met.

"Close to dawn. I set the alarm for you because I assumed you had to work today." She grinned. "Though if you're your own boss, you can arrive late anytime you damn well please."

"That's right. I can."

"You've inspired me. I'm going to paint today until I fall over."

"Save at least a little energy for later." Kennie couldn't stop herself from grinning wickedly.

"What did you have in mind?"

"Anything you want." She kissed Lily again, marveling at how perfectly their bodies melded together, even with the palette floating around somewhere to her right. She broke the kiss, breathless. "You working on something new?" She gestured toward the painting, but she could only see the back and side of the easel.

"Yes, but I don't want you to see it yet." Lily slipped out of Kennie's arms. "Leave me at it, and come back later today. Maybe after your shift is over?"

"I can do that."

With a crooked smile, Lily lifted her face and accepted another kiss. "Later, then," she said.

AFTER SHOWERING AND dressing in a fresh uniform, Kennie sat at the guard desk, aware in the back of her mind that minutes were passing, but having no conscious regard for anything. Instead of the coherent and linear thought patterns she was used to, her mind offered up snapshots of the night before. Tastes and textures and smells completely undermined her ability to think cogent thoughts. She and Lily had made love for hours, their bodies so close, skin so on fire that she was surprised they hadn't consumed one another completely.

She hadn't felt this way in so long—not since the first few years of the relationship with Janeen. She'd had a great sex life with Janeen, full of love and emotional passion, but she saw now that their lovemaking had been simple. No toys, no skin-heating lubes, no talking dirty. In one night with Lily, Kennie had let herself go in ways she never had before.

And why hadn't she ever let loose like that? Her brain wouldn't compute the question. She looked down at her hand, opened the palm, and studied her fingers. Just hours earlier these hands had touched Her, Kennie thought. "Her" with a capital *H*, because Lily was surely a goddess.

She roused from her stupor when someone rang the back delivery door. As she walked down the hallway to the rear of the building, she thought about what she might take up to Lily later on.

A nice bottle of wine, perhaps some sandwiches, fruit, cheese. Was there any food left from the caterers the night before? She had no way of knowing, but even if there were leftover chicken, potatoes, and vegetables, it would all require too much preparation, even just to heat it. Foods that could be eaten in bed, picnic items, were what Kennie thought would work best. She didn't think Lily, engrossed in her painting, would pay any attention to meals today, so Kennie resolved to feed her.

Kennie accepted delivery of a dozen five-gallon containers of paint, and once she directed the guys to where they should stack them in the basement, she headed back to the guard desk. The elevator door was just closing. She caught a glimpse of a dark blue suit, but didn't pay it any attention. When the door reopened a few moments later, tiny Virginia Quist stepped out. She didn't look a day over sixty, but Kennie had it on good authority that she was pushing eighty.

"Miss Quist, good afternoon."

Dressed in an old-fashioned tweed coat, nylons, and leather walking shoes, the woman from 6A came to stand at the counter. She held an umbrella and a dark brown fedora trimmed with bright yellow crochet. To Kennie, she always looked like a character straight out of an Agatha Christie novel, right down to her tiny mouth and crooked lower teeth. Only the tops of her shoulders and head showed, so Kennie rose, then realized too late that now she was towering over the little lady.

With a scowl, Miss Quist tipped her head up and said, "Now, Kennie, I like to enjoy a good night's sleep as much as the next person, but it's difficult when I have an artist living overhead."

As the words sunk in to Kennie's slow-moving brain, she felt heat suffuse her face. Had Miss Quist heard every move, every thrust, every thump of Lily's bed against the wall? Oh, Lord. How embarrassing.

"Is there any way you might minimize all the racket coming from the penthouse after ten p.m.? I swear, that woman never sleeps. She's walking and squeaking and thumping and bumping nonstop all night."

"I—I see..."

"As I've mentioned in the past, some decent carpeting on that expanse of space above my apartment would cut down on all the creaking and stomping."

With sudden clarity, Kennie imagined the layout of the Allen Arms. Miss Quist's apartment was below the ballroom, not anywhere near the bedrooms. "Let me see what I can do. I'll talk to management."

With a curt nod, Miss Quist turned and donned her hat. Kennie beat her to the door and opened it for her.

"Thank you, dear. That's such a heavy door. Squeaky, too. This whole apartment building certainly has auditory character."

Kennie watched the little bird of a woman pick her way carefully down the stairs and stride confidently along the sidewalk. A bubble of hilarity burst in the back of her throat, and she laughed out loud. If Miss Quist was truly nearing eighty, how did she get so lucky to have the hearing of a baby? She made sure the door shut completely. What the hell would Kennie do if the tenants in 6B could hear what went on in Lily's bedroom? Oh, my. Maybe the carpeting in the master bedroom muffled the noise? Well, they'd never complained before about any nocturnal activities up in Lily's place. But the building was old, and the floors did creak. She didn't think there was much she could do about that, carpet or no carpet. The thought of ruining or covering up the ballroom floor was out of the question, and monkeying with the ceilings below to add a layer of Quietrock soundproofing would cost enormous sums and not do much to solve the problem.

After making a cup of tea and a sandwich, Kennie settled in behind the desk again. People came, people went, she greeted them all, but her mind was somewhere else. If emotions had colors, she'd be swirling in rainbows of happiness.

The afternoon passed slowly, but Kennie didn't care. Around five p.m., a flurry of tenants popped in from the rain and hurried to the elevator, obviously eager to get out of their rain-drenched clothing.

The elevator opened, and a tall woman in a dark blue suit exited and stepped aside to allow the herd to enter the elevator. White-cold shock hit Kennie, as if someone had grabbed her and immersed her in an avalanche of snow. She staggered to her feet, the muscles in the backs of her thighs tight and sore. She met the other woman's eyes at the same level so the woman couldn't look down upon her at the guard desk.

The suit fit her marvelously, but the tie was askew, and she looked slightly rumpled, as though she'd just bedded someone. She cast a haughty glance at Kennie and gave a satisfied-looking smile as she passed.

How had Lily's lieutenant gotten past Kennie—and when? And what was up with the snarky smirk?

WHEN SIMMS ARRIVED to relieve Kennie—late again, as usual—she let him have it about his tardiness.

"Christ, Kennie," he said. "What bug do you have up your butt?"

She held her breath and stood tight-lipped for a moment before she whirled and stalked off. She let the door to the efficiency slam a little bit harder than she meant to, stomped through to 1A, and paced in the living room.

What did she have to fear? So what—the lieutenant had obviously been up to see Lily. It probably meant nothing, right? But what was that Cat-Who-Ate-the-Canary look she'd received from the evil bitch?

She fretted and worried for several moments before finally changing into jeans, a t-shirt, and tennis shoes. The hell with food. She needed to see Lily. She needed to touch Lily, to reassure herself that the future she'd already begun to imagine could be a reality.

As she rode the elevator up to 7A, she tried to get back the happy feelings of earlier in the day, but her stomach was too tightly tied into a big ball of knots.

Lily answered the knock dressed in tan paint pants and an unbuttoned men's white shirt with quite a few red splotches on it. The t-shirt underneath was also marred.

Kennie met those bright blue eyes, and in an instant, she knew the truth. The look on Lily's face said it all. Kennie took a gulp of air and stepped back.

"Please," Lily said. She lifted a hand, as if to reach out, then let it drop. "I can't help it. I have to try. With her, I mean."

"Did you tell her about you and me?"

"Yes. I had to. I don't want to hurt you. I thought it was over, that she, that I, we didn't—"

Kennie held up a hand, palm outward. "No. I don't want to know." She turned and pressed the elevator button. The damn thing was gone. She held back the tears. She hadn't heard Lily leave or close the door. She dared not turn back for fear she'd either pick up the fainting couch and throw it through the window or fall to her knees and beg.

The elevator wasn't coming. Someone must be holding it on another floor. She stepped to the stairwell door, turned the stiff knob, and punched it open. As she let go, she glanced back to see Lily weeping in the doorway.

Glad to be wearing tennis shoes, Kennie stomped all the way down to the second floor, cut down the hall to the back stairs, exited through the service door, and emerged into a steady rain. She half-ran, half-walked at least a mile before bending over, hands on knees, and letting out a yowl of pain that caused people at the bus stop down the block to step out of the glass enclosure to see what was happening.

Chapter Five

THE NEXT DAYS of spring were rain soaked, and the persistent showers matched Kennie's mood, adding to her depression and sadness. Not a day went by without tears on her morning run and crying herself to sleep at night. She felt like a great big mushball, but she couldn't stem the tears, and they weren't so much about the loss of Lily but about the end of hope, the end of the dream she'd always had of being partnered, in love, happy with a soul mate. She thought after Janeen she'd never have another soul mate; after Lily there wouldn't likely be another lover. She couldn't afford to let that happen.

It was bad enough that the lieutenant stole the girl right out from under Kennie, but she seemed to delight in rubbing it in. She never said a word, though. She didn't have to. When she came through the lobby during Kennie's shifts, she always wore a smirk—a wolfish, self-satisfied expression that infuriated Kennie. She wanted to smash her face in. She tried to stop herself from thinking of all the ways she could kill the exultant cop, but sometimes it just felt good to let her imagination run rampant. Her current fantasy involved high bridges and a gunnysack.

Even worse than the lieutenant's periodic visits was being on duty during Lily's comings and goings. Kennie had to give Lily credit. If she'd been in her shoes, Kennie would've come down the elevator to the second floor, taken the back stairs, and departed through the loading dock area. She would never be able to get back in the building that way, but she could have at least reduced the awkwardness for half of the time.

But Lily came resolutely up and down the elevator or the grand staircase, and she didn't avoid Kennie's eyes. She didn't speak either, but she generally nodded to acknowledge her existence. Kennie thought it took guts for Lily to face her everyday—because they'd had something, hadn't they?

So whenever she saw those trim legs descending the stairs, if she could manage it, she marched down the corridor away from the lobby so she didn't have to see Lily. Who was the coward then? At least Lily had been straight-up with her and was behaving with dignity. Kennie merely fumed and paced...and thought about all the ways she wanted to kill the mean-spirited cop.

After a time, Kennie simply ran out of energy. She couldn't take it anymore, sitting at the guard desk, accepting deliveries, helping tenants with groceries, hearing complaints, doing the same thing every day, feeling the same pain.

Simms was more than happy to switch to the day shift. And for the time being, Kennie engaged the services of a temp agency who sent her a laconic older man who rarely left the guard station, but Kennie didn't care. He was there if anyone needed him, and he kept excellent notes about complaints and problems.

The relief she felt was literally visceral. Not seeing Lily hurt her in a strange, broken way, but avoiding the smug lieutenant was a lifesaver.

The third anniversary of Janeen's death passed, and Kennie marked it by taking a drive to the rocky Oregon coast and staying right on the beach in a ramshackle cabin with clunking baseboard heaters and no water pressure to speak of. She spent most of the weekend out wandering the beach, picking up shells, throwing rocks into the surf, and trying to come up with even the slightest idea of what she wanted to do with the rest of her life. If age forty marked the midpoint, she still had another forty years to go. Shouldn't she figure out a way to enjoy her life, to live more fully and happily?

She had no idea how many miles she walked alone on the cool, sandy beach, but by the third day, she had found a sweet solace in the salty ocean winds where no one bothered her and seagulls cried in the same key as the closing of her heart.

Chapter Six

"WELL, HELLO THERE."

Kennie had just hauled a clanking ladder and a bucket of paint gear into 2D, and Mr. Faulkner's voice startled her.

He stood in the hallway, one hand behind his back. "Long time, no see," he said. "I can't believe it's already June. How come you're never at the front desk anymore?"

She leaned the ladder against the wall and set down the bucket filled with brushes, rollers, tape, screwdrivers, and an extension pole sticking out awkwardly. "I'm not working the desk anymore, Mr. Faulkner."

"I figured. Well, I'll be. You sure are doing a nice job in here," he said with appreciation. "Mind if I step in and look around?"

"Be my guest."

While he wandered through the apartment making more ooh and aah noises than a gay man at an interior decoration store, Kennie set up the ladder and popped the top off a five-gallon bucket of ceiling paint.

"Look what you've done to this kitchen." He stepped inside and gazed at the ceiling, which had a bright new light fixture. He pointed at walls from which Kennie had painstakingly removed years of wallpaper. "How'd you get that horrid crap off the walls?"

"A lot of special solvent."

"And no small amount of elbow grease, I bet."

He moved out of the kitchen, and Kennie eyed the empty bottle of Jim Beam dangling in his hand.

He noticed and held up the empty. "I try to sneak 'em out when Evelyn's napping, so she doesn't catch on to how often I like to imbibe." He reddened slightly. "Even after fifty-six years of marriage, she's still nagging about that."

"Just toss it in that trash can there, Mr. Faulkner, and I'll take it out to the recycling bin for you." Kennie knew exactly how much he drank. Every month, one case of Jim Beam was delivered to the back of the Allen Arms by the nearby liquor store, so apparently he downed twelve bottles a month. If she did the math, she was pretty sure that qualified him as a problem drinker, but who was she to judge? Lately she'd gotten into the vodka a lot more than ever.

"That's real nice of you," he said as he dumped the bottle on top of piles of old wallpaper. "Don't you think it's about time you started calling us Norm and Evelyn? Even if you're an employee here, you're still a fellow tenant."

Kennie squatted down and stuck a paint stirrer in the paint, then hesitated, but in keeping with her new vow to be honest wherever she could, she said, "I was never an employee, Norm. I own the Allen Arms."

He went still, frowning. "Really? Huh. I didn't see that coming." He hitched up his polyester pants and tucked in his golf shirt as though suddenly he needed to appear presentable. "Guess that saves me a call to the management company. I can appeal directly to the owner."

She rose, slightly concerned. "You're giving notice?"

"Oh, no, not exactly. I like what you've done to this apartment. Once you've got the paint on the walls and new carpet installed, this place is going to be a wonder. It's the same layout as our place, and I'd like to rent it. Is that possible, or is it already promised to someone?"

"I haven't advertised it yet, but you need to know that the rent for this unit is going up."

"How much?"

She'd just looked at the rent checks the day before, so his current rental rate popped into her head. "Kind of a lot. Four hundred dollars more per month than what you pay now."

"Two hundred."

"What?" she asked.

He smiled. "I'm a retired accountant and day trader. You've got to at least dicker with me."

"Oh. Okay. Three-seventy-five."

"Three hundred."

"Three-fifty?"

"You drive a hard bargain, Ms. McClain. Okay, three-fifty it is."

"That's quite a jump from your current payment. Are you sure it'll be okay with Mrs. Faul—uh, Evelyn?"

"Who cares about money anymore? We've got a lot in the bank, and between us, we're 153 years old. We've been in that dark, smoky apartment for over twenty years. Time for a change."

"Smoky?"

He rolled his eyes. "Yeah, she made me quit smoking when I retired, but the damage had been done. You'll be able to clean it all up in a jiffy for another tenant, and we can start over in this pretty place."

"What about the friends you wanted to move into the building?"

Grinning, he said, "I guess they can take over our old unit or some other one that comes open." He made tracks for the door, turning to say, "I promise we'll take care of this place. No smoking, not ever. I won't even need new address labels. I can just change 2A to 2D. Wait'll I tell Evelyn. She'll be down here before day's end wanting to help pick out carpet colors and make arrangements for movers. Hope you've got some flexibility."

He shuffled down the hall, moving along at a much faster gait than she'd ever seen. Kennie gazed after him, amused by his attitude. She had planned to get a new renter in the building who'd add a big chunk of change to the overall gross. The rent would be fifty dollars less than she'd figured, but actually, that would work out fine. She could get the Faulkner's place refurbished fairly quickly, and that'd be one less unit needing work. And she could tack the fifty bucks on there.

By early evening, she'd finished rolling the ceiling with flat white. She was sitting cross-legged on the floor to trim the baseboards when the first of a string of tenants showed up. Tiffany Dale from 5C tapped on the doorframe and hovered just outside the door, wanting to know if she could have the next refurbished unit. Before she finished her pitch, Virginia Quist from 6A stopped to inquire whether the folks in 6B might be vacating so she could take over their unit. "Or, in the alternative," she said, in her precise way, "perhaps I could make special arrangements for my household, take a holiday, and you might revamp my apartment while I'm gone?"

The Halliwells from 3C, the youngest tenants and only in their thirties, appeared then. The husband barged right on in and said, "Congratulations on buying the building, Kennie. Quite a coup."

His wife said, "From security to super. Not sure I'd want to be in your shoes."

Kennie heard more voices in the hallway, and Evelyn Faulkner squeezed through, using a cane in place of her walker. "Oh, it's lovely. So bright. So sunny. Let's do blinds on the windows instead of those stuffy horrid curtains all the apartments were outfitted with back in the Sixties."

Kennie opened her mouth to respond, but her paintbrush threatened to drip. She scraped it on the edge of a paint bucket. When she looked up, Lee Nguyen from 4B, an elderly Asian man who dyed his hair an unnatural shade of blue-black, piped up to say, "Congratulations on owning the Allen Arms. You're going to be a great landlord."

Tiffany Dale, her voice rising with excitement, said, "Oh, my God, I didn't even know you'd bought this place, Kennie. Now we have someone on site who really listens."

Kennie couldn't get a word in edgewise, so she wasn't able to remind them she'd lived in the Allen Arms and been the landlord for quite some time, so she had always been available to listen. She put the paintbrush in a safe spot away from the madding crowd and got to her feet.

Adam Vendrick elbowed his way through the crowd. He was a little younger than Kennie, and a lot shorter. He might even be labeled diminutive. She always felt like an Amazon next to his tiny frame. He was fond of sky blue and often, like today, wore silk shirts that color, probably because they set off his cornflower blue eyes. His blond hair was parted down the side with a swoop reminiscent of Hermey, the Misfit Elf dentist, who was Rudolph the Red-nosed Reindeer's friend. Every time she saw Adam traipsing down the stairs from 2C, she had to restrain herself from asking if he'd ever considered being a dentist.

As far as she could tell, Adam was the only gay man in the building. He owned a pet store, and he occasionally smuggled ailing animals in to nurse them back to health, but Kennie and Simms always looked the other way. An occasional ill kitten or injured puppy wasn't enough to complain about. Besides, he and a few friends ran a catering company on the side, and he often shared some delicious leftovers.

He clapped his hands together and said, "People, people, calm down. I have a suggestion that you all must hear. In honor of the big changes around the Allen Arms, I propose we have a party. A celebration in honor of Kennie."

"Oh, no..." she started to say, but everyone crowded into the living room and roared their approval.

Adam turned to her gleefully. "How about two weeks from Sunday? Mid-June all right for everyone?"

Before she could reply, the various tenants were pulling out Blackberries and Dayplanners and clicking or scribbling. Evelyn Faulkner just flat out said, "We'll be there with bells on."

Everybody looked so happy Kennie didn't have the heart to disappoint them.

"Excellent," Adam said. "I'll get some invitations made up. Any special requests, Kennie?"

"Requests?"

"For the menu, silly. Any special dishes? Or is there a particular type of cake you like?"

"I'm not really very picky. Except, maybe you could skip serving chicken?"

"All right, anything else?"

"Let's not have chrysanthemums."

Adam flopped a hand her way. "Goodness no. We'll have much classier accents than chrysanthemums. Come along, people. We've got decisions to make, a budget to finalize, a timeline to..."

And with that the room cleared, leaving only Mrs. Faulkner behind. She turned kindly eyes on Kennie. "You look a little shell-shocked, dear."

Kennie had to agree. She wasn't sure what had just happened, but it sounded positive, so she wasn't going to complain. "So your husband wasn't kidding. You really want to move into this unit?"

"I'd love to." She beamed at Kennie, her soft face all wrinkled with joy. "I'd like to get the window coverings and carpeting to match my decor. Will you let me select them?"

"I think so. If what you choose fits the budget."

"I'm more than happy to cover any extra costs."

"Why don't we take a trip to the store tomorrow, and you can pick what you want?"

"I'd be delighted to." She leaned heavily on the cane and limped to Kennie to throw an arm around her shoulder. "I'm so glad to have this opportunity."

Kennie blushed. "Seems like good timing all around. Watch out that you don't get any paint on you, Mrs. Faulkner."

"Oh, nonsense. This is just an old housecoat, and I don't care. It's more important to hug people than to worry about how we all look. And go ahead and call me Evelyn. Norm told me about your conversation earlier." She gave Kennie a quick squeeze. "I'm glad to see you're recovering. You looked so bereft there for a while."

"Uh..." was as much as Kennie could get out.

Evelyn patted her hand. "No need to talk about it, dear. I could see what happened, but don't worry. I'm sure there's not another soul in the building who has a clue. Not even Norm. He's just as oblivious as the rest. Just know that you'll get over her eventually, and someone new will come into your life. Just mark my words. You're too good a catch to be single for too long. You're taking good care of yourself, right? Not working too hard?"

Kennie nodded, deciding that silence was the best course of action. How else was she supposed to respond to any of that emotionally loaded statement, much less the questions? Better yet, how had Evelyn Faulkner tumbled to those facts?

As if she could read her mind, Evelyn said, "I'm sorry if I was intrusive, Kennie. I don't usually talk much. I was once a counselor, and I still spend a lot of time observing people. I couldn't help but notice you and Lily. I had seven kids, boom boom boom all in a row, two of them gay, and I got such an amazing education watching them get their hearts broken. Now they're all seven in relationships, and I've got great-grandchildren. You remind me of one of my granddaughters." She stepped to the side and used the cane as a fulcrum to turn. "I'll leave you be now. You still look a little overwhelmed. I see you're a Jim Beam drinker like Norm."

She pointed at the nearly full trash bin. "Have a couple of shots, and you'll settle right down. Seems to work for him."

As soon as Evelyn was safely in her own apartment, Kennie shut the door to 2D and slid down against it. She pulled her legs up and wrapped her arms around her shins. Holy Mother of God, she thought, I'm never leaving the hall door open again when I work in an apartment.

Chapter Seven

THE DAYS TOOK on a new drift now that Kennie had let go of everything but the building. She remembered the name of a poem she read in high school, "The Hollow Man." Hollow described her state of being quite well. She felt empty inside most of the time and only experienced a little satisfaction when she finished some part of the remodeling of the various apartments.

In the quiet, lonely evenings, she anesthetized herself with television shows she'd DVR'd so she could skip the commercials. Everyone on TV had interesting lives full of drama and excitement, and when they had emotional troubles, they were either resolved within the forty-two minute program or else the problems worked themselves out over the course of the season. If only her own issues could be boiled down to a mere season of twenty-two chunks of time.

Every day she took off on a run, sometimes three miles, sometimes five or six. Being on foot in Portland offered her much to look at. She discovered the running paths through Laurelhurst Park and the steep hills and stairs up around Mount Tabor. One day she saw a sign for wine-tasting at a woman-owned winery called Hip Chicks Do Wine. She wasn't too sweaty, so she dropped in and ended up ordering two hundred dollars worth of the best port she'd ever tasted.

She jogged by lots of microbrewery pubs and cafés and charming-looking bistros filled with boisterous, laughing people. She raced past these places, ignoring the emptiness that other people's happiness evoked in her.

She'd always considered her neighborhood to be generally safe, though nobody dared leave anything valuable about. If possessions weren't nailed down or the car was left unlocked, petty thieves were more than willing to relieve their owners of whatever they could find. Tenants didn't have to worry about assault or the drug trade, but theft was a growing concern. That was part of the reason Kennie employed security in the Allen Arms. Especially after dark, she had no intention of letting anyone into the building who could rip off any of her tenants.

The owners of the grand homes and the apartment buildings in the area had formed an association long before Kennie's time, and Kennie and some of her tenants had joined it. They met quarterly to share information, and the Neighborhood Watch was a vigorous group of landlords and tenants who watched out for each other. They'd recently foiled a bicycle-theft ring by communicating with the elderly renters who kept an eye on neighborhood activities. She wouldn't say she'd become complacent, but Kennie felt comfortable in her neighborhood.

So after a long run, she wasn't at all prepared to round the corner to the back of the Allen Arms and find a scruffy guy in jeans, t-shirt, and ball cap, kicking someone curled up on the ground.

"What the hell?" she called out as she backed way up. She'd sprinted the last block and had trouble catching her breath.

Scruffy looked up, and she very clearly saw his pocked face and dead eyes. "Fuck off," he said. He stood over his victim, the toe of one shoe tucked under the body.

Kennie was bigger than he was, and after a moment's hesitation, she balled up her fists and advanced, shouting, "Get the hell out of here before I kick your ass."

His face looked grayish, as though he hadn't been healthy for some time. When he opened his mouth to snarl more epithets, she saw that what teeth he still possessed were mottled with ugly brown decay.

She reached into the pocket of her shorts for a nonexistent cell phone. Actually, she didn't carry a phone, just her ring of keys pinned inside the pocket. "I'm calling the police. Now."

That was all it took. He backed away, bringing up hands to display his middle fingers for her viewing benefit. "I'll be back. Nobody steals from me. You hear me? You owe me."

He loped away with an awkward gait as though his legs didn't fully bend at the knee. She hoped he'd fall down and break both of them.

Still winded, she bent to check on the kid lying curled up on the ground. His dirty brown hair was cut short, and he wore a red long-sleeved shirt, torn jeans, and worn, scarred, used-to-be-white Nikes.

"Hey, are you okay?" she asked.

A fist came up without any force behind it. She dodged back. The kid wheezed out, "Stop. I haven't got 'em. Stop." Blindly the youth swung an arm around, but the effort was so feeble that Kennie easily avoided it.

She grabbed a shoulder. "Calm down. I'm here to help. I'll get an ambulance."

"No!" The kid uncurled and groaned and tried to crab-walk away from her. Kennie looked at the face and realized that "he" was a "she." Her face was too heart-shaped, her features too fine to be a boy's. She looked to be fourteen, maybe fifteen. Her brown eyes, wreathed by a mess of stringy unkempt hair, were unfocused, and there was so much blood on her face that Kennie gasped. One arm buckled, and the girl sprawled back on the pavement.

Kennie grabbed a ripped-up tennis shoe. "Wait, you're hurt. Please don't run. You need help." She tugged at the girl's foot. "I won't hurt you, I promise."

The girl's body went limp, and she lay crying, her scrawny chest heaving silently. Kennie rose and went to her Jeep Commander, unlocked the passenger door, and tipped the seat back. She returned to the girl and squatted down. "Can you get up on your own?"

The girl tried, but she couldn't get her feet under her. Kennie picked her up and gently carried her to the SUV. She didn't cry out until Kennie tried to belt her in.

"I'm sorry. So sorry."

"It's okay. O-kay, o-kay..." the girl said, panting. She grimaced in pain and bit her bottom lip.

Kennie patted her leg. "Hang in there. It won't be long."

As Kennie shut the door, she met the girl's eyes, and what she saw reminded her of a dog she'd owned as a teenager. Bucky had gotten hit by a car right in front of the house, and Kennie had seen the same kind of fear and resignation in Bucky's eyes when she lifted him up to take him for medical attention. After an initial struggle, he whimpered and showed her a hopeful look—just before he went slack and died.

THE DISTANCE TO the hospital was short, maybe only two miles. Kennie sped when she could while trying not to jerk her passenger around. During the entire trip, streams of tears tracked through the blood and dirt on her face. She only spoke once to whisper, "Hard...to breathe."

Kennie stepped on it and pulled up to the ER. She got out of the car, ran for the entrance, and called out, "I've got someone in the car who can't walk."

A nurse just inside heard her and shouted for a gurney.

When Kennie went back to the car, the girl had gotten the seat belt off and the door open. One leg on the ground, the other still in the foot-well, she started to lean precariously.

"What the hell are you doing?" Kennie asked as she steadied her.

"Away," she gasped. "I—I can't..."

"You need a doctor. What's your name?"

"No money. I can't..."

"Yes, you can. What's your name?"

The girl said, "Max."

The gurney arrived, and before the kid could manage an escape, she was strapped down and two nurses wheeled her inside.

Only then did Kennie notice how hard her heart was beating and how out of breath she was. Shaking, she slid into the driver's seat and tried to get her breathing under control. She still hadn't managed it when a vehicle pulled in behind her and beeped the horn. She saw the flashing lights of an ambulance, so she started her SUV and hastened away from the ER entrance.

It took a long time to find a parking place. She ended up wedged into a spot on the street several blocks away. The hike back to the ER took five minutes. By the time she arrived, she was shivering, sweaty, and her stomach hurt. It'd been a long time since she'd eaten, and she never properly cooled down from her run. She took a deep breath and resolved to check on the kid, then head home as soon as possible.

Inside the hospital, she stopped at the first nurse's station and asked for the status of the red-shirted girl brought in a few minutes earlier.

The nurse held a license in her hand and was filling in a form. From upside down, Kennie saw that she'd written Elizabeth Maxine Wallington. The nurse didn't look up from her paperwork and just said, "You family?"

"Nope, just the good Samaritan who found her and brought her in for help."

"Then you know I can't tell you anything significant."

"I just want to know if she's going to be all right."

The nurse sighed and met Kennie's gaze. She looked tired. And a little bit suspicious. "So you're saying you can't go to the business office and fill out the paperwork? You actually don't know her?"

"No, I don't. She was beaten up by some thug behind my building. I chased the guy away and brought her here. Never saw her before in my life."

The nurse gave a little nod, as if she found that explanation acceptable. "She's with the trauma docs now. It'll be awhile. You can sit down the hall in the waiting room."

Kennie looked down at her shirt. For the first time, she noticed she had blood and dirt on her left shoulder. "I live close by. I'm going to jet home and get clean clothes. I'll be back."

"Uh-huh."

Kennie turned to walk away, but she heard the nurse mutter, "That's what they all say."

KENNIE MADE IT back to the Allen Arms in record time, parked in front, and rushed in the front door past Simms.

"Hey, Kennie!" Simms said.

She turned but kept walking backwards.

"What's happening? Why the rush?" He hastened toward her. "Jesus, is that blood all over you?"

She quickly described what had happened as she unlocked 1A.

"Did you call the police?"

"No, I didn't. I think the hospital staff will do that."

"You're going back?"

"Yeah, I feel I should. You hold down the fort."

"Aye aye, boss. You got it."

She closed the door and went to the bathroom to take the world's fastest shower. She had to chuckle a little about Simms. Ever since he'd found out she owned the building, he'd taken to calling her "boss." She kept telling him to stop it, but she figured it was his way of making sure he kept their respective roles in mind. After all, he'd been employed by the former owners, and at the very least, he must have thought of her as his equal, if not that he outranked her in terms of longevity.

Out of the shower, she brushed her hair without looking in the mirror. She had no desire to see her wan face. She dressed in a long-sleeved Henley shirt, khakis, and tennis shoes, and grabbed her wallet. In the kitchen, she quickly assembled and downed a turkey, cheese, and tomato sandwich. Thirty minutes later, with some snack crackers, a banana, and a couple of energy bars in a paper bag, she left the apartment and headed back to the hospital, noting with chagrin that there was blood all over the passenger seat of the car. She made a mental note to clean that later.

A different nurse was on duty at the desk, and Kennie debated telling her she was a relative, but she squelched that idea after thinking about issues of liability. She strolled back to the empty waiting room, prepared to settle in for the duration, but before she even dropped into a seat, a doctor clad in blue scrubs and carrying a clipboard skidded into the room.

"Wallington?"

She didn't bother to waste words identifying herself. "Is she okay?"

Consulting his clipboard, he said, "Broken finger, fractured ribs, possible cracked clavicle, lacerations, deep bruises consistent with quite a beating. She doesn't appear to have internal injuries, but without an MRI, we'd need to keep her for observation to be sure." He stared at her through silver half-moon eyeglasses, which looked ridiculous on his face since Kennie estimated he was all of about twenty-five years of age. "She wouldn't give us any information about the injuries or assailants, and she refused to allow us to call the police."

"What? Call them anyway."

He gave her a withering look. "Obviously you're not conversant with the requirements of HIPAA."

"No, you're right. I have no clue what you're talking about."

"HIPAA protects a patient's right not to have medical data released against their will. If she'd been stabbed or shot, we would have been authorized to call the police, but her injuries are such that she can and did refuse to allow it."

"That's ridiculous. She's obviously been beaten."

He pulled a pen out of the pocket of his white jacket. "You're next of kin?"

"No, but I wanted to make sure she's all right."

He frowned. "What's your name? I'm Doctor Ankeny, by the way."

She introduced herself and gave him a quick summary of the assault.

The doctor made a few notes and said, "We need to find someone responsible for her. Who can we call?"

"I can't help you there. Let me speak to her. Maybe I can convince her to tell you her parents' names."

"I'll see about that." As quickly as he'd appeared, he bolted back out the door and down the hall.

After a few minutes, Kennie rose and looked out the window at the busy traffic. She'd sat in far too many waiting rooms in clinics and hospitals while Janeen had been ill. Sometimes she was able to be with her, but during the surgery and then later with radiation, she could only wait impatiently, pacing the hospital hallways and drinking bad coffee from the machine. She didn't find hospitals a grim place like so many people might after they'd been through what she had, but being inside this one brought back the hollowness with a vengeance. She didn't know whether to burst into tears or throw a raging fit. Finally, she sat down and tried to remember how to breathe regularly again.

She wasn't sure how much time passed before a nurse came and escorted her to a curtained bay in a quiet emergency room. "Where the heck is everyone?" Kennie asked. "Isn't the emergency room usually a lot busier?"

The nurse said, "Calm before the storm. All hell will break loose anytime now." She slid open the curtain, and Kennie saw the alarmed expression on Max's face before the kid looked down and away.

Paper bag in hand, Kennie stopped alongside the bed. "Hey. How're you feeling?"

Max tried to shrug, then winced in pain. Big brown eyes were framed by a pallid face that looked like its owner had been in a prizefight. No doubt she was going to have double black eyes. Her brow was pink and swollen, bruised in multiple places, and above her right eye were stitches that disappeared into her eyebrow. Matching stitches, though fewer of them, ran down the center of her bottom lip and half an inch to the side.

"They cut my clothes off," the girl said dully.

"I suppose they had to. If you've got broken ribs, it would have hurt something awful to try to get a shirt off over your head."

"Got nothing else to wear."

Kennie wasn't sure what "nothing else" meant. Nothing else at all, period? She changed the subject. "You want to tell me what happened behind my apartment building?"

"Not really."

"Who was that guy?"

The girl looked down and seemed to shrink a little, as if that were the only way to protect herself.

"Okay, let's start with something easy. Your name is Max, Max Wallington?"

She nodded.

"How old are you?"

"Eighteen."

Kennie couldn't stop a huff of disbelief. She composed herself. "You don't look eighteen."

"And you don't look like my guardian, so I don't have to talk to you." She closed her eyes and turned away.

"I didn't mean it that way." But she had. She would never have guessed her to be more than fifteen, maybe sixteen at a stretch. The kid was near emaciated. The skin on her face stretched tight over fine bones, and since Max probably wasn't much over five-two, she appeared childlike and fragile. Behind the hospital gown, her frame was stick-like, a real testament to the old skin-and-bones cliché.

Kennie tried again. "So you have a guardian?"

"No. I'm on my own."

"Are you out of high school already?"

"You could say that."

"Where are you living?"

"Nowhere. Everywhere."

Great, Kennie thought, a homeless teenage kid who's sullen and fearful. This doesn't sound like it'll go well. "Look, I'm only interested in helping. I'm not here to judge you or tell you what to do."

The girl opened her eyes. "Why do you care?"

"Well, for one thing, that guy could have killed you, and he could've killed me, too. For another thing, you're a human being. I wouldn't have wanted what he did to you to happen to any person.

Seeing people in pain isn't fun for me."

Max relaxed back against the pillows with a sigh.

Kennie hadn't been aware Max had been so tense, but now she looked all in, as if she could just curl up and die. "Did they give you some pain meds?"

"Yeah."

"You're feeling sleepy?"

"Totally wasted."

"Before you close your eyes and rest, who should I call? Is there a parent we can contact?"

Max closed her eyes. "No. No one. My dad died a long time ago, and my mom joined him last year."

"No sisters? Brothers?"

"That *was* my brother," Max said in a weak voice.

"Who?" For a moment Kennie cast about, trying to figure out who she referred to, but then she had a frightening realization. The attacker—he was slim and fine-boned. Cleaned up, he could definitely resemble Max and be related.

"Oh, Max, I'm sorry. Are you protecting him?"

The girl's eyes popped open, and for a moment, Kennie could see the fury there. Without warning, her eyes went glassy and dull. "No protection for him. He should...be in...jail."

"Why not let the hospital call the police then?"

Max let out a sigh and was gone.

Crap, Kennie thought. She's conked out on the meds. Now what do I do? This isn't really my problem, but the kid's all alone.

Chapter Eight

KENNIE HAD NEVER wanted to be a parent. After her own dismal childhood as a periodic playmate for her teenage sister and never being quite worthy enough of attention from her mother and father, she doubted she could do a decent job raising kids. She felt ashamed to admit it, especially since such a large number of women in the lesbian community had children now. Whenever she went out running, she regularly came across women who set off her gaydar, yet had infants nestled in BabyBjorn carriers or tiny tots in backpacks or sleeping kids in strollers. As far as she could tell, the lesbians of east Portland had a regular baby boom going on.

So driving Max Wallington back to the Allen Arms twenty-four hours after her hospital admittance was not something she'd counted on volunteering for. The kid was a mess, and she needed a lot more than rest and medical care. Max was probably every bit as emotionally traumatized as she was physically wounded, although her physical state was rather frightening. The passing of one night had fully revealed the mess the beating had made of her delicate face. The skin around the stitches over her eye was a swollen, bloody-colored line. She had two black eyes, and her face was blue and purple and seemed to be swelling even as they drove.

Worst of all, she seemed vacant, hopeless. Ever since Kennie showed up in the late afternoon with sweat pants, a t-shirt, and some fresh socks, Max hadn't been able to meet her eyes. Clearly, she didn't want to come with Kennie, but where else was she to go? She'd continued to refuse to give any information about herself or her family, and because she didn't want to give a police report, the authorities hadn't been called.

Kennie looked over at her nervously. How was she supposed to take care of this kid? Obviously the girl wanted nothing to do with her.

Getting her in the SUV hadn't been so hard. Max came out in a wheelchair, and a hefty male nurse helped. Max was weepy and clearly suffering. Her arms were in double slings, her left pointer finger sported a clunky splint, and the pain meds only served to make her weak-legged. So getting her out of the SUV without jostling her broken ribs and collarbone seemed practically impossible. She was so small that the step out of the passenger seat was a long way down, and the angle was so awkward that Kennie didn't want to try to carry her out. She finally unlocked the back door to the Allen Arms, called for Simms, and headed back to the Jeep.

"Kennie?" Simms called from the doorway. "What's going on?"

"Need you to help me here."

Simms clattered down the stairs and came to a stop next to the open car door. "Whoa. What happened to you, kiddo?"

Turned in her seat, feet on the side running board, Max looked at him blankly.

Simms said, "Okay, how do you want to do this, Kennie?"

She described what she thought would work.

He said, "But once we get her inside, where're we going?"

"To the efficiency."

"Hadn't I better go in and unlock it first?"

"Good idea."

Max said, "Why are you doing this?" Her words came out slurred.

"Where else do you have to go?"

Max closed her eyes and wobbled a little, so Kennie leaned in and got an arm around her. As she stood waiting for Simms, a tan BMW convertible whizzed into the lot and came to a stop in a swirl of dust.

"Shit, just what I need," Kennie said under her breath.

Lily's lieutenant unfolded up and out of the car. As she moved across the lot, she hit the lock button on her keyless entry, which made an irritating *baloop* noise. Kennie rolled her eyes. Locked doors in an open convertible were going to stop a thief? What a moron.

The lieutenant was dressed in a lime green polo shirt, dark gray shorts, and tennis shoes. She was lean and tall and muscled, not unlike Kennie, with the main difference being her smug half-grin.

She stopped twenty feet away and frowned. "What's going on?"

"None of your business." Kennie couldn't help responding with animosity in her voice. The taller woman took two steps toward her, and Kennie straightened up. She kept a hand on Max's shoulder, but faced the cop.

The woman scowled. "You know I'm a police officer. I have every right to ask what's happening."

"Nothing illegal, and let me remind you that you're standing on my property. Move on, or I'll have you removed."

The lieutenant made a harrumphing noise and started to say something, but Simms came hurtling down the stairs and jogged toward them. "Ready," he said, with a curious glance toward

Lily's girlfriend.

Kennie resolved to ignore her. "Okay, Max, get ready. We'll be as gentle as possible." She and Simms got their arms around her and grasped hands under Max's knees. "On three, Simms..."

Max whimpered as they lifted her out, but with the addition of Simms's steady grip, they didn't jostle her too much. Carefully, they made their way to the staircase. As they reached the top of the steps, Kennie heard a car door slam and looked back to see the lieutenant had shut the Jeep door and was now hastening toward them. Kennie sped up.

"Hey, slow down," Simms said. "You're going to hurt her."

Shut up, she thought. All she wanted to do was get away from the self-satisfied cop on their tail.

Once they got Max into the built-in bed in the efficiency, Kennie hurried to close the apartment door. The cop had paused out in the lobby, a puzzled look on her face. Kennie hoped she'd go away soon, maybe fall down the stairs and be paralyzed—or worse. She knew she shouldn't think that way, but she couldn't help herself. All she felt was relief when she looked out a moment later and saw the cop taking the stairs two at a time. Her footsteps faded as Simms asked, "What happened to this kid?"

Kennie explained the events of the day before, and Simms was outraged. "Maybe we need a camera out back. What if this lunatic had beat up on one of our residents?"

"It wasn't random. I think it was a rare event, not likely to be repeated, I hope."

"How can you know that?"

"Family matter. Her brother was the attacker."

"Jesus."

From the bed, a tiny, faraway voice said, "You know I'm awake, right? I can hear you."

Simms gave her a glance and said, "I better get back to the desk. Let me know if you need anything else."

When he pulled the door open, Kennie saw the lobby was still empty. Thank God, she thought. Good riddance to Lily's moronic lover.

She untied Max's scuffed shoes and removed them. "Are you cold?" When Max nodded, she busied herself tugging the covers out from under her and arranging pillows. "Does that feel okay? Can you shift upwards and get comfortable against the pillows?"

Grimacing, Max wormed her way under the covers, all the while making small mewling noises.

Kennie smoothed the quilt over her. "I'll be right back."

She left and pulled the door nearly shut. Simms looked up from behind the desk. "Keep an eye on her, will you? I've got to run to the Jeep." Outside, she was happy to see the BMW was gone.

She was back inside quickly, carrying a paper bag filled with the tattered remnants of Max's clothes and a package with medication in it. She'd shelled out forty-eight bucks for the prescription, but she couldn't begrudge the kid.

An examination of Max's worldly possessions revealed she carried eighty-eight cents in change, half a pack of Lifesavers, a gold crucifix necklace, and a worn leatherette business card case. The case contained two one-dollar bills, a driver's license, and a bent photo of two smiling dark-haired adults with four children: a girl in braces who looked twelve or thirteen, a boy about ten, and two little girls who were much younger. The two littlest wore their light-colored hair in pixie cuts, and both were dressed in navy blue turtlenecks and red-and-blue-plaid jumpers. The mother and father held the two youngsters on their laps, and all six family members looked thin. Not just thin, but tiny, Kennie thought, like a family of elves.

Back in the efficiency, she found Max still awake. "I'll make you some soup whenever you want. You're due to take another pain pill in a little while. You shouldn't take it on an empty stomach."

"Is this your apartment?"

"You could say that. I actually spend all my time through there." She pointed to the open door that led to 1A. She rose and moved an end table nearer the bed, then poured a cup of water and brought over a box of tissues. "Can you think of anything you need?"

"Sleep. If I could just sleep for a while, then I'll get out of your way."

"I don't think that's a good idea. Remember, the doctor said someone needs to monitor you. If you feel any chest pain or shortness of breath, you have to let me know. Or if you get dizzy or start sweating. Please tell me, okay?"

She grabbed a ladder-back chair and pulled it over close to the bed. "You can stay here as long as you need to. I can't say I'm a very good nurse, but I don't mind keeping an eye on you until you're feeling well enough to go back to your regular life."

Unshed tears glistened in Max's eyes. "I don't have a regular life."

Kennie didn't know what to say. What would make Max feel better that wouldn't be offensive? With no clue, she didn't speak. She remembered after her parents died, she'd been tossed from one relative to another. First to an uncle and his third wife, then to an elderly cousin. It wasn't until she went to live with Aunt Clara that she felt she'd found a home, someplace she could be herself. In truth, Aunt Clara had been there, but not really *there*. She had provided Kennie with a room of her own, food in the cupboard, any clothes she needed, and a regular meal on the table each night, but that was about it.

When Kennie turned sixteen, Aunt Clara sent her alone to the local used car dealership to pick out a car, and she went back later to make the final arrangements on Kennie's behalf. Which was how Kennie began her lifelong love affair with Jeeps. Her first had been a used, but lovingly cared for, 1980 Jeep Renegade.

When she needed clothes or school supplies or anything else, she told her aunt or left her a note with an estimate of the amount needed. Within a day or two, she'd find a sheaf of folded-over bills on the entryway hall table beneath the glass jar full of marbles.

Aunt Clara assigned no chores, had no curfew requirement, and never pried. The few times Kennie tried to discuss anything serious — difficulties with a dreaded teacher, problems with a rude classmate — her aunt had half-listened, then responded with comments such as, "Well, dear, I'm sure you'll work it out."

As far as Kennie was concerned, she had raised herself after her parents died. Sterling and Suzanne visited occasionally, but her siblings were so much older that nobody ever found common ground, and how long could they discuss the weather?

It wasn't until she was a senior in high school that Kennie understood her aunt had never recovered from the death of her husband and that she drank herself to sleep every night. Aunt Clara had been very sneaky about it, too. The vodka was never out in the kitchen, and since she never asked Kennie to take out the garbage or recycling container, it had taken quite some time for Kennie to tumble onto that reality. They had a maid once a week to make sure the house was tidy, the gardener kept up the yard, and Aunt Clara spent most of her time in her little sitting room watching soap operas and nighttime dramas. Kennie had her own TV in her bedroom.

As she thought about her past, Kennie realized she *had* had a regular life — it just wasn't particularly normal. Max, on the other hand, might once have had a normal life with her smiling elf parents, and now she had no one. With no regular life to send her back to, Kennie was at a loss as to how to help her. The one thing she could do was provide safe haven for a while and make sure she was fed and rested. She wasn't sure why, but it felt like the right thing to do.

"I — I'm sorry," Max said.

"About what?"

"Messing up your day."

Kennie shrugged. "I didn't have much going on anyway."

The girl's face changed from dead pale to pink.

"What's the matter?" Kennie asked anxiously. "Are you all right? The bathroom's right through that door. Do you need some help in there?"

"No, no, I'm okay." She swallowed and closed her eyes. "I know you told me, but I can't remember your name."

"Kennie. Kennie McClain."

"Okay, thank you, Kennie McClain." Max let out a sigh and fell asleep.

THE NEXT COUPLE of days were busy. The Faulkners moved from their unit to the newly remodeled one, and Kennie took stock of their old apartment. She wondered if there was ever any call at local museums for pristine, circa 1960, olive-green shag carpet. Surely the rugs in 2A were antiques. She didn't even bother to pull it up herself, but hired carpet-layers to do that for her. She would have them come back later to install new industrial-strength rugs when she had the chance to finish repairs, upgrades, and painting.

The plans for the Sunday party were still underway, and occasionally she'd run into Adam Vendrick or Miss Quist or the Halliwells, and they'd flash knowing smiles at her as if they all shared an amazing secret.

When Max came out of her drug-induced stupor, she settled into a bitter mode and sat fuming every time Kennie knocked and entered the efficiency. Even when Kennie showed up with a couple hundred dollars worth of socks, underwear, t-shirts, and pants, Max didn't react positively. She said thank you, but that was the extent of it.

At first Kennie thought Max was angry at her, but after observing her for a while, she came to the conclusion that Max was upset about something she had no way to express. What that was Kennie had no way of knowing, and she couldn't pry it out of her with a shoehorn. Her every attempt to elicit information was turned away, and after a while, she left Max to watch endless game shows and reality contests on TV and didn't expect more than a cold thank-you when she provided snacks or meals.

One afternoon three days later, Max shuffled out through the foyer and onto the small stone porch that overlooked the street. A three-person glider took up nearly half the porch, leaving just enough room for the heavy-duty exterior glass door to open. Kennie liked the front porch. With the shrubbery coming up high, and all the climbing vines on trellises, it felt like a little sanctuary. Apparently Max felt the same way. She sat out there for hours.

Later, Evelyn Faulkner joined her. Next time Kennie came

down from the second floor, she spied Max sitting on the glider, her head on Evelyn's shoulder, and the older woman patting her maternally.

After that Max brightened up. She was still quiet, but she didn't emanate the rage and fury anymore.

Was a motherly presence what Max needed all this time? Some affection? Kennie felt like a failure, but she reminded herself she hardly knew the young woman. Max wouldn't let her in. Kennie had asked and asked and asked, to no avail. Max was a closed vault.

And then one minute with Evelyn, and the kid looked like she was spilling every secret she knew.

"YOU READY FOR the hijinks, Kennie?" Norm Faulkner emerged from the elevator just as Kennie came in from a run, and he stood beaming at her.

She paused, sweating, and nodded. "You bet. What's the appropriate attire for this bash?"

"Well, there's the dunk tank to navigate." She must have flinched because he laughed. "Just kidding." He lifted his hands up and out. "You can't go wrong with quasi-golf attire." He wore a white polo shirt, neon yellow pants, and the kind of cracked, white leather shoes that old duffers so often dressed in. On his head sat a jaunty-looking, newsboy-style cap in olive green. It reminded Kennie of the carpet in his old apartment.

She said, "I'll have to come up to your place and pick out some of your golf attire."

He raised a finger and shook it. "Now you know your legs are far too long to fit in my stubby little outfits. Just dress casual."

With a smile, she headed back to 1A and let herself in. The party was supposed to start in two hours. She had no idea what to expect.

After a shower, she dressed in khaki pants and a short-sleeved cotton shirt she'd just finished ironing. She was still barefoot when someone knocked on the door. Shoes in one hand, she pulled the door open.

Lily stood there, her blonde hair falling down to her shoulders in lustrous waves. She wore white linen slacks and a shiny gold and black vest unbuttoned. The white blouse underneath was open far enough to show cleavage. Her eyes were still the most captivating aspect of her face, but Kennie could hardly meet them, much less open her mouth to say anything. She felt like an idiot. Shouldn't she be mad? But she couldn't muster up that emotion. Instead, she felt unsettled.

"Could I come in for a moment?" Lily asked. "There's something we need to discuss."

As if in a fog, Kennie dropped her shoes and stepped back to allow her entrance, leaving Lily to close the door.

"Look," Lily said, leaning back against the door, "I thought I'd better tell you I'll be at the party later on today."

Kennie found her voice and choked out, "Okay."

"I don't want things to be weird between us or for you to feel uncomfortable."

"Okay." She felt her face heating up. Was that all she could say — okay?

"Every time I've seen you lately, Kennie, you've gone running the other direction. You've never given me the chance to explain...to apologize."

"That's not necessary."

"Yes, it is," Lily said, with some heat in her voice. "I started something with you that I intended to be a good thing, to be more than — than, you know, just the one night. But PJ came back the very next day. I thought I was over her, I thought I'd mourned her leaving. But obviously I hadn't, and I had to give us a chance. It was four years, Kennie." Her voice took on a pleading tone. "Four years we'd been together. I just couldn't — "

Kennie raised a hand to cut her off. "I get it. You don't need to say another word."

Lily closed her eyes, and her face took on such an expression of pain that it caught Kennie entirely by surprise. For a brief flash, an iota of time, she had the impulse to go to her, pull Lily into her arms, and comfort her.

But Lily opened her eyes and soldiered on. "You're a good person, and I in no way meant to hurt you. I need you to understand that. Under different circumstances — "

Kennie cut her off again. "Please. Say no more. I understand. I do."

Lily studied her face a moment, long enough for Kennie to blush again.

"I'll be just fine, Lily. And if you give me some time, you and I will be fine, too."

"Really?" She didn't appear particularly hopeful.

"Sure. I'm sorry I've been so touchy. It's not just you. I've had a lot of issues in my life lately. Personal stuff, stuff like, well, you know..." She trailed off awkwardly, not able to unearth anything of consequence.

"No need to go into detail." Lily plastered a smile on her lips, and Kennie suddenly couldn't look away. She remembered kissing those lips, cupping that face in hungry hands, nuzzling Lily's neck, which smelled like flowers and sunshine.

Lily's eyes widened.

A shock of longing coursed from Kennie's heart all the way to her groin, promising to overwhelm her ability to stand. For a moment she couldn't breathe.

She stepped back.

Blushing furiously, Lily fumbled behind her for the doorknob. She managed to get the door open, and when she turned back, she looked confused and nervous. "I'll see you at the party then." With that, she fled down the hall, her heels clattering on the marble.

Kennie had never been so grateful to shut a door in her life.

What the hell was that? She felt like a lunatic, her emotions swinging back and forth like a crazy person's. She bent to retrieve her shoes, then made her way to the couch and sat heavily, waiting for her rapidly beating heart to settle down.

If Lily had expected to make nicey-nice and have them go back to the way they'd communicated before Kennie's birthday, back when they had a passing acquaintance and chatted freely, before things heated up, well, she was obviously clear now that it wouldn't happen. The only comfort Kennie could find was that Lily hadn't been playing her. She *had* shown real feelings for Kennie. That was clear from her reactions today.

Kennie thought the situation would be a lot easier if Lily wasn't such a good-hearted person. If she'd just used Kennie and tossed her away when she was done with her, then a certain level of animosity would be easy to cultivate. Betrayal would ultimately lead Kennie out of the feelings of loss and into a different place of understanding.

Instead, she felt as though she were imprisoned by feelings she couldn't express to Lily, and having the strange experience of discovering that Lily reciprocated—at least in some way—made it all the more painful. How could she escape when she kept hearing a tin cup incessantly banging against the metal bars of her heart's jail cell?

THE EVENT WAS already underway when Kennie crossed the hall to the party room at four p.m. The gabbing of excited people had already reached a dull roar. The older tenants were parked on the three couches and in the various wingback chairs around the room. The rest stood around chatting.

Kennie stood in the doorway just a moment, amazed at the variety of decorations. Someone had strung gold and purple crepe along the back arches and in swoops to the corners of the room. Gaudy, shiny CONGRATULATIONS signs hung on all three walls, and bunches of dark blue and yellow balloons festooned the ceiling in the back corners of the room, clashing miserably with the purple and gold theme.

A long table toward the back was covered in an elegant white cloth. Upon it sat punch bowls on either end and a 3-tier cake in the middle (remarkably similar to the wedding cakes for which Adam Vendrick's catering partners were famous). The silverware, which appeared to be solid gold, was arrayed on the table in a perfect fan.

A disco ball dangled from the center chandelier, and anybody much over five feet tall would have to navigate carefully or get smacked in the head.

She hadn't thought Adam would come up with such a strangely jarring color scheme. The man himself separated from a knot of guys off to the side and came toward her with a look of misery on his face.

He grabbed her by the arm, pulled her out into the hall, and leaned toward her conspiratorially. "I am *appalled.* I had a lovely decorating plan, and these uncultured fools have muffed it up completely."

Kennie hid her smile. "It's the thought that counts, Adam."

"But who would ever hire my services if they thought I had anything whatsoever to do with such wretched ornamentation? I can only hope to God that no one I know shows up to see this dismal collection of trailer-trash frippery."

Kennie laughed aloud at his description. "Don't worry. The weekend guard isn't going to let anyone in who shouldn't be here."

"I should hope not." He ran a hand through his blond hair and flipped the bangs back.

The Halliwells came down the hall. Harry cradled a bottle of champagne in one arm, and his wife, Ingrid, clutched a bouquet of pink and yellow roses.

Under his breath, Adam said, "And now we've got mismatched flowers and fourth-rate champagne to add to the mess."

"Kennie," Ingrid called out. "Congratulations. These are for you."

Adam intercepted her and swept the flowers out of her hands. "I'll just go get these in a vase."

"Thanks for coming," Kennie said. "Looks like we're going to have a rollicking good time."

KENNIE KNEW THE moment Lily entered the party room. Though she stood with her back to the door, chatting with the ever-precise and ever-boring Virginia Quist, Kennie felt something change in the atmosphere, like the taut, electrical feeling that occurred sometimes before a lightning storm. Maybe she caught a whiff of Lily's perfume. Or maybe the men in the room suddenly went on point like bird dogs seeking a particularly attractive quail.

Whatever it was that alerted her, she couldn't resist inching back and to the side to scan the room. Sure enough, Lily was stepping around three chatty women to get to an arrangement of easy chairs in the middle of the room. There she greeted Lee Nguyen, who was talking with Norm Faulkner and the new guy in 5A whose name Kennie couldn't remember.

When she turned back to Virginia, the older woman's eyes were narrowed. "Lovely woman," she said, "but so noisy in the night. Have you figured out a solution to the creaking noises? It's the only detraction from the complete comfort of my apartment."

Kennie felt a tug on her arm and was thankful for the interruption. Evelyn Faulkner, both arms leaning on her walker, stood grinning behind Max.

The girl looked quite different in a pair of brand-new black jeans and a white button-up, long-sleeved shirt. She'd gelled her short hair back, and for once, she looked relaxed—perhaps even happy. Her face was still a mess and one arm was in a sling, but the bruises had faded away. Since the stitches had come out, the cuts over her eye and on her lip weren't quite as noticeable.

"Hey, Kennie," Max said. "Evelyn invited me."

"Excuse me, Miss Quist," Kennie said, relieved to get away from her. She ushered Max to the side, and Evelyn followed. "Technically you live here, Max, so it's fine that you came to the tenant party. I should have thought to invite you, but it totally slipped my mind."

"That's what I told her you'd say. See," Evelyn said to Max, "you belong here."

A clinking noise rose over the din of excited voices. Kennie looked to the front of the room. Adam held a glass high to which he was gently applying a spoon. "Attention, ladies and gentlemen. Thank you for coming to the first-ever tenant party at the Allen Arms. Kennie come on up front. Come on—"

A polite round of applause interrupted him, and Kennie made her way around the crowded room to stand next to him in front of the cake.

He said, "Today we want to honor our new owner and thank her for all the work she's done to keep the place up. Kennie, the building hasn't been so lovingly cared for in the ten years I've lived here."

Kennie half-listened to the accolades Adam heaped upon her, but her gaze went to the wingback chair near where Lily stood. Out of her peripheral vision she could watch Lily — or at least make out her shapely form. She went to a place of peace. For a moment, she had the feeling that everything would be all right. Then Lily and the others were clapping, and she snapped out of her reverie. As she started to look away, a tall black-haired woman sidled up to Lily.

All the good humor Kennie was feeling drained away. So much for the guard keeping the riff-raff out, she thought. The woman Lily had called PJ smiled down at Lily, then turned her attention to the front of the room. She met Kennie's gaze, and once again, she wore that smug expression, as if she'd won every round of Texas Hold 'Em and was enjoying Kennie's bankrupt status.

"...and as a token of our appreciation..." Adam said. He stepped around the table and picked up a rectangular object wrapped in brown paper. The room erupted in applause. "From all of us to you, Kennie. And be very careful. This is quite fragile." Adam set the gift on the arms of a chair, kept a hand on the upper corner, and motioned for her to open it.

The whole room fell silent, everyone waiting with expectation. With slightly shaky hands, Kennie tore away the paper to expose a painting — a real painting on canvas, not a print. The scent of oil paint wafted up, reminding Kennie of the smell in Lily's ballroom.

The canvas itself was perhaps thirty inches tall and fifty inches wide. Framed in mottled gold with a rope pattern all around, it was double matted, one mat a deep, rich purple and the other an oatmeal color. The brush strokes were thick and textured. Kennie moved back to let others see and to allow the colors to blend in her own vision.

In the foreground, in shadows, a woman stood, facing away from the viewer. Her short hair was a deep brown, her shoulders broad and hips slightly flared. One arm was up, and the hand shaded her eyes from all the brightness reflecting from the rest of the scene. Kennie might have thought the figure to be Lily's lieutenant, but epaulets on light-gray uniformed shoulders convinced her the artist had drawn Kennie.

In the background sat a building, very clearly the Allen Arms, radiant with light from every window and rendered so that Kennie felt she could reach out and touch the brick, stone, awnings, porch, dormers, and chimneys. Clouds overhead seemed to be dissipating, and a rainbow forming in the sky suggested that a storm had just passed. A tree that didn't actually exist in front of the real building was filled with birds and squirrels, and an old-fashioned rope swing with a wood seat hung from a low branch. A garden, replacing the real Allen Arms's lawn, was filled with bountiful flowers in a riot of rainbow colors, and every petal seemed to dance in the breeze.

Instead of a busy public street, a path meandered through tall grass between the woman and the building. There was no reason Kennie should feel anything ominous about the composition of the painting, but still, she had the feeling that the figure was debating whether to take that path. She half expected her to suddenly turn and run from the painting.

Someone in the room whistled, and someone else said, "You outdid yourself, Lily."

The truth of the painting's provenance smacked Kennie upside the head like the proverbial two-by-four. Who else could have painted this? She felt like an idiot for not immediately putting that together.

Norm Faulkner rose from a nearby chair and pointed at the painting. "This is great, Lily. Amazing. Simply amazing. Kennie, it would look wonderful hanging next to the elevator by the staircase. Don't you think so?"

All Kennie could do was nod. She cast a glance over her shoulder at Lily, but it wasn't her eye she caught. Her gaze halted at the lieutenant's face, which was nearly scarlet.

Uh-oh, Kennie thought. Trouble in paradise. Little Miss PJ must not have known about Lily's art project. Laughter bubbled up, and her reaction served only to enrage PJ, who leaned down and said something sharp in Lily's ear. Kennie could tell it was less than pleasant because Lily frowned and moved away from PJ like the other woman was kryptonite.

Kennie used her own amusement to energize her. The tenants were all talking at once, everyone trying to get a closer look at the artwork. She went behind the table, grabbed a bottle of champagne, and called for a toast.

During the time it took to distribute plastic cups and pour a bit of bubbly for everyone, she watched Lily and PJ out of the corner of her eye and was thrilled to see that some sort of spat was in full swing. Lily kept trying to shut it down, but PJ wasn't letting it go.

"I want to make a toast to all of you," Kennie called out. "Thank you for your help and your support and for being good-natured about repairs and remodeling. I've never owned a building before, but I don't think I could ask for a better group of tenants. Cheers to you all."

She took a big swig of the champagne, and if it was fourth-rate, she didn't mind it. A series of kind remarks were made by various tenants, and she raised her glass and sipped more champagne after each. When the gaiety died down, she finished off the drink and moved toward the punch bowl, which she hoped was spiked with something seriously alcoholic. "Max!"

The girl wore a guilty expression on her face.

"Yeah, you know what I'm going to say." She grinned and shook a forefinger in the air. "No more drinks for you what with all the pain meds."

Max raised her cup. "Bottoms up with this one, since it's my last." She gulped it down, then set it on a side table.

A horde of people surrounded Kennie then, everyone talking excitedly. Somewhere along the way the cake got cut, and somebody handed her a piece which took forever to eat because of all the people talking to her nonstop. It turned out to be spicy with cinnamon and yummy, and she hoped there'd be a lot left so she could take a couple pieces back to her apartment for later.

After what seemed like hours, the party started to wind down, but when Kennie looked at her watch, she was shocked to see it was only a quarter after five. Not enough time had passed to scare the lieutenant away, though. She stood glowering near the door, checking her watch periodically and staring at Lily, who was chatting with the Halliwells.

Max sauntered over and stopped next to Kennie. "Good cake," she said nonchalantly.

Kennie nodded. "I agree. Looks like we'll have some leftovers."

"Can I ask you something private?"

"Sure." Kennie leaned in so Max could speak quietly.

"Who's the psycho by the door? She doesn't live here."

Kennie glanced up, saw PJ staring daggers their way, and laughed. "No, she doesn't. You can bet I didn't invite her."

"How'd she get in then?"

"With someone else who does belong here."

"She doesn't like you at all, does she?"

"Nope. And the feeling is mutual."

Max shifted the sling she wore and stepped back.

Adam called to Kennie from over at the serving table and asked if she wanted to take the cake. Kennie grinned and nodded enthusiastically. She was unprepared for a hand to clamp down on her shoulder. Whirling, she found PJ in her face, one paw squeezing the muscle that ran from her neck down to her shoulder. She also had hold of Max, and the girl looked like she was going to faint from pain.

"Get your hands off her," Kennie said. "And you can let loose of me, too."

"Surely, you know I'm a cop."

Kennie twisted out of her clutches. "Let go of her. You have no right."

"Sure I do. I just watched you serve alcohol to a minor."

Face flushing, Max said, "I'm not a minor."

"Yeah, right," PJ said. "What are you — twelve?"

Hands balled in fists, Max said, "Eighteen."

"Sure you are."

Max's face was very red. "I am eighteen. I have ID."

"Doesn't matter. As I said, you're not the legal age to drink. I can arrest you right now."

Their little triangle was expanded by the addition of another person. The new tenant from 4D said, "Folks, I couldn't help but overhear your discussion. My name is Pete Ackerman, and since I'm a lawyer, I thought I'd weigh in on your dispute."

Kennie smiled at him gratefully. He was new enough in the building that she hadn't even remembered his last name, but she wouldn't ever forget him now.

Pete said, "The legal age to purchase and consume alcohol is 21. However, a parent or legal guardian may provide alcohol to minors for whom they are responsible if they are in a private residence."

"This isn't her kid," PJ said. "More like her boi toy."

Kennie said, "How dare you. You are so out of line — "

Pete interrupted to calmly ask if Kennie was Max's guardian.

Loudly, Max said, "Yes. Yes, she is."

Kennie whipped around and gave her a surprised look.

Max shrugged. "Well, you are."

"Oh," PJ said, "guardian – is *that* what they call it nowadays?"

"Get out," Kennie said, hot fury in her voice. "Get out and don't return to my premises or I'll call the police and lodge a formal complaint."

PJ laughed. "Uh-huh. You just go ahead and do that and see where it gets you. Hmmm...let's see. Oh, yeah, that's right — I'm the one who processes citizen complaints." She laughed again, but Kennie thought it sounded forced.

Pete took a deep breath and raised his chin. He didn't look like a particularly brave man, but what came out of his mouth next endeared him to Kennie forever. "I daresay that a citizen complaint filed by a practicing and decorated member of the bar along with a commercial property owner and a young woman such as this one here typically will find credence, especially if it were hand-delivered to your commander. I suggest you meet Ms. McClain's demands and remove yourself from the building before you find yourself in a lot more trouble than you can massage away by conspiring with your cronies."

The lieutenant turned on her heel and stomped off, beckoning Lily to follow her to the door, but Lily shook her head and indicated she wasn't done speaking to the Faulkners. PJ steamed out the door like an out-of-control locomotive.

Kennie had been holding her breath, and apparently so had Max and Pete, because they all three released heavy sighs at the same time, then broke into nervous laughter.

"Jesus, Kennie," Max said, "what'd you ever do to her?"

She glanced at Pete. She didn't know him at all, but she spoke the truth anyway. "We went after the same girl, and she's still sore about it."

"Because you won the gal?" Pete asked.

"On the contrary. She did."

He shook his head. "Still insecure, I suppose." He pulled out his wallet and extracted two business cards. "If either of you find you need an attorney for any reason, let me know. I'm not cheap, but I'm good. I specialize in criminal law, but I also take on a number of family-law matters, and my two partners cover many aspects of civil and personal law. The only thing we don't focus on is business-related matters, but I can refer you to excellent representation for that should you ever need it."

"Thank you, Pete," Kennie said. "I can't tell you how much I appreciate you intervening. That was going to get ugly real quick."

For the next few minutes, a flurry of departures occurred. Some of the people shook Kennie's hand, others hugged her. Evelyn hugged Max, too, and the kid followed her new friend out the door, waiting patiently for Evelyn's every slow step with the walker.

While Adam and the Halliwells busied themselves with cleanup, the last guest finally came over.

"There," Lily said, "that wasn't so bad, was it." She said it as a statement, not a question.

"If you mean regarding you, then of course it wasn't bad at all. However, you may have some real issues tonight with your girlfriend."

Lily frowned. "What do you mean?"

"I guess you'll see."

"She did leave in a huff. I wondered about that."

"Let's just say she's not welcome anywhere near me, Lily. Keep her reined in."

Lily's mouth dropped open, as if she had no clue what Kennie was referring to. The expression on her face was so surprised that Kennie concluded Lily didn't have any idea about the inappropriate challenges and subtle hazing her lover had engaged in ever since the morning after Kennie's birthday.

Lily recovered enough to change the subject. "Did you like the painting at all?" she asked shyly.

"Are you kidding? It's the most beautiful work of art I've ever owned. If the tenants weren't all hot to trot to have it out in the lobby, I'd haul it off and hang it in my apartment. Maybe worship before it."

Lily gave her a perplexed look. "I'm glad you like it."

"When did you paint it?"

"I've been working on it for" – her face went red, but she forged on – "for a long while. I just finished it the day before yesterday. In fact, the paint isn't dry through and through. That's why you're going to have to be very careful with it, and you shouldn't hang it right away."

"Really? Why not? It looks dry."

"Maybe on the outside, but not under the surface. Oils don't dry by evaporation like latex paints do."

"How the heck do they dry then?"

"It's a kind of oxidation reaction. I guess the chemical equivalent would be a slow, flameless combustion. There's ionization and the creation of a network of polymers." She paused as if gathering her thoughts to launch into lecture mode, then thought the better of it. "It's complicated. And boring."

"Okay. So should I lay it flat or against a wall or what?"

"Put it somewhere safe and dry—perhaps on its back on a table. I'll let you know in a couple of weeks when it's ready for unveiling. Maybe we can have cake and punch in the lobby again, and PJ can bring her winsome personality for all to enjoy."

Her eyes twinkled, and Kennie couldn't help but smile back. "I think we can just settle for a quick installation and call it good."

Lily grasped Kennie's forearm for a brief moment, then let go. "I'll go smooth things over. PJ can be a hothead, but she's really not a bad person. She's a terrific police officer and has been decorated numerous times for bravery."

Kennie wanted to respond by saying "if you say so," but she held her tongue. The touch to her arm had made her weak in the knees. She had no desire to reveal how close she was to her new painting's slow, flameless combustion.

Lily bid farewell, and Kennie watched her cross the room, feeling a depth of want that shook her so much she had to turn away lest Adam or the Halliwells notice. But Kennie knew exactly when Lily left the room. It was as if a light went out, leaving her in a much sadder, darker place.

Chapter Nine

BELLS WENT OFF and loud rapping penetrated Kennie's consciousness. She awoke with a start. As she propelled herself out of bed, she saw her bedside clock showed 4:54.

"What the hell?" she muttered.

The doorbell rang, and the rapping at her apartment door continued.

"Just a minute! Hang on."

She scrambled around the room, looking for a shirt and shorts to put on over her regular nightwear, which consisted only of a pair of sleep shorts.

In the front hall, she looked through the peephole and frowned when she saw cops. Who was in trouble now?

She opened the door. "Are my tenants all right? What's going on?"

"The tenants are fine."

"Then what's the problem, officers?"

"We have a report of child endangerment. May we come in?"

"What? What are you talking about? There're no children here."

Both cops were young, one not quite her height and wiry, the other much taller and more heavily muscled. The big cop said, "We'll be the judge of that." He stepped forward.

"Wait a minute. You can't just come barging into my place without a search warrant."

One hand on his holster, he disregarded her comments and pushed past. The other officer said, "Please, ma'am, don't make this any worse than it already is. Please just wait here with me while my partner does his job."

Fuming, she stood inside the doorway, arms crossed. She felt so confused. At first, all she could think was that a mistake had been made and they had the wrong address. But then the truth dawned on her. Only twelve hours earlier she'd had the run-in with Lily's lieutenant. Could this be some sort of retaliation? Wait, wait, she told herself. Don't get worked up now. These cops aren't responsible. I'll kick her ass later.

The big officer returned. "All clear. Nobody here." He stood on one side of her, and the officer in the doorway the other, so she backed up to the entryway wall in order to see both of them.

"Are you Kendra McClain?"

"Yes."

"And you've resided here for how long?"

"Ever since I bought the building."

"You own the building?"

"That's what I just said. I mean this with all due respect, officers, but get out of my house."

The big cop ignored her and took a pen and small notebook from his breast pocket. "Who lives here with you?"

"I live alone."

"Who are your recent visitors?"

"I've had no recent visitors."

"We received a viable report that a youngster lived here with you, someone possibly being abused."

"I'm going to kill her," she said under her breath.

"Pardon me, ma'am," he asked. "What was that?"

"Nothing. Am I under arrest?"

"No, not at this time."

"Then get out," she said with more venom than she intended.

The officer put away his notebook and pen. With a last suspicious look, he sauntered toward his partner. Over his shoulder he said, "Thank you for your time, ma'am."

She shut the door quietly, then staggered over to the couch, her heart beating hard. That bitch! I can't believe she did that. She sat in a state of disbelief for a couple of minutes until she felt calmer, then rose and found shoes and socks. After applying a hairbrush to her unruly locks, she found her keys and peered out the back door to the parking lot. Sure enough, she saw a tan BMW convertible with the top up.

Fueled with indignation, she went up the elevator to the penthouse and rang the doorbell. After a moment, the door swung open, and Lily stood there, palette in hand, and dressed in paint clothes.

She frowned. "Kennie, uh, hello."

Kennie opened her mouth to speak just as the lieutenant, clad in full dress uniform, stepped around the corner from the kitchen hallway, a coffee mug in hand. Her self-satisfied, superior expression infuriated Kennie.

"You...you..." She stopped herself because Lily stepped back, looking alarmed.

"What's going on here?" Lily asked.

"Ask your...your...ask her!" She pointed at PJ as a wave of shame and anger rolled over her. She couldn't even find cogent words to explain her level of rage or her feelings of embarrassment about the cops showing up at her door to pry into her private domain.

PJ came up behind Lily and put a proprietary hand on her shoulder. "You're out of control. I think you'd better back off."

Kennie felt like she could spit nails, and she wished she had the ability to do so. "You're a nasty-minded ass. What's your last name?"

"None of your business."

"Oh, yeah, it's my business." She crowded forward, through the door, and leaned around Lily.

"Kennie!" Lily gasped. "What's wrong with you?"

The lieutenant back-pedaled, but not before Kennie got close enough to read the gold nameplate on her breast pocket. JARRELL. Kennie lurched back, outside the doorway, and debated what to say. Suddenly PJ wasn't looking quite so smug. Kennie squinted at PJ, taking in the proud face and piercing eyes. For the first time, it occurred to her that PJ was probably only about thirty. Her brown hair was styled in a professional-looking bob, and her skin was healthy and lightly tanned. With her height and broad shoulders, Kennie thought she was a very handsome woman. Too bad she was such an asshole.

Kennie took a deep breath and met Lily's gaze. Even with her hair in disarray and a smudge of red paint on her cheek, Lily was mesmerizing. Kennie let out a huff and forced herself to focus. "Lily, I apologize for barging in so early. I'm glad to see I didn't wake you, though I'm sorry to interrupt your painting."

"What in the world is going on?"

"Your lover there decided it'd be funny to sic her cop friends on me, apparently for statutory rape."

"What?" Lily looked up at PJ. As she turned slightly, the hand holding the palette came toward Kennie and she saw half a dozen swirls of various shades of reds, pinks, and whites. Valentine's Day flashed into Kennie's head.

"PJ? What have you done?" Lily said ominously.

The lieutenant removed her hand from Lily's shoulder and stood ramrod straight. "You can't blame me for doing my job." With a sneer, she went on. "She's robbing the cradle. That kid she's with now can't be more than fourteen or fifteen."

Lily's mouth dropped open as she looked back at Kennie. "You're sleeping with Max?"

"No, I am not," Kennie ground out through gritted teeth. "I'm old enough to be her goddamn mother. I have never ever had any inappropriate contact with her. And by the way, she's eighteen. I've seen her ID, and PJ was very clearly informed of that by an attorney yesterday at the party." She knew she was stretching the truth, but Max was eighteen.

Lily glanced back at PJ who shrugged and said, "How was I to know? I've got to do my job, and it seemed to me there was some child endangerment there."

"So you decided to report Kennie to the department? Without determining the circumstances first? Without even touching base with me?"

"Well, I—I..."

Lily put a hand on the middle of PJ's chest and shoved her gently, then whirled long enough to say goodbye to Kennie as she slammed the door shut.

Kennie stood in stunned silence for a moment, then leaned closer to the door. She couldn't quite make out the words, but she heard their voices arguing. The higher voice escalated, and she thought the words were "How could you!" The other voice, slightly lower, seemed to be making noises of appeasement, but they must have moved into a different area of the apartment because the sounds gradually faded.

Back on the elevator, she debated her next action. Should she call the police department—or visit—and swear out a formal complaint? And what should she tell Max, if anything at all? She thought it possible Max was gay, but that was her business to sort out on her own, in her own time. Still, it wouldn't be pleasant or fair if she got blindsided with all of this. It wasn't Max's problem. The whole mess was hers and hers alone.

From their brief discussion with Pete Ackerman at the party, she thought Max understood that she was gay, but just in case, she needed to make sure it was clear, and it seemed like she ought to do it pretty damn soon.

KENNIE SAT AT the desk in her second bedroom, a room she used primarily as an office. Bills covered the desk surface, and she struggled to keep her focus on paying them. She was still fuming every time she thought of the stunt PJ had pulled. She wished she could key her car or pop her tires—but that would be stooping to PJ's despicable, childish level and she couldn't allow herself to go there.

She let out a sigh and stretched. Her neck and shoulders were stiff and sore from moving what seemed like an unending bunch of window air-conditioning units from basement storage to various apartments, and she wasn't done. The building didn't have central AC, and now that the summer weather was heating up, many of the tenants requested the window units.

She heard a faint knocking, rose, and unlocked the door that connected 1A and 1B, as the efficiency apartment was now labeled. Max stood on the other side barefoot, in shorts and t-shirt, looking overheated.

"I'm roasting."

"Join the club. Everyone in the building is."

"I saw you wheeling around air conditioners."

"Don't worry, I'll get you one."

"Actually, I had an idea. Why don't you let me help you?"

"Help me what?"

"With the air conditioners."

Kennie repressed a smile. Max couldn't possibly weigh much over a hundred pounds, though she seemed to have filled out a little in the short time she'd been at the Allen Arms. The splint on her finger was gone, and her face was healing nicely. The broken ribs and collarbone didn't seem to be paining her as they first had, and she no longer appeared so skeletal. Still, she wasn't ready to be lifting anything. "Not sure what you can do. The units are almost too damn heavy for me to carry."

Max frowned, looking uncertain. "There must be something I can do. It's time I earned my way and paid you back somehow. I can't stay here forever. I guess I better get a job. I just thought maybe there was some way I could help. You know, until I get some money and pay you."

"Come in." Kennie swung the door wide and ushered Max into the living room

Max slowed to look around. The room was furnished with comfortable easy chairs and a large couch in front of a mammoth-sized television.

"Holy shit, Kennie. That's the hugest TV I've ever seen."

"Have a seat."

Max slipped out of her tennis shoes and angled herself into the corner of the couch with her stocking feet underneath. "I'm surprised I've never heard your TV."

"Just because the screen is big doesn't mean I have to have it blasting." Kennie pointed to free-standing speakers on various tables and shelves. "I've got surround-sound, but it doesn't have to be up loud to sound good."

"When I grow up I want to be just like you."

Max grinned, and Kennie was struck by how much calmer and more settled she seemed. But what did she know about her? And what was she going to do with her?

"Let's talk about what you want to do next."

Max's expression went serious. "Okay."

"So...what do you want to do with yourself?"

With a smile, Max said, "I don't even begin to know."

"Before your life got turned upside down, what did you want to do? Go to college? Work in a particular industry?"

Max shrugged, then winced. She moved her shoulder gingerly.

"You sure you didn't ditch the sling too soon?"

"No, it's okay."

"All right then. Tell me about you. Just start anywhere."

Max took a deep breath. "My dad died when I was ten. He was drunk and got in a head-on collision. Killed a bunch of people in other cars and my sister, too."

"Your sister was in the car with him?"

"He picked Yvonne up kind of late at night after an away basketball game. She was in the front seat of the car. They both died later at the hospital."

"That must have been awful."

"Yeah, well, nothing to do about it now."

Kennie noticed how tense Max had gotten. She thought she'd be tense, too, if she had to share the events of her earlier life with someone who'd been a stranger until so recently. "You want a Coke?"

Max nodded.

From the kitchen, Kennie called out, "How many kids originally in your family?"

"Four."

She came back with two tall glasses and handed one to Max, put hers on the coffee table, then settled in at the other end of the couch. "Who's the oldest in the family?"

"It went Yvonne, Derek, me, and Olivia."

"So Olivia's still a minor. Where is she?"

Max's eyes filled with tears. She struggled to fight them back. "I don't know. When my mom died last Thanksgiving, Social Services came in and took her."

"There wasn't any family to help?"

"No."

"What about you? You weren't eighteen yet. Why didn't you go with your sister?"

"I ran away. Before my mom died. I mean, when she was going to die. I couldn't deal."

She looked so ashamed, so crestfallen, Kennie wanted to give her a hug, but the way Max was wedged into the corner of the sofa, she could tell it wouldn't be welcome. "What did your mom die of?"

"Cancer in her uterus."

"Jesus." Kennie rose and walked to the window. The parallels in the kid's life were too similar, too striking. She felt sick to her stomach. With her back to the couch, she said, "So where is your sister?"

"I don't know. Derek was on drugs, so they couldn't trust him, and he's such an asshole. If he got an address, he never said. I don't know where Olivia ended up."

"Have you considered going down to Social Services and finding out?"

"I did. I went and applied for finances — what's it called?"

"Some sort of aid?"

"Yeah. But the money people wouldn't give out the info, and the social workers wouldn't give me the time of day 'cause I wasn't old enough. I went a week before my birthday to get the application going and make sure the money started when I turned 18. Derek told me to do that."

Kennie paced by the window. "So Derek was smart enough to tell you about how the welfare system works, but not smart enough to stay off drugs or to keep track of his own flesh and blood."

"Yup."

"Then what?"

"I went to see the worker to get the card they give for groceries and money, but there was some sort of mix-up. They told me to come back the next day."

"And did you?"

"No. That was the day Derek beat the shit out of me."

The light went on. What had her brother been saying? Something about Max stealing from him and that she owed him. "Derek beat you up because you didn't give him the funds from the county?"

"Yeah, and he wanted my mom's wedding rings to sell. I told him I didn't know where they were. He wouldn't believe me about that or that I hadn't gotten any money yet. He went crazy."

"No shit, he was crazy. Every time I go outside I worry he's coming back." Kennie hadn't wanted to admit that, but it was true. She had the security guards on alert and had reconsidered putting a camera out in the back lot to discourage trespassing, theft, and any other misdeeds. She was still debating.

"He *will* come back."

Kennie paused, then sat on the couch. "What do you mean?"

"My brother may be a failure in almost every way, but when it comes to money he thinks he's owed, he won't fail to collect. If he had my ID, I bet he would've sent someone to the aid office to get the money."

"So his plan was to steal your benefits?"

"No, I was just supposed to give 'em to him."

"For room and board, or what?"

"He wasn't paying for our house. It was being repo'd. He just figured he had a right to the money. Don't ask me why. He's always been like that. Selfish. Everything's all about him."

"Where is the house?" Max reeled off an address over in southeast. "Has it been repossessed now?"

Max shrugged. "I don't know."

"Is there anything in it you want or need?"

"Probably not."

Max looked so wistful then that Kennie wanted to press her, but she forced herself to sit still, to wait. Max sucked down half the glass of Coke, and another few moments passed before she finally turned to face Kennie. "It's the pictures I want and some of the old mem...mem...what do you call them?"

"Mementos? Memorabilia?"

"Yeah. That. Mostly the photos though. Derek ripped off everything else that could be sold. The furniture. A bunch of the kitchen stuff. My dad's old tools. But nobody wants our old picture albums. Nobody 'cept me."

"Do you have a key to the house?"

"Not on me, but I hid one on the porch and another in the yard. I can get in, even if I have to break a window. I could be in and out of there real fast. Get the photos, some of my special things, maybe my clothes, and I'm gone."

"So you have some short-term goals—get your stuff, and find Olivia. What about long-term goals?"

"I've never been able to think that far ahead, not since Mom died last year. I didn't even finish my last year of high school."

"If you had the chance to go back to finish your senior year, would you?"

"But I'm eighteen. That'd be embarrassing."

"You're in a different school district here, kid. Nobody would have to know. And besides—no offense—but you're small enough to pass for younger than eighteen. I bet not a single person would even notice your age. I don't know how many credits you still need, but you might not have to go the full year. Maybe you just show up for the first term, get the classes you need, and be done with it."

"Maybe. But I didn't really go to school at all as soon as my mom got sick. I'd probably get stuck doing the whole year."

"You have the summer to make that decision. In the meantime, we can work on your two short-term goals, and you can also start doing some in-kind labor for me."

"Like a job?"

"Sort of. But first, there's something you need to know."

Max gazed at her expectantly, looking for all the world as though she trusted Kennie completely.

"You do understand I'm a lesbian, right?"

"No duh."

"So you figured that out."

"Soon as I saw you acting weird around the lady from the penthouse, I was totally clued in."

"What do you mean, acting weird?"

"Hey, don't get all freaked out. I don't have to be a genius to see that you and that cop are fighting over her."

Kennie laughed ruefully, even though Max's blunt assessment bothered her. Was she so obvious? First Evelyn Faulkner, now Max, had noticed. Was everyone in the building paying attention? She sure as hell hoped not. "I just wanted you to know under no uncertain terms that I'm gay, Max, so there are no surprises. You have the right to know who you're hanging around."

Max's face scrunched up in concentration. "You're not asking if I am, are you?"

"No."

"Good, 'cause I really don't know, and I don't want to think about it."

"That's totally your prerogative. One of these days, you'll meet some guy or girl and you'll figure it out. In the meantime, my intentions toward you are honorable. You don't have anything to fear from me."

Max stared at her as if she'd grown a third head. "I never thought I had anything to be afraid of."

"Good. Because you don't. Now let's get back to business. If you think you can work with me, then I suggest we start doing some projects around here."

"To make up for all the money you've spent on me and the cost of the apartment I'm in?" When Kennie nodded, Max asked, "How much would the efficiency apartment cost to rent?"

Kennie named the amount, and Max's mouth fell open in amazement. "Shit, I could never afford that." As if in shock she said, "The bigger apartments here must cost a fortune."

"Leasing an apartment isn't cheap, and the Allen Arms units are larger and more swanky and upscale than a typical apartment. You could get a place for considerably less in other parts of the city. Hey, take the defeated look off your face. Things will work out, Max. I'm not prepared to hire you as an employee, not yet anyway, but you can work with me around the building, and I'll be able to see if you can develop the skills needed. You'll have a place to stay for a while. I promise."

"You're kidding!" Max came out of the corner of the couch and put one foot on the floor while the other remained tucked under her. Her energy level had gone from zero to sixty in three seconds.

"Nope, not kidding. Right now, most of the apartments need new air conditioners installed. Actually, the penthouse gets two, and so does 6B."

"What about 6A?"

"Miss Quist doesn't let anyone in her place. She's always said she didn't need or want one."

"Bizarre. Whatever. I'm happy to help however you want me to."

"If you feel up to starting today, I could really use your help with the air conditioners. I suspect they're too heavy for you to lift, but there's a whole raft of them downstairs that need to be uncrated, wiped down, and then tested to make sure they work. That part's been taking me forever. I'm not dragging a unit all the way up and installing it, only to find out it's defective. If you prep them, I can take them one at a time on the rolling cart up to the various apartments, and that should speed things up. After that, I've got some gym equipment to put together. I want to turn that one open area in the basement into a workout center."

"Cool. I'll do it. I'll work real hard, too. I won't let you down."

"I know you won't. Go put on some old jeans. It's dirty down in the basement where the AC units are stored, and I don't want you to get cut on any sharp surfaces anywhere."

Max shot up off the couch and nearly ran to the connecting door. Before she got there, she skidded to a stop, came back, and pointed at her glass. "Can I take the Coke with me?"

"Sure."

And she was gone like the character in the Road Runner cartoons.

Now that was more like it, Kennie thought. A kid Max's age ought to be a lot more interested in drinking soda pop, buying clothes, hanging out with friends, and figuring out what kind of phone and texting plan she wanted. Instead, Max possessed nothing and didn't have much hope for the future. It wasn't supposed to be that way for kids. Out of the blue, Kennie realized it was now important to her to see that Max was taken care of. She had to shake her head. Maybe her maternal instinct had finally surfaced after all these years.

Chapter Ten

AS THE DAYS rolled by, Kennie did all she could to remove herself from the emptiness of her life by working sunup to sundown on projects in the Allen Arms. As she painstakingly scraped up crappy old linoleum from the bathroom of one of the vacant fourth-floor apartments, her anger bubbled to the surface. Why had she let herself get sucked in by Lily? Why hadn't she been more careful? Lily had given her hope. Now she realized she actually wanted a companion, someone to love her and to spend time with, and the person she was most attracted to in the whole world wasn't available.

If only they'd never made love. If only they'd never had dinner. If only she'd never flirted.

She could "If only" herself to death, and it wouldn't help. Instead of feeling better, she just recognized her loneliness at an even deeper level.

She stabbed at the linoleum with her flat shovel, then erupted in a flurry of furious effort.

Shit.

Chips came off instead of the sections that should be peeling away with ease. None of the other bathroom floors had been this difficult to remove. She wondered who had laid the tiles. She bet a tenant had done it on the sly, somebody who didn't know what the hell they were doing. They had to have used gallons of adhesive, especially along the walls.

Despite wearing gloves, her hands were starting to chafe. She slid down against the wall, the shovel handle against her thigh, and peeled off the gloves. Her palms were red and felt bruised. Maybe this was it for the day.

Once she'd sat in place for a few minutes, she was overcome with the most amazing wave of exhaustion. Abruptly, she heard Janeen's voice rattling around inside her head.

Work, work, work... It didn't "work" for me, Buttercup. Find a new gig to make your life have meaning.

Kennie's eyes filled with tears. Janeen's voice—she still heard her inside her head at times. How weird was that? That was one thing she didn't tell anyone. She didn't want people to think she was crazy. But when Janeen died, where else did her essence have to go? Kennie felt like she was still carrying a little bit of it around. Or maybe all of it.

All that maniacal energy...Janeen had focused it on her work, and it wasn't until the end that she finally dropped everything to attend to her health. But it was too late. Too damn late.

Buttercup. She had almost forgotten how Janeen used to call her Buttercup, after the girl in the movie, *The Princess Bride*. It had nothing to do with how Kennie looked and everything to do with early in their dating when Janeen had once ordered Kennie to do something. With mock reverence, Kennie replied with the line, "As you wish," as Princess Buttercup had so often said to her lover, Wesley. Little did Kennie know that Janeen would never forget that. She often called her Buttercup in public just to jerk her chain. And in bed to tease her.

The tears came in earnest now, and Kennie didn't bother to wipe them away. They ran like acid down her face, reminding her of the bitter weeks after Janeen's funeral when every moment of every day felt like she'd been dipped in something corrosive. The pain wasn't merely psychological. Her whole body hurt as though she'd been boiled and flayed alive. Every nerve ending zinged a message of anguish to an already overloaded system.

Oh, God. She thought she'd got past this ache, that she'd used every bit of her skill and strength to fold up that circus tent full of crazies and trapeze terrors until it was small and boxed up, put away on a shelf deep inside her, never to be opened again. But no, every so often the insane ringmaster escaped and reminded her of all she'd had with Janeen. The listening ear. The laughter. The lightning strike fights followed by lots of soul-soothing, make-up sex. The amazing dinner parties they threw. Reading to one another: Anne Tyler novels and erotic short stories and Lee Lynch's "Amazon Trails." The cuddling in bed on cold Sundays with flavored coffee and lots of homemade cookies.

She hadn't drunk coffee very often since Janeen died. It went down like acid, and the last thing she needed was the bitter ache she felt on the outside transmitted inside, too.

Why did this have to hurt so bad? She felt like a big whiner, and yet, there was nothing she could do about it. Her grief had a will of its own, like an insistent storm. No amount of running allowed her to escape the thunder and rain.

But like all storms, eventually her internal tempest passed and left her even more exhausted. She chucked aside the shovel and rose, turned off the lights in the apartment, and went to the elevator. The doors opened, and she stumbled in, grateful she didn't have to walk down to the first floor. Instead of the downward motion she expected, though, the elevator went up.

No. Oh, no. She hastened to wipe her face. Oh, shit. Double shit. She backed into the corner of the elevator and squeezed her eyes shut.

The elevator dinged and opened, and she kept her eyes closed, postponing the moment when PJ would mock her. She heard an intake of breath, then felt a hand on her arm.

"What's the matter?" Lily asked.

Kennie peeked through half-closed eyelids and shook her head. No way in hell would she allow herself to spill her guts, not here, not now, not to Lily. But as if she were a bit of metal attracted to a very powerful magnet, she allowed Lily to lead her out of the elevator and over to the fainting couch at which point she balked. "I'm not going to faint."

"I know that, you idiot. Just sit down for a few moments."

Kennie lowered herself to the couch. With elbows on her knees, she took her head into her hands and looked down at the ground. The hand Lily put on her shoulder felt comforting.

Lily said, "Please tell me there's nothing wrong with your health."

Kennie finally looked up, frowning. "No, my health is perfectly fine."

"Whew. Glad to hear that." She rummaged around in a shoulder bag tucked under her arm and came up with a packet of tissues. "Here. Take this."

Kennie accepted a couple of tissues. She wiped her face and blew her nose, feeling stupider than she had in a long time. She had no idea what to say, how to explain.

Lily saved her the trouble by saying, "I wanted to apologize for the other day, for what PJ did."

"Shouldn't PJ be the one apologizing?" Kennie rose and for some childish reason felt better to tower over Lily.

"PJ doesn't apologize."

"Why doesn't that surprise me?" She meant to go on, but she saw the expression of sadness on Lily's face and stopped herself.

"Her actions were uncalled for, and I'm sorry she caused trouble for you. I hope you know I had no idea she would do that."

"Lily, if there's one thing I know about you, it's that you don't have a mean bone in your body."

Eyes flashing, Lily said, "You have no idea. None at all." As fast as the anger glinted in her eyes, it died back down, leaving her somehow reduced, as though someone had sucked out half the energy she desperately needed. "You can rest assured it won't happen again."

"I better go," Kennie said. She stepped around Lily and punched the elevator button. She turned back as she waited and had no idea what to say.

Lily clutched her bag and wouldn't meet her eyes. When the

door opened, Lily pulled her keys out of her purse and said, "Go on. I just realized I forgot something."

Kennie backed into the elevator, watching Lily fumble to get her key in the doorknob. As the elevator door closed, she could swear she heard Lily sob. She floated down to the first floor smelling the faintest scent of sunshine and flowers, the essence of Lily.

Chapter Eleven

"ARE YOU READY for this?" Kennie asked.

Max sat in the passenger seat of the Jeep, arms crossed. From across the street, she and Kennie surveyed the avenue, yard, and house where Max used to live. Three nights in a row, she and Kennie had driven over and parked to wait and watch. Third time was a charm. Just after dusk, as the neighborhood settled down and the crickets started up with their singing, Max's brother emerged from the front door and descended the stairs looking like a character from a zombie movie. He meandered off down the street.

Max didn't answer Kennie until her brother was out of sight. "All right. Let's try it." She picked up a flashlight from the dash and opened her car door, but Kennie reached across and grabbed the long sleeve of her black t-shirt before she could get out.

"What?"

"The phone I gave you is on, right?"

"Yeah," Max said, sounding slightly irritated. "Just keep watch outside. Call me if you see him coming back."

"I'm going up on the porch with you."

"Really, it's not needed."

"What if someone's in there?"

"The whole house is dark."

"Good Lord, for all you know the power could be turned off now. He could have a whole bunch of drugged-up meth-heads hanging out in the dark this very moment."

"I'll ring the bell first."

"I think I should come in with you."

"No, not a good idea. I'm sorry, Kennie. I need to do this myself. You can come up to the porch, but please stay out."

In response, Kennie opened her car door and got out. She left the car unlocked and followed Max up the walk. Some of the cement stairs were crumbling, and all were chipped on the edges. She waited halfway up while Max dug around in a planter filled with dead weeds.

"Aha." Max scurried over, opened the screen door and put the key in the lock. "Jeez, is he an idiot or what? He didn't even lock up."

She opened the door, slipped inside, and pushed the door nearly shut, but not before Kennie got a look at the mess and a snoot full of something rancid. She went up the remaining stairs and stepped behind a pillar on the porch to look in through curtain-less windows. Despite being shrouded in shadow, there was enough light to see pizza boxes, crushed beer cans, fast-food wrappers, and wadded-up trash. They'd both worn dark clothes, so she almost didn't see Max move by. Her dark shape passed through the living room and disappeared into the shadows.

As her eyes adjusted to the darkness, Kennie saw two single mattresses stacked on top of one another toward the back of the living room. They were heaped with clothes. Or was that a body? She sucked in a deep breath of alarm then decided it wasn't a person. She didn't want it to be a person, so therefore it wasn't.

The interior walls were scarred and marked with strange symbols Kennie couldn't make heads or tails of. The exterior paint was peeling, and nobody had done anything to the grounds for a very long time. She turned away to watch the street. The grass was knee high and the yard littered with garbage and old car parts. Once upon a time, the place had been a home, and now it was nothing more than a trash receptacle.

She clicked on the light on her watch. Max had been inside for about four minutes. Did she have all the time in the world? Or would Derek be back soon? She hoped he was out for the night, but he could have gone down to the 7-Eleven. Or maybe he just wandered Belmont Street and mugged people so he'd have money for more drugs.

At the six-minute mark, Kennie started to get nervous. How much time did it take to find a couple of photo albums and some clothes?

After eight minutes, her stomach hurt from nerves. This is why I never became a criminal, she thought. No way could I handle this stress.

Down the street she heard a whistle. It could be anyone, but somehow she knew it was Derek. She hit speed dial on her phone and slipped down the steps and behind the overgrown bushes to the left of the porch.

"Pick up," she whispered. "Max, where are you? Pick up." The phone went to voicemail. She redialed. Same thing.

"Aw, shit."

She could see Max's brother ambling along, two houses down, a paper sack clutched to his chest. He wore a backwards baseball cap and draggy-ass basketball shorts. As he neared, she saw his white t-shirt was stained with dark splotches. He sauntered along, head down, in cheap flip-flops that didn't fit correctly so that his heels were half on, half off the ends.

She dialed again, desperate to reach Max but she didn't pick up. Had she dropped the phone? Was she hurt? Maybe there was someone inside after all who'd gotten the drop on her.

Derek turned up the walk, humming tunelessly. Kennie took a deep breath and stepped out of the bushes.

"Whoa, dude!" Derek nearly dropped the bag, but managed to corral it at waist level. His voice was raspy, as if he'd been smoking nonstop. "Who the fuck're you?"

Before she could answer, he came toward her and pointed a finger. "I 'member you. Fuckin' bitch, got between me an' Max. Where's she?" His jaw dropped open, and he gazed dully like some sort of stupid aquatic critter. "Oh, I get it. She's here to rip me off, that's where." He raced up the front steps surprisingly fast, considering he was tripping on something.

"Wait!" she shouted.

He only paused a moment, then rushed the door.

Pocketing the cell phone, she went up the stairs after him, only to nearly fall backwards when he stepped back abruptly.

Max shoved the screen door open, which knocked him out of her way. The only thing that stopped him from falling down the stairs was Kennie. He flailed and shouted. She pushed him from her, and the paper bag fell to the porch with a clunk.

"Well, if it isn't the little sis," he snarled. "Got us a family reunion, and you ain't leaving."

"Oh, yes, I am."

He didn't lose his footing despite the ridiculous flip-flops. "You little bitch. What're you taking?"

"My stuff." She had a death-grip on a brown grocery sack with the top rolled down. "Stuff you couldn't get any money for, so it'll be no great loss to you."

Kennie stepped back a stair, letting Max slink down the stairs on the other side of her. "She's got a right to her clothes and things," Kennie said. "So back off."

"She aban...aban...she left her shit. Mine now."

He slurred his words. Kennie was grateful he was under the influence of some kind of downer. His reflexes weren't good, and he wasn't thinking fast. She backed down the stairs, watching intently, but he was so stoned he just stood staring and teetering back and forth ever so slightly.

She reached the sidewalk and half-turned, keeping an eye on him but making tracks behind Max. At the Jeep she waited for Max to get in, then sat heavily in the driver's seat. "Shit, that was close. I thought something was wrong when you didn't pick up."

"I had my hands full."

"Of what?" She started up the Jeep.

"Wait. Just drive around the block, then come back and park up a ways. I hauled a bunch of stuff out back, next to the garage."

"Huh, I wondered how you got everything in that small grocery bag."

BACK AT THE Allen Arms, Kennie helped Max carry in the various boxes and plastic bags they'd snagged behind the house. They dropped off the photo albums in the efficiency, but Max wanted a chance to look through the rest and make sure they weren't bug-infested before bringing them into the apartment. The clothes all smelled, as Max said, "odorific," and needed laundering. So did what she was wearing. They tromped down to the laundry room. Even in the muted light, Kennie saw Max's clothes were streaked with dust and dirt.

"How the heck did you get so filthy?"

"Crawled into some pretty disgusting places. But I think it was worth it."

They dumped clothes into a pile on the floor, and Kennie said, "It's great you've got so many pairs of jeans."

Max got a strange look on her face. "Some of them aren't mine. I went ahead and took most all my mom's clothes, too."

Kennie picked up a pair of worn Levis. "Will these fit?"

"Might be a little big in the butt, and I have to get the length shortened, but yeah."

"Good score then."

Max turned her back and bent to separate darks and whites into different piles. "I think I'll feel odd wearing Mom's stuff...but maybe good, too."

"What did your mom do for a living?"

"She worked at the DMV."

"In the office? At the counter?"

"She was called an examiner and went out on the road to give people their driving tests, you know, for licenses."

"I see." Kennie backed up to the counter that ran along the wall across from the washers and hitched herself up to sit on it. She leaned her shoulders against a corkboard that posted a sheet of contact information in case the washers or dryers acted up.

"It's kind of funny that she worked for the DMV," Max said, "since we didn't have a car for the last two years or so. Derek wrecked it, and we couldn't afford to get it fixed. She had to junk it, and what a rip-off that was."

"Lucky we can get around Portland pretty easily."

"Yeah, but I'm going to get a car as soon as I can save up for it." She picked up a box from the floor. Setting it on the counter for folding laundry that ran down the middle of the room, she said, "I hid this box good."

Carefully, she lifted out something bulky wrapped in a towel, set it aside, and removed half a dozen smaller items wrapped in terrycloth washrags. "I can't believe he never found all this."

Kennie didn't want to seem nosy, but she squinted to see from her perch at the side of the room. An old pink towel came off the big item, and from a distance it looked like a red-colored box about nine inches wide and six inches deep. Max lifted a lid, and Kennie couldn't bear the suspense anymore. She hopped down and stood on the other side of the table. "What is it?"

Max spun it a quarter turn, and Kennie saw it was an old lacquer jewelry box filled with a pile of tangled chains, watches, and tiny, black, velvety-looking earring boxes. On each end of the jewelry box were decorative brass handles. One long drawer ran across the bottom front with two drawers half that size above. The drawer pulls were brass maple leaves each about the size of a penny. Max pulled on one leaf, and the drawer came completely out. Two rings rattled around. She did the same with the other small drawer. It held a ring as well.

She grinned up at Kennie. "My parents' wedding rings, and somewhere in here are rings from three of my grandparents. We never got Grandpa Dave's. His sister took 'em."

"Where did you hide this so Derek never found it, if I may ask?"

"There's a crawl space in the basement. Every foot and a half or so is a gap under the floorboards with some open space down below—just enough room to get little bundles in. Before Mom died, I crawled all the way to the back with these things and hid 'em."

"Hence the filthy clothes. "

"Yup. It was a bitch getting the box in and out, but I managed."

"I have to say Operation Recovery seems to have worked out pretty well, even if your brother did show up."

Max gave a perfunctory nod and focused on unwrapping one of the other items. She leaned around the table to toss the washcloth in the nearby trash then stopped herself. "This isn't very dirty. I could wash these and use them."

"You could."

Kennie looked at the shiny, multicolored item left on the table, not sure what it was for a moment, then the visual clicked in. Christmas ornament. A glittering and plump Santa carried a giant green bag full of dolls and toys and tin soldiers and gingerbread men.

Max pulled some more cloth-wrapped items out of the box. "Christopher Radko made these, and every year from when I was in first grade until...until Mom died, she gave me one for Christmas."

Her voice broke. She continued unveiling the bright-colored glass items: a snowman, a red-plaid stocking stuffed with goodies, a pretty golden puppy with a present between his paws, Santa by a Christmas tree, and more. Eleven total.

"They're beautiful, Max."

Max lifted a package wrapped in green and white Christmas paper out of the box. "I never opened the last one," she choked out. "I found it after she died."

Her hands shaking slightly, she ripped the paper away and opened a box a little bigger than what a softball would fit in. "Nicholas Gnome," she read.

White bearded with a pink face, the little gnome wore brown and gold shoes, a red and white coat, royal blue gloves, and a green hat circled with a red belt and buckle.

"He's really cute," Kennie said. "I've never seen anything like him." When she glanced up, she saw tears tracking down the girl's face. "Oh, Max." She came around the counter and enclosed Max in a hug, patting her and making soothing noises. Max sobbed, her thin body shaking in Kennie's arms. "Go ahead, let it out. It's good to cry. I know you miss her."

After a few moments, Max relinquished her hold and backed up, her head down. "Sorry. My life is real fucked up here."

"Join the club."

"Your life is fine."

Kennie snorted. "You have no idea, kid. Don't believe anything you see from the outside."

Max wiped her face on her sleeve, and Kennie winced. "Oooh, I don't think you should have done that."

"What?" Max looked at her blankly.

"You just wiped a significant amount of the crawlspace across your face."

"I don't give a crap. I need a shower anyway."

"Why don't you take these things upstairs and put them someplace safe, where you can enjoy seeing them, then get in the shower. Throw your clothes outside the door, and I'll get your laundry going."

"You don't have to—"

"Dammit, Max, I feel bad enough about how things have been for you. Let me do this one little thing. When you're cleaned up, come over to my place and I'll make you a grilled cheese sandwich and tomato soup."

Max's face brightened for a moment, and she busied herself with the ornaments. "Will you carry up the jewelry box for me? Then I can put all the ornaments here in the bottom and leave the washcloths in the wash pile."

"No problem."

Thankful for the maximum-load washers, Kennie further sorted the clothes and got the laundry started. All of Max's clothes plus her mother's items barely filled two of the four washers. The kid sure didn't have much.

Chapter Twelve

DAYS WENT BY and the Fourth of July approached, one of Kennie's least-favorite holidays since she'd bought the building. Every kid in a mile radius started setting off firecrackers several days before and didn't stop after the blessed event was over. Everyone ended up with five or six nights of interrupted sleep. She was surprised Miss Quist didn't come down every night to complain.

The workout center in the basement was coming together. She'd had a treadmill and elliptical machine delivered, and both were up and running. Now that summer had arrived, the heat was sometimes relentless. Some days Kennie enjoyed not having to go outside to run. The basement was cool and private. She got in the habit of working out before dinner at the height of the day's heat. Now if she and Max could finish putting together the Universal gym, she could lift weights as well. She'd put down a sixteen-by-sixteen-foot square of carpet for stretching and yoga, and a variety of hand weights sat on a rack in the corner. All in all, she was delighted with the progress.

Where was Max? She needed her to hold the tension wires so she could set up a stack of weights and make sure the machinery was calibrated properly. The kid had run upstairs to the bathroom fifteen or twenty minutes earlier. Oh, well, Kennie thought, I'm thirsty anyway. I'll take five and go see what's keeping her.

She set down the book of complicated assembly instructions and headed up to the lobby. As she traversed the back hall, she noted that the door to Max's efficiency was open, so she paused in the doorway. Fighting back tears, Max stood holding one of the photo albums she'd rescued from her old house.

"Hey," Kennie said softly.

With a guilty expression, Max snapped the album shut and set it on the coffee table in the middle of the room.

"I was just checking to see what the holdup was."

"Sorry. I'm ready now." She stalked past Kennie and out into the lobby.

"Where's Simms?" Kennie asked.

"Bathroom break. I told him I'd keep an eye on things for a bit."

"I'm curious about something, Max. What are you going to do about Olivia?"

Max spun and glared. "What do you mean?"

"Have you done anything? Looked her up, tracked her down, whatever?"

"Uh, no."

"Do you need help with that?"

"I wasn't really—I don't know."

"Don't know if you need help, or don't know how to go about finding her?"

"Jesus, Kennie, lay off."

Kennie was taken aback. "I'm sorry. I was just asking questions."

Max trudged over to the stairs and sank down. She put her elbows on her knees and her head in her hands. "I haven't been ready. I don't have any money. So I just haven't done anything."

"What do you need money for?"

Max gaped at her as though she thought Kennie was the stupidest person on the planet. "To take care of her, what else?"

"I thought you said she'd been placed with a family."

"Some family—not our family. She should be with her own people."

"At the risk of sounding overly logical here, her own people are, number one, currently a chronic drug-using abuser, and number two, an eighteen-year-old just getting back on her feet after a lot of tough experiences. Do you have any other family—aunts or uncles? Somebody else who could help you and Olivia?"

Shaking her head, Max looked completely defeated.

Kennie crossed the lobby and sat on the stairs next to her. "Here's what I'm thinking. Up until your mom died, Olivia had a mother, a sister, a brother, and suddenly, she's on her own. She's probably with a perfectly nice family, but just like you're wondering and worrying about her, she's probably fretting about you and Derek. You're not required to do anything, but it might make you feel better, and your sister, too, if you tracked her down and figured out a way to see her on a regular basis."

When Max looked up, there were tears in her eyes. "I feel responsible, like I let her down."

Kennie let that float in the air for a moment, weighing her words. "Circumstances have let her down. You had no control over the loss of your mom. Your dad either. But I hope you can look at this a little bit differently. It isn't all or nothing. You don't have to support and raise your sister or never see her again. There's a middle ground."

Norm Faulkner pushed open the front door and held it for his wife. She came in, red in the face and leaning heavily on her walker. Her face perked up when she saw the two of them, but that was quickly followed by a frown. "Kennie, are you picking on Max?"

"No, of course not." Kennie rose and greeted Mr. Faulkner, then turned back to Evelyn. "Didn't you previously work with the county?"

"Yes, twenty-eight years as a social worker."

"Do you know anything about foster care and placements?"

"Some. I mostly dealt with elders, but I worked alongside colleagues who had foster care caseloads. Why?"

"Max would like to locate her younger sister."

She explained the circumstances, and Evelyn nodded with a thoughtful expression on her face.

"Max," Evelyn asked, "have you called anyone at the county yet?"

KENNIE WENT BACK to the basement, happy that Evelyn had taken Max with her and Norm to their apartment for a strategy session regarding locating Olivia. The assembly of the gym machine would be easier with another set of hands, but she constructed all the parts she could alone. She felt impatient to get the unit put together, but she knew it was best for Max to sort things out with Evelyn's help.

When she got as far as she could, she knocked off for the day. She washed her hands in the laundry room, stashed her tools in the workshop, and locked up. With a sense of satisfaction, she mounted the stairs whistling an old Madonna tune. She headed toward the lobby, intending to go out to the front porch and sit on the glider for a while.

The front door was open, and a taxi driver was rolling two pieces of red luggage out. She wondered which of her tenants was leaving for a vacation.

The elevator dinged and out stepped Lily followed by Simms, who held a carryon bag. He dragged out a matching red suitcase even bigger than the two the taxi driver had taken out.

Lily wore brown Capri pants, tennis shoes, and a tan and blue blouse. She had a lightweight sweater over one arm and a purse-sized backpack in the other hand.

"Uh, hi," Kennie said, then got a look at Lily's face. To say it was strained was an understatement. She looked like she hadn't slept for days.

"Hello, Kennie. I've already given instructions to Brian regarding the penthouse."

"Brian? Oh, you mean Simms." Kennie felt like a bumbling idiot. "Uh, where are you going?"

Simms practically bowed as he came toward them. For a moment, he reminded Kennie of those ingratiating butlers in English period pieces. He said, "I'll just get your bags to the taxi, ma'am."

"Thanks, Brian." Lily glanced nervously at Kennie. "I'm going to Barcelona."

"Spain?" The word came out louder than Kennie meant it to, but at least it wasn't prefaced with "Uh."

"Yes, that's where Barcelona is located."

Kennie saw a hint of amusement in Lily's eyes, but in the next instant it was gone, replaced with an expression of sadness and exhaustion. "How long will you be gone?"

"Don't know. I'll keep you posted."

Kennie stood mutely, mortified that she had no idea what to say or even how to say goodbye. Lily put her head down and said, "So long," as she headed for the door.

When Simms came back he said, "What a great tenant. One thing nice about Lily Gordon — she never skimps on tips." He held up a ten-dollar bill.

Kennie wanted to tell him to shut up. Instead, she whirled and stomped back to her apartment. Seeing Lily around the building hurt — but the prospect of not seeing her felt like a knife in the heart.

Chapter Thirteen

"WHY IS HE looking at this?" Max asked. In the corner of the ballroom in the seventh floor penthouse, she leaned from side to side, her feet causing the floor to make almost imperceptible squeaks and groaning noises. "It's really not that bad."

"Maybe not up here, but below us, Miss Quist is probably going insane." Kennie watched the workman down on hands and knees as he tapped with a rubber mallet and occasionally pounded with his fist. "It's bad enough. If it can be fixed for a decent price, I want to get it done."

"Ah, I see. Special present for one Miss Lily Gordon?"

"Noooooo, it's—"

"You got a lot of play under the wood," the workman called out. He sat back on his heels. For his age, which Kennie guessed to be around sixty, the guy was pretty limber. No way would her knees take kneeling like that for long periods of time. The thought of it made her kneecaps ache.

With Max following, she ambled toward him. "What do you think is causing it?"

"Could be the subfloor moving against the nails as people's weight comes down on it. Or if the floorboards weren't nailed fully or if they loosened over the years as the building settled, then they might be rubbing and making all those creaking noises."

"Lots of wear and tear over the years," Kennie said.

"Yup. The worst possibility is if the cross-bracing beneath the subfloor was installed wrong and the old braces are rubbing."

"The building was finished at the turn of the century, Jake. If it's lasted this long, they must have done something right."

"Yeah. It's probably the cross braces wearing down over the decades. Only way to fix that is pull up the floor and chisel or sand down the bad spots. Big waste of time, you ask me."

"What can we do?"

"We can't work underneath, right?"

Kennie shook her head. "I don't think I want to go so far as ripping out the ceiling below."

"Well, then," he said, hitching up pants which seemed constantly ready to fall off his thin frame, "we can shoot some finish nails or small-headed screws through the floor and into the subfloor. That might hold it."

"I don't want to scar the wood."

"Not a problem. I drive the screw or nail below the floor surface and hide the holes with a wood filler that matches. We don't even have to sand and refinish the whole floor. I can do that to the holes, and nobody's ever the wiser."

"Any other option?"

"Lay a great big thick rug that muffles the squeaking."

Kennie laughed. "It's not the tenant on this floor who's complaining. It's the lady who lives below."

"Oh. Well then me and my guys can work a section of the floor and see what happens."

"All right, let's give it a try."

"Seems to me this section in the middle is the worst. How about I start there? And if it doesn't work, we'll know in a couple hours and you won't be out much money."

She gave him the okay and led Max out to the elevator, feeling such a sense of sadness that multiplied with every minute spent in Lily's ballroom. She didn't know where all the paintings were. Before she left, Lily must have stored them somewhere. They could be anywhere in the penthouse, but Kennie wouldn't pry to find out. With the exception of the stacks of chairs in the corner, the room was bare. Only the faint scent of oil paint would alert anyone that a painter had once worked magic there.

"How'd you learn all this, Kennie?"

"All this what?"

"About building and repairing stuff?"

"You thought I knew something about wood floors? Ha. That's why I had to call Jake in."

The elevator dinged, and they got on. "But you still know lots of stuff."

"I worked on a paint crew in college, and I used to repair stuff around the house with my dad. Nowadays, I look up procedures and information on the Internet. When in doubt, I call someone in."

The elevator stopped at six and opened to reveal tiny Virginia Quist. Her face was white, and her eyes sparkled with anger. She wore black-and-white saddle shoes, a dark tan tweed skirt, and a jacket over a button-up blouse with a wing collar. The outfit made Kennie feel tempted to look around for hounds and an English walking stick.

"Just the person I'm seeking," Miss Quist said. "What is that God-awful racket in the penthouse apartment?"

Kennie stepped out of the elevator and looked back at Max. "You coming?"

Max shook her head slowly, and Kennie could tell she was holding back a grin. "I've got that thing to do. See you in a bit."

The doors closed but not before Kennie caught the gleeful look on Max's face. When she caught up with Max later, she'd administer a nice wedgie or noogie.

"I should have spoken to you, Miss Quist, but the woodworker I've been trying to get in here to look at the floor came early because of a cancellation, so I didn't expect him today." Kennie punched the elevator button. "He's bringing up some guys to repair the ballroom floor. I'm hoping to stop—or at least minimize—the creaking. I'm sorry you're bothered by the noise."

Miss Quist huffed but calmed down. "Thank you. That would be a real benefit, and I suppose I can put up with the racket for a while. How long will it take?"

"He's going to do some further experimenting. You may hear a lot of banging for the rest of the day, I'm sorry to say."

Miss Quist sighed. "Oh, well, perhaps it's for the best. I think I shall move up the timeline for my luncheon and depart shortly."

"Thank you so much for your understanding. I'll let you know when he'll be finished, as soon as the worker gives me an idea." The elevator returned, and Kennie stepped into the car to descend, all the while feeling she was escaping from a 1940s English movie. As the door shut, the words *Miss Quist Gets Pissed* came to mind and she laughed.

When she reached the first floor, she tapped on the door to the efficiency. Max opened it and giggled. Kennie wanted to give her a friendly smack, but she realized Max actually looked happy. The cuts on her face had faded so much they were no longer the first thing you noticed. With a grin, Kennie said, "You're absolutely incorrigible."

"Okay, not that I even know what the heck that means."

Kennie faked a punch. Max let out a shriek and darted inside to the other side of the couch. For a moment the two of them dodged one way and the other before Kennie backed off laughing. "You're in good spirits today."

"Yes, I am."

It was a tribute to the resilience of youth that Max had so quickly healed physically and that she might be on the way to emotional balance again as well. Max had changed clothes, and Kennie commented on that, then said, "You're quitting for the day? It's only eleven a.m."

"Me and Evelyn have an appointment. Don't you remember?"

"Oh, yeah. Flat forehead moment. I forgot. No wonder you're so up. When you get home, no matter what happens, come over and tell me about it."

"Absolutely."

Kennie studied Max's face, seeing sparks of hope. "Not to be a spoilsport or anything, but please don't let your expectations run too high. The appointment is preliminary, and this could be a long, dragged-out process."

"Yeah, yeah, I know. Evelyn already schooled me all about that."

"Who's driving you?" For a brief moment, Kennie had a frightening vision of myopic Evelyn Faulkner behind the wheel, but Max disabused her of that notion.

"Mr. F is. He's going to drop us and come back when we call."

"So you're putting the cell phone to good use?"

"Don't worry. I won't go over the minutes. I haven't got a soul to call."

"No," Kennie said, exasperated. "I didn't mean it that way. I just want everything to work out for you."

"It will. It has to."

Considering the desperate cast her face suddenly took, Kennie hoped she was right.

KENNIE KEPT BUSY all afternoon mudding and sanding a wall she built in the basement to separate the workout center from the storage area. But her thoughts kept coming back to Max and her situation. She didn't know much at all about how the social services system worked, and that was a tribute to her Aunt Clara. When she considered how easily she could have ended up in a bad situation after her parents died, she felt grateful.

What kind of home had Olivia ended up in? For Max's sake, Kennie hoped the foster parents were nice people. It wouldn't be easy to take in a traumatized fifteen-year-old whose world had been turned upside down.

The afternoon passed far too slowly for Kennie's liking, but eventually, she put away the sander and hauled her dusty self up for a shower and meal preparation. She was in the kitchen putting the finishing touches on a big batch of Baked Hawaiian Chicken when the doorbell buzzed.

She stuffed the pan in the oven, wiped her hands on a towel, and went to the door to invite Max and Evelyn in. Evelyn, in a pair of forest green polyester slacks and a knit top, came forward slowly with her walker, her shoulder bag flopping against her side. From Max's demeanor, things hadn't gone well.

Evelyn commented on the apartment and how good it smelled. "What are you making that smells so delicious?" She settled heavily into an easy chair.

"I'm making Hawaiian Chicken and baked potatoes. I was thinking maybe you and Norm might want to eat with Max and me."

"That would be terrific. But Norm won't be home for half an hour or so. He dropped us off and headed to the cleaners to pick up his shirts for our trip."

"Perfect. It'll be ready around then." Kennie glanced at Max who had slipped out of her shoes and curled her feet under her on the couch. Kennie didn't like the sullen silence. "So? What happened?" She lowered herself to a seat a few feet from Max and turned to the side with her arm along the back of the couch.

"It went well," Evelyn said.

"Not really," Max said.

"Now, now, dear, the outcome is going to be in your favor."

Max crossed her arms and looked so cranky that Kennie resisted teasing her. The subject was too serious to risk upsetting the poor kid. "Tell me everything. Spare no details."

"I was able to track down old colleagues," Evelyn said. "Well, they were young pups back when I worked there, and now they're all older and have advanced in seniority. One in particular I had trained many years ago—Sheila's her name—and she was so helpful. She looked up the information on the computer. When I started work in Multnomah County, we kept paper records and racks of files. It was ever so crowded and tended to be dusty, and nowadays with computers—"

"Evelyn!" Max said.

"I know, I know, get on with it. Anyway, we had to wait quite some time for this Cindi Valdivia, the caseworker. Unlike Sheila, she wasn't very forthcoming, and we had to have a long conversation with her, then with her supervisor."

Max said, "They were pissed I'd escaped their clutches. I tried to tell them I skipped because I couldn't deal, but they didn't care. They told me I was unreliable and untrustworthy."

"Yes, they were pretty cut-and-dried about it," Evelyn said, "but we just kept hammering away at our point. At first I thought we might have to get an attorney—"

"I threatened them with Pete Ackerman. I showed them his card."

Kennie imagined Max—naïve, idealistic Max—holding out the card like it was a magic talisman. She suspected the social workers weren't very impressed.

Evelyn went on. "As they say, push came to shove, and Max and I were prepared to make a scene. But another social worker showed up, and between him and Cindi and the supervisor, they decided to schedule a supervised visit between Max and Olivia. First they had her sign a release allowing them to do a background check."

"Like I was some kind of common criminal."

"Now dear, what if just any-old-body showed up and wanted to find your sister?"

"What if it was Derek," Kennie asked, "and he wanted to get his hands on Olivia or whatever her foster family provides? That wouldn't be good, would it?"

"I s'pose not, but I just didn't like how suspicious they were of me."

Evelyn nodded. "I know that was irritating, but once they clear you, all will be well. You told them you've never been arrested, and there are no financial records out there to show you've run up thousands in debts."

"I sure hope not," Max grumbled.

"So Olivia's scheduled to meet Max at the social services building a week from Friday. The only problem is that Norm and I will be down in Arizona visiting David and Donnie. So I can't go with her. Can you do it instead, Kennie?"

"Sure."

"Someone needs to be with Max, to advocate for her."

"Okay. I guess I can do that." She glanced at Max who wore a strange expression. "What? Did you think I'd say no?"

"No, it's not that. It's the smell. I haven't eaten since breakfast, and I'm dying here."

"You didn't eat lunch? Silly girl." Kennie rose and strolled toward the kitchen. "I should have offered you both snacks and drinks anyway. I was just too curious about what happened. Lemonade? Iced tea? Soda?"

Evelyn said, "Oooh, I'd love an iced tea with a bit of sugar."

"I'll have a Vodka Seven," Max said.

Kennie laughed. "Yeah, right. Like that'll happen."

Chapter Fourteen

FOR THE FOURTH straight time, Kennie lay in bed far into the night, unable to sleep and with her mind racing. Some of her fretting was productive. She thought of To-Do-List items to add to her punch list, and she pondered over repair and replacement ideas for various units. But most of the time she thought about her life and what a mess she'd made of it. What was her life worth, anyway?

Jewish people had a saying that to be successful in this life, one needed to plant a tree, raise a child, and write a book — none of which Kennie had ever done. In her old life with Janeen, they'd contributed to the neighborhood recycling efforts, and once they'd worked for Habitat for Humanity. Janeen donated time to feminist nonprofits that needed computer systems or websites, and she had possessed enough money to donate liberally in both of their names to many causes. Some of those organizations had found Kennie all the way across the country and were still sending mailings addressed to her and Janeen. For a long while, every time she got one, she felt like her heart would explode.

Other than donating funds here and there, what good in this life had Kennie exerted to influence others and to live on after her days on earth were done? She had no intention of writing a book, and at her late great state of age forty, no way was she bringing a child into the world. She could go out to the front yard of the Allen Arms and plant a tree — but how would that make any major difference in the world?

What is my purpose? she wondered. Am I supposed to merely live a quiet life of desperation and expire later on down the road after I've used up X amount of goods and services? Why am I even here?

She glanced at the bedside clock. Nearly half past two. She was going to be tired again in the morning. Actually, make that exhausted. As she turned over, she heard a thump. Then another. Muffled, sounding far away, she heard muted cries. Was that Max? She sat up and threw the sheet off her legs. Was she crying again? Even with the tearful and loving reunion with her sister, Olivia, things had been hard for the kid lately. Olivia couldn't live with Max, and the foster family, though lovely people, wanted to take Max's association with her sister slowly. Max's mood had been upsy-downsy: angry one day, weepy another day, and then buoyant every time she got a call from Olivia. Obviously, her misery was getting the best of her tonight.

Kennie rose and made her way to the adjoining door to Max's apartment. She tapped a few times, then opened it, leaned her head in, and said, "Hey, you okay, kiddo?"

A giggle. Someone shushed someone else.

Max cleared her throat. "Um, really, I'm just fine."

"Oh, crap," Kennie said. "I'm sorry. I didn't realize. I'll go—"

"No, no, it's okay." Max's feet hit the floor, and her figure materialized, wrapped in a sheet and appearing gradually more solid in the low light seeping in through the closed blinds. "I'm really sorry we woke you." She bent and turned on a ginger-jar table lamp that cast a weak golden light, only illuminating the sitting room area. In the built-in bed across the room, someone huddled, but Kennie couldn't see the person clearly in the dimness.

"You didn't wake me at all. I couldn't sleep."

"Us neither." Max sounded embarrassed. "I'm really sorry. I have a guest who I, uh, you know, didn't clear with you."

"Oh, Max. We need to talk. Maybe in the morning?"

For a second, Kennie thought Max was going to faint. Even though the room wasn't well-lit, it seemed her face went pale.

"I'd rather talk now, if you don't mind," Max mumbled. "Get it all out on the table."

"Why don't you and your friend throw on robes or whatever and pop over to my place. Can I make you a snack?"

Max shrugged.

"Come on over. I could use a snack myself."

In the kitchen, Kennie wondered how to play this situation. Max seemed really freaked, but Kennie didn't care what Max did next door as long as it wasn't illegal and didn't disturb the other tenants. Was that too cold-hearted? Max was only a kid. But she was eighteen, and Kennie didn't feel she had the right to boss her around about who was allowed to visit. Or did she?

Kennie opened up the fridge and pulled out fresh strawberries, which she knew Max liked. She had half an angel food cake and plenty of Cool Whip, and she got out plates and napkins and nice flatware.

Max trudged in followed by a slender blonde girl who, if possible, looked even younger and thinner than Max. They both wore t-shirts, and the girl had on baggy green shorts. Max was barefoot and in tight, skinny jeans.

"Pull up a stool," Kennie said.

Kennie loved how she had remodeled her kitchen. Instead of retaining the dining and cooking areas that came standard in all the Allen Arms apartments, she'd knocked out the wall between the two areas and increased the room size substantially. A built-in counter with cabinets underneath, eight feet long and five feet wide, graced the center of the room. Both sides had drawers and cabinets below a gray-and-white-speckled synthetic stone countertop that had an overhang on two sides and tall four-legged stools tucked underneath. Max and her friend pulled out two stools on the opposite side of the built-in. Quickly arranging them, they clambered up and sat close to one another.

Kennie introduced herself, and the blonde girl said, "I know. Max told me all about you. I'm Renae."

"Good to meet you, Renae. You know the old saying: Any friend of Max's is a friend of mine."

Kennie slid place mats, silverware, and napkins across the counter, which Renae set out in front of the two of them. Kennie kept up a patter of innocuous comments about the berry season and how excellent the fruit had been lately. Every time her gaze rested on Max, she thought the kid looked more miserable and upset. She prepared a dish of strawberry shortcake the way she knew Max liked it and asked Renae if she wanted the same.

"I eat pretty much anything." She smiled and leaned to the side until she bumped Max who jumped. Though Renae's arms were below the edge of the counter, Kennie could tell she'd put her hand on Max's knee or thigh. She wondered why Max was so freaked about the whole situation, so she didn't waste anymore time.

"How did you two meet?"

Max picked up a fork and stared down at her dessert, not making a move to dig into it.

Renae, on the other hand, answered with her mouth full. "I work at Siggy Starshine's Café down on Belmont. Max came in a couple of weeks ago, and we got to know each other."

Kennie stopped herself from observing out loud that they sure had hit the sack quickly, partly because she realized she was guilty of the same thing. In fact, she had slept with Lily on the first date. Besides, who was she to judge?

Renae said, "I've been living here and there, staying with friends, you know, whatever, since I came up from Salem after I graduated. Max offered to put me up for a while, and these last couple of days have been amazing. Love your apartment. I love the whole building." She gazed around the kitchen. "I spend all day in and out of a really disorganized kitchen at work, so it's nice to see one looking clean and neat."

"I'm not cooking for the masses," Kennie said. "Makes it a lot easier."

"You're right." Renae took another bite. "Good cake and really great strawberries. This is way yummy."

Max had yet to sample hers. Obviously, she was nervous and upset, and Kennie didn't want that. "Max. Hey. Earth to Max."

"Huh?" She didn't meet Kennie's eyes.

"Listen to me. Your life is your life. Your apartment is your castle. I apologize for barging in on you two. I didn't mean to invade your privacy."

Max mumbled, "It's okay."

"No, it's not. I keep forgetting you're a full-grown woman, and I've got to stop treating you like a teenager. Actually, you are a teenager, but you're not a kid. You're an adult now."

Max looked up, eyes filled with misery. "I thought you'd probably want me to pack up and head out."

"Why? Why would I want that?"

"I didn't ask permission for Renae to stay with me."

Kennie let out a sigh. "You aren't listening to me. Your apartment is your castle to live in as you please."

"Not really. This is all a temporary thing."

"Do you want it to be a temporary thing?"

"Don't know."

"Do you have other options?"

"Not really."

"Do you like it well enough to stay here?"

Max looked like she was holding back tears. "Uh, yeah."

"Okay, that's something to work with." For herself, Kennie dished up a small helping of angel food cake and a liberal pile of berries, no Cool Whip. She pulled out a stool and carefully stayed at the corner of the built-in, giving Renae and Max their space across the way. "Seems like it's time to formalize your working and living arrangements. And since Renae has joined you, she probably should be part of this deliberation. You think you're clearheaded enough even if it's the middle of the night?"

"Yeah."

"How about you, Renae?"

"Okay, I guess."

Kennie did some quick calculations in her head. "How about this? I hire you as a three-quarter-time employee to work around the building, serve as a caretaker periodically, and do security coverage when I need it. Your hours would be flexible, agreed upon by you and me on a weekly basis, and I pay you an hourly wage."

She named an amount, and Max's eyes widened.

"Don't look at me like that. For what you'll be doing, that's not too much. If anything, it's a little conservative."

Renae poked a strawberry with her fork, swept it through some whipped cream, and held it up for a moment before popping it into her mouth. "Pretty good deal, Maxie," she said. "That's a lot more than I make. 'Course, I get tips, and you won't."

"Actually," Kennie said, "sometimes the tenants slip tips to security, and many of them drop some nice checks and gifts your way at Christmas. But it's nothing regular. As for your living circumstances, I'll deduct your apartment rent in even portions out of your twice-a-month pay, and I'll set the rent at a reduced rate to make up for the fact that when you're home, you could get called upon by tenants. A reduced rent fee would take into consideration that you might sometimes be interrupted and have to do some troubleshooting." Kennie was making it up as she went along, but with every word, Max sat up straighter on the stool and appeared increasingly relieved.

"What about me?" Renae had finished her bowl-full and was picking at Max's. Max looked down, and said, "Hey, that's mine."

She sounded so shocked that Kennie laughed out loud. She hooked the bowl of berries and slid it over to Renae, followed by the plate of cake and Cool Whip. "Help yourself to more, Renae."

Max took her first bite of the dessert and followed that with another.

"I hope you're remembering to chew," Kennie teased.

"I am," she said with her mouth full. "It's good."

"I'm glad you like it." She turned to Renae. "I think you and Max need to sit down and decide how she wants to handle your presence and what funds the two of you want to devote to your in-common household."

"You could charge me whatever is fair," Renae said to Kennie.

"If you guys don't mind," Kennie said, "I'd prefer you work out the details with one another. The apartment is, technically, Max's. Keep in mind that it's small. Might be that sometime down the road you'll want to move to one of the other apartments in the building."

Max shook her head. "I could never afford that."

"You'd be surprised. At some point, you might even decide to move somewhere else." At Max's look of disbelief she said, "Don't look so shocked. Eventually you might want to move near a particular community or closer to the café or even buy a house. Also, have either of you thought about going to college this fall?"

They looked at one another, and for the first time, Kennie observed solid signs of their affection for one another. Now that Max had relaxed, she gazed at her girlfriend with open warmth and not a little of what Kennie could only describe as lust.

Renae said, "I came up here to go to Portland Community College, and that's my plan."

"Me, too," Max said enthusiastically. "Once I get my high

school diploma, I'd also like to take classes there."

The rest of the conversation was lively, and by the time Kennie sent Max and Renae off yawning, she was weary as well. As she headed back to bed, she thought about how tired she was going to be in the morning, but the fatigue seemed worth it. Maybe it was her lot in life to take in stray kids and help them get their lives on track. She sure as hell couldn't come up with any other purpose.

Chapter Fifteen

THE CALL CAME in the middle of the night, as such calls often do. Aunt Clara probably had no idea that 7:30 a.m. in New York equaled 4:30 a.m. in Oregon. Kennie awakened completely once she heard her aunt's voice.

"It's the end for me, dear," Kennie's aunt said in a tone that sounded like she was reporting that dinner was ready.

"What?"

"I just wanted to...say goodbye...and wish you well." After the first strong sentence, her voice had gone faint and wispy, as though she'd run a distance and couldn't catch her breath.

"Wait a minute, Auntie. What are you talking about?"

"Heart attack. No hope."

"What happened?" Kennie was already out of bed, pulling clothes out of her dresser, ripping shirts off the hangers.

"Doesn't matter. But I didn't...want to go...without saying...goodbye."

"Where are you?"

"Watertown...General."

"I'll be there. I'm getting on a plane."

"No, dear. It's all right—"

"Just let me do it. I'll see you as soon as I can get there."

She heard some fumbling, and then a male voice with an Asian-sounding accent came on the line. "This is Kim, nurse of your aunt. She ask me to tell you she fine."

"I beg to differ," Kennie shouted. "She just told me she's near death!"

"Hold on, please." There was a long pause during which Kennie pulled on clothes and shoes. She gathered up her bathroom essentials and dumped them into a travel bag. When Kim came back on the line, he must have left the hospital room because now he spoke candidly. "I hear her tell you she dying. Is probably accurate. We taking good care of her. I lend her my phone because she say only you are left for family. She want to say goodbye."

"Tell her to hang tight. I'll be there later today."

"Yes, ma'am."

Kennie ended the call. She dialed Max's cell number and asked her to come through the connecting doors immediately.

She gathered her clothes in record time and was stuffing them in a suitcase when Max called out from the living room. Dragging the bag behind her, Kennie met Max and Renae, both hair-mussed and sleepy-eyed.

"I need you guys to look after this place. I don't know for how long. And I need a ride to the airport."

Max said, "Okay. What's wrong?"

Kennie filled her in as she gathered her wallet, cell phone, and keys.

Renae asked, "Do you want me to get you a flight to New York?"

"I'll do it at the airport."

"Not a good idea," Renae said. "Really. You'll end up running all over the place there. Let's go online, get you a good deal, and book that way."

"I don't have time," Kennie said, embarrassed to find herself tearing up. "I don't care how much it costs."

"Take me to your computer. Give me a credit card number and where you want to go, and Max can drop you at the airport. When you get there, call me. I'll tell you where and when."

Kennie led her into her office and turned on the computer. She opened her wallet and removed a card. "Take this. I've got another one if I need it while I'm gone. When you're done, put it in the drawer there. And please, don't use it for anything else."

Renae's face took on such a hurt expression, that even in her frantic state, Kennie knew she'd wounded her. "I'm sorry. I didn't mean that how it came out."

"It's okay. I'm fine. I promise I'll use it only for this flight."

"I know you will." She typed in her computer password and grabbed a piece of scratch paper to write down the name of the airport. "Have at it. Watertown, New York. Where'd Max go?"

"Maybe to get dressed? She'd look awfully funny out at the airport in that long t-shirt and underwear."

Kennie hadn't even noticed what either of them was wearing. Now that she paused for a moment, she thought it might be a good idea to go look at herself in the mirror and it was lucky she did. Her short-sleeved shirt was buttoned crooked, and she hadn't brushed the mangy batch of hair sticking up all over her head. She shut the bathroom door and took a moment to use the facilities, brush her hair and teeth, and wash her hands and face. She let go for a moment and wept, before wiping her eyes and putting on her game face.

When she emerged from the bathroom, Max was standing over Renae, pointing at the screen. "That's shitty, Ren. Too many connections."

In an irritated voice, Renae said, "There's no other way to do it."

Kennie said, "I know I have to take a short-hop from Albany."

Max said, "And you'll have a connecting flight in Chicago."

"So be it. Let's go." She grabbed her suitcase and dragged it toward the front door, Max trailing behind.

Renae hurried after them. "There's a flight leaving in a little over two hours from United. I just figured out I can't book the flight online because it leaves in less than four hours, but if you go directly to United, they'll get you on. Here—take the credit card back."

Kennie paused long enough to stuff the card in her wallet and impulsively gave Renae a hug. "Thanks for your help."

Before Renae had a chance to answer, Kennie turned on her heel and sped out the door.

THE RIDE TO the airport was tense. Kennie found she couldn't quite think clearly, and Max was obviously nervous about driving the Jeep. For five in the morning, traffic seemed heavy, but Max soldiered through and, with a sigh, delivered her safely to the drop-off zone.

"Max, make sure you tell Simms and Thomason why I'm gone and that I'll call them later with instructions when I can think. You can call me on my cell if you need anything, but I trust your judgment. Just take care of the place."

As she opened the door, Max grabbed her arm and said, "I'm sorry this is happening to you."

"Yeah, me, too." She got out and hefted her suitcase from the backseat, then leaned in. "Use the Jeep as you need it, Max. Be extra careful."

"You got it."

Head swimming, Kennie went to the United desk to make flight arrangements. She was glad she'd brought her driver's license as well as her passport. Apparently they looked upon last-minute passengers with extra suspicion, perhaps because she was heading toward New York, the Terrorist Target of the World. The ticketing process seemed to take forever, but at last she dumped off her bag. Armed with a ticket that had set her back almost eight hundred dollars even with an allowance for family emergency, she made her way through security feeling strangely naked. She hadn't brought a jacket or a backpack or anything but the wallet and passport in her back pockets and cell phone in her shirt pocket. Max had her keys, and she hadn't even remembered a pen. Few times in her life had she ever felt so unprepared and out of sorts.

She had sixty minutes to kill so she bought a magazine, a mystery novel, and a bottle of water. As she moved robotically down the concourse, she saw a purse and luggage store. On impulse, she purchased a miniature sling bag with a shoulder strap and tucked her purchases in there. Now she didn't feel quite so vulnerable and unprepared.

GETTING FROM PORTLAND to Chicago to Albany took all day. At Albany, she paced in the terminal for forty-five minutes before the airline personnel finally loaded the plane for Watertown. The plane was a tiny, jam-packed, turbo-prop Cessna. They hit turbulence along the way, slowing the flight and causing more delay.

Kennie landed in Watertown seventy minutes after takeoff, sick to her stomach. The queasiness didn't go away during the ride from the airport to the hospital. As the taxi approached the medical center, Kennie was struck with a sense of *déjà vu*. How many times had she taxied to this very spot while Janeen was dying?

It was full dark when she paid off the cabbie and walked into Watertown General. She'd fallen asleep on the first leg of the trip but hadn't been able to sleep since. After the interrupted sleep of the night before, she felt as though she were traveling through a surreal *Alice in Wonderland* world. The neon lights of the hospital's overhead sign sparkled and blurred, and she realized she was teary-eyed again. All day long, every time she thought of Aunt Clara, she did so with such remorse. Why had she never come out to visit her since she'd moved? She'd sent her a birthday card the month before, but she could have sent flowers, a gift, something. She wanted to bring something up to the hospital room, but it was late and the gift shop was closed. Just as well, she thought. She shouldn't delay if Aunt Clara was that ill.

Pulling her wheeled suitcase, she asked directions for the cardiac care unit. She stood in the elevator wondering if she could feel any more exhausted. The door opened, and with every step she took, she felt as though she lost air until she barely had enough breath to ask for Kim at the nurse's station.

A plump black woman shook her head. "Kim went off shift. Won't be back until tomorrow morning at six."

"Of course. I wasn't thinking. I'm here about Clara McClain." When she mentioned the name, the nurse rose and bustled around the counter. "Oh, dear," she said. "She passed, hon. Only happened a little bit ago. She's still in her room. Do you want to see her?"

What little air she had left went out of Kennie. She felt like she was going to faint. Next thing she knew, the nurse had her in a death-grip under the elbow, forcing her to walk over and drop into a nearby chair.

"Put your head down for a minute," the nurse said.

Kennie leaned forward and sucked in a long breath.

The nurse said, "There, that'll make it better," and patted her rhythmically on the shoulder.

As if in a dream, Kennie breathed in and out, letting the weariness overtake her. The plane was late leaving, late arriving, and her baggage had taken forever. If not for that, she could have been here on time, she could have said goodbye. She felt a sudden irrational rage toward the airline. She knew it wasn't their fault, but still, she was so furious she couldn't stop clenching her fists, barely breathing, barely containing herself.

Chapter Sixteen

SHE SHOULD HAVE known Aunt Clara wouldn't leave her in the lurch. She had instructed the nurses to hand over her purse, and Kennie must have been convincingly heartbroken because they did it without even questioning her identity.

Clutching the purse to her chest, she arrived at the house feeling hollow and wrung out. She had looked in the purse at the hospital, and the house keys were zipped in the outer side pocket, the same place her aunt had kept them in all the generic purses she'd had all through Kennie's teen years.

She let herself in the darkened house, shoved her suitcase in the door, and groped for the light switch in the front hall. A vase of still-fresh pink roses and white calla lilies stood at attention on the hallway table next to the old-fashioned dial-style telephone, the only phone in the house. The glass jar of multicolored marbles sat where it had all the years Kennie had lived there. Otherwise, the hall was in disarray. The oriental rug was bunched up against the wall and folded over on one end, and several plastic bags were tossed here and there. A gauze pad dotted with blood lay next to the rug. Her foot skidded on a plastic cap, some sort of medical cover. She bent to pick it up and had no idea what it was.

A wad of something dark blue sat on the bottom stair. She fingered the familiar style of cable-knit sweater her aunt liked to wear and picked it up to find a jagged slice down the middle that severed it in half. Never to be repaired again. She dropped the cardigan on the stair and sank down next to it, head in hands.

KENNIE'S TOUR THROUGH the house after tea and Cheerios the next morning revealed that little had changed. The toaster was twenty years old, few furnishings had been replaced — much less moved — and Aunt Clara still had the same layout in her TV room. She had a wide-screen TV, though, and a new recliner of a deep forest green that contrasted nicely with the impeccably-clean tan Berber carpet.

The back wall contained a rolltop desk and a side table where her aunt had paid bills and answered correspondence. Kennie had been told in no uncertain terms that she was never to touch her aunt's papers, though she was allowed to use the typewriter that sat on the table. She'd typed many a high school essay there, and in deference to Aunt Clara's wishes, she'd never once opened a drawer or lifted the rolltop.

In all the years she'd lived with Aunt Clara, Kennie had never sat in her recliner. She lowered herself now and surveyed the room. This was the view her aunt had spent the majority of her waking hours looking at. The TV, a painting of some sort of Egyptian marketplace, two fake-looking candle sconces—all on a wall only about twelve feet wide. She picked up a nearly full bottle of Black Velvet whisky from an end table to the right of the chair. Always careful of the furniture, her aunt had used a plastic tray to set her drink and bowl of ice cubes on, both of which sat in a puddle of water now. The ice had melted. The drink was ruined.

She picked up the tray and its contents and took them to the kitchen sink to wash. When she was done, she poured herself another cup of tea and slid into a chair at the kitchen table.

Before she'd gone to bed the night before, she'd opened her aunt's rolltop desk and found a neatly organized set of file folders labeled WILL, INSURANCE, HOUSEHOLD, and FINANCES. The folders lay on the kitchen table, and she reexamined the contents.

Two fifty-thousand-dollar insurance policies, both in Kennie's name. Banking statements, bond and stock certificates, contact names for a financial planner and lawyer. Household bills, each marked *paid* with the amount, date, and check number. Her aunt was nothing if not organized.

The copy of the will surprised Kennie the most. She had expected she might be a beneficiary, but not *the* beneficiary. Aunt Clara had left Kennie's older brother and sister a thousand bucks apiece, and the same bequest went to Uncle Harold's two great-nieces. Three local charities had received modest bequests, but everything else—the house, its contents, the car, the bank account, the stocks and bonds—all went to Kennie.

She'd already called the mortuary and left a message at her aunt's lawyer's office. She wasn't sure what to do next. Her appointment with the funeral director wasn't until three p.m. Perhaps she ought to find her aunt's address book and start calling people.

The doorbell rang.

On the front porch, dressed in an off-white linen ensemble that accented lustrous long black hair, stood Kennie's sister, Suzanne. In her middle-fifties, she hardly looked Kennie's age, and it registered with Kennie that Suzanne had to have had some major face-lifting done.

Kennie managed to choke out a hello before Suzanne swept past her into the foyer. "I heard, I heard, and it's so terrible. She wasn't even seventy."

"Seventy-eight, just last month," Kennie said as she closed the door.

Suzanne looked around the foyer briefly and stalked into the living room. "She hasn't changed a thing." She steamed through the room, into the kitchen, and into the back den where she stopped to give the room an appraising eye. "Well," she said with a huff, "this'll have to be cleared out and repainted."

Kennie stood in the kitchen doorway, looking down the hall. Though she towered over her sister, she'd always felt small and insignificant in her presence. When was the last time she'd seen Suzanne? Four years ago? Five? They'd spoken by phone a few times since then, but with so little in common — and the issue of Suzanne's homophobia — Kennie hadn't missed seeing her in person.

Now Suzanne turned to face Kennie, a frown crumpling her otherwise lovely features. "Why didn't you call right away?"

"I just arrived late last night."

"I had to hear about Auntie's death from a friend of a friend who happens to work at Gaylord's Funeral Home."

"Sorry about that. I'm still in a bit of shock." Kennie told her about Aunt Clara's final call and how hard she'd tried to make it to the hospital before their aunt died.

"I can't believe she didn't call me or Sterling. How ridiculous that she wasted your time when one of us could have been down to the hospital inside half an hour. She may have been a little off her rocker at the end."

Kennie clamped her lips and didn't respond. Aunt Clara had always been a very intentional person. If Suzanne wasn't on the list of those to be contacted in the event of an emergency, then that's what Aunt Clara had wanted.

"Where are her legal — oh, here we go."

Kennie darted forward and picked up the files before Suzanne could get to them. "She named me executor. I've got a call in to the attorney."

Hand on one hip, Suzanne narrowed her eyes and stared at Kennie. Somewhere in the gene pool someone must have had Kennie's brown eyes, but Suzanne's — and Sterling's as well — were ice blue like their parents' eyes had been. When Suzanne turned them on anyone with malice, her expression was almost frightening. As a child, Kennie had run away from her. Now, despite Kennie having grown into a tall, strong adult, her sister was still trying to intimidate her.

"I get it, little sis. I see. You're making a play for all the goodies."

Kennie's face flushed hot. Before she could answer, her cell phone rang, and someone from George Zimmerman's law office asked her about scheduling an immediate appointment.

TWO HOURS LATER, Suzanne showed up, uninvited, for the meeting at the lawyer's office. Kennie's initial discomfort from Suzanne's earlier visit to the house moved to full-fledged irritation. Before Suzanne had stomped out of Aunt Clara's in a complete hissy fit, Kennie had tried to tell her she had no call to horn in on things, but her sister had a mind of her own. Now she stood in the waiting room insistent about attending the meeting.

They sat, tight-lipped, in opposite corners of the room until the attorney's administrative assistant called them into his office. He recorded some standard data and took copies of their driver's licenses, then ushered them into George Zimmerman's spacious office, which contained a gigantic desk and credenza, both bigger than any Kennie had ever seen. Oak bookshelves lined two long walls in one-half of the room, and a variety of other furniture was arranged in the other half.

Zimmerman greeted them and introduced himself. Rather than have them sit in visitor's chairs at his desk, he summoned them to a perfectly squared-off set of four burgundy leather sofas. A dozen people could sit there comfortably, more if they were good friends.

The attorney sat in the middle of one sofa and opened a thick file on the wide wooden coffee table in front of him. Kennie and Suzanne sat across from him at opposite ends of the couch. Zimmerman probably hadn't missed the significance of that. Kennie glanced over at Suzanne. Her sister sat back on the sofa, one leg crossed casually over the other, with her hands in her lap and fingers laced together. She seemed to be nodding, ever so slightly, to some silent music only she could hear.

"Ms. McClain," Zimmerman said.

Suzanne said, "Yes," with an engaging smile, her face lit up and welcoming. It was an expression Kennie remembered well. With a job in real estate, Suzanne had never had any trouble meeting and captivating men. She had never married, though ever since Kennie was a small child, she'd had a string of handsome playboys in her life. Suzanne had never lacked for male companionship, that was for sure. Now she was doing her best to charm the lawyer.

"Ahem, yes, well," he said, "it's the other Ms. McClain I refer to. As the executor, disposition of all the property is up to her."

Suzanne's smile froze a little. "Am I provided for at all?"

"Your aunt left you a specific bequest."

Suzanne smiled Kennie's way. "How wonderful. Are you at

liberty to go into detail?"

Zimmerman looked over-warm, definitely sweating in his expensive suit. He removed a handkerchief from his breast pocket and dabbed politely at his forehead. "It's preferable that it come from the executor. I would like to brief her at length, so at this time, your presence isn't required."

Suzanne's expression reminded Kennie of the time in kindergarten when she'd brought home a fluffy white kitten, a gift from one of the neighbors, and the kitty had taken a nap on Suzanne's bed. Unfortunately, her sister had laid out a snazzy little black cocktail dress for a college soiree she was to attend, and the cat had shed all over it. The expression she wore now mirrored the look of horror and disgust on her face then.

"I—I don't understand. I'm a member of the family, one of only three close family members left."

"There are some private matters pertaining solely to Ms. McClain here. I'm afraid they're confidential, and therefore I can't permit you to hear them at this time. Once I brief your sister, you and I can speak, or you may find she can give you the details. Here," he said, fumbling in the breast pocket of his suit jacket, "please take my card and call me in a few days if you're not satisfied with the situation."

Face red, eyes sparkling with indignation, Suzanne rose, accepted the card, and stomped out of the office without another word.

Zimmerman eyed Kennie, and she shook her head. "Don't even ask me about her," she said. "My sister is a real piece of work."

"I suspect we'll need to prepare for legal action once she discovers the extent of your aunt's bequests. I presume you've been through the documents she kept on file at home?"

"Yes, sir, I have."

"Let's not stand on ceremony. Please call me George. May I address you as Kendra?"

"Kennie. Just call me Kennie."

"All right then, Kennie. Let me go through the details of your aunt's estate."

As the lawyer flipped through many pages of materials and discussed extensive stocks and holdings, Kennie zoned in and out. Meeting with this lawyer in an over-decorated office that smelled of old cigar smoke brought back memories of the excruciating experience she'd had with the attorneys after Janeen died. This time she felt considerably less overwhelmed. With Janeen's death, she'd felt like her own life was coming to an end; with her aunt's death, she merely felt sad.

"...and there's one more major matter to attend to, Kennie, and this one's a little delicate."

She snapped out of her meandering. "Oh?"

"Your aunt left a letter for you, and she wanted you to read it here, in my office, should there be any questions."

He handed a cream-colored envelope across the wide coffee table. "I'm going to make some tea. Would you like some? Or I could get coffee."

"Tea would be great, George. Thank you."

She examined the envelope. Her full name *Kendra May McClain* was written on the front in Aunt Clara's inimitable cursive. She was glad she'd never had to forge her aunt's name for school excuses or permission slips. No way could she have duplicated the fancy slant, curlicues, and decorative loops. If the letter inside was written in this script, no wonder the lawyer had left the room. She'd be spending a lot of time reading.

She broke the seal and removed three off-white sheets of paper monogrammed with her aunt's initials, *CMM* – for Clara May McClain. For years, she hadn't thought about the fact that she shared her aunt's middle name.

The letter was typewritten and dated two years earlier. Kennie remembered the old IBM Selectric her aunt kept in her TV room. The lowercase *a* had always been slightly off, as it was in this letter, so she knew where the letter had been typed.

My Dear Kendra,

Since you're reading this now, I have obviously departed this earth. Whatever the circumstances of my demise, I'm sure it's been stressful for you, and I apologize for any problems or heartache I may inadvertently cause.

Every family has secrets, and ours is no different. I've carried this secret for nearly four decades, and I promised never to reveal it as long as I lived. But I no longer live, and I cannot in good conscience take this matter to my grave.

The great tragedy of my life and the downfall of my marriage was that I was barren. During Harold's and my early years, we tried so hard to conceive, but at long last, the doctors determined I was infertile. The loss of that dream dealt a crushing blow to both of us and to our marriage. Harold desperately wanted children. I wish you could remember him. He was an uncommonly charismatic man, one who had mood swings and melancholy like I'd never seen. I loved him desperately, as I've never loved anything or anyone before or since.

Kennie finished the page, wondering why her aunt had needed to share this. Uncle Harold and Aunt Clara's childlessness and their desire to have children had never been a secret. The passion of her attachment was news, but Kennie had been too small to know Uncle Harold, and her aunt had been so private.

She set the first page aside and continued reading page two.

Still, I was shocked when he embarked upon a relationship with your mother. Though the affair was short-lived, it had one lasting result: You.

What? Kennie sat back against the leather sofa; her brain had ceased to compute. After a moment of trepidation about what else the letter might contain, she lifted the sheet and read on.

The man you have always thought of as your father was your uncle, and Harold was your birth father. Your mother never told Harold's brother, the man you consider your father, and Harold begged me never to tell anyone.

But you have a right to know that and to understand that "Uncle" Harold didn't die of a heart attack. His mental issues and his guilt and grief over not being able to claim you as his own were too much for him. He committed suicide while you were still a toddler. Even though he wasn't faithful to me, I loved him very much, and I think you know I never got over losing him. If there's a heaven, I hope to reunite with him when I die.

These are heavy facts, and I'm trying not to be melodramatic. Perhaps you shall wish I hadn't told, but after years of agonizing, I feel I must be forthright. Please know that one thing remains clear — I have always loved you and especially loved the part of Harold I've always seen in you. You have his smile, and you have his eyes — deep, dark, and full of warmth and love. Your presence in my home during your teen years was a gift to me, and one I can never repay. If he were alive, Harold would want you to have our worldly goods, and I feel the same.

Please forgive me if my letter upsets you or causes you undue anguish. That's not my intent. Please take the proceeds of my estate and do with them what you will. You've always been such a sensible girl. I'm sure you'll figure out how to enrich your life to do something useful with the funds.

Thank you for not forgetting me all these years. Your cards and letters and occasional photographs have meant more to me than you will ever know. I have always been proud to be your aunt. You're the child I wish I had birthed myself, and I hope you go on to live a life full of joy and contentment. Most of all, I'm happy that a little bit of Harold lives on.

Love Always,
Aunt Clara

Stunned, Kennie set aside the page with tears in her eyes. In fifty thousand years, she would never have come up with this scenario. She reread the letter. Wow. She had no idea how to absorb it. All she could do was sit in silence.

After a few minutes, George and his assistant bustled in and set a teapot, mugs, napkins, containers of milk and sugar, and a selection of tea bags on the coffee table. Kennie watched with dawning comprehension as the two men worked together to lay out an attractive arrangement.

"There you go," the assistant said as he smiled at George Zimmerman.

"Thanks, Rob," George said.

Rob gave Kennie a sympathetic look as he left the room, and that was all she needed. She understood there were no secrets, legal or otherwise, between the two men. Somehow that was comforting to her.

George set to work pouring the tea water, and once they both sat dunking teabags in their mugs, he said, "I trust you're as surprised as I was?"

"Yes." She struggled to find words. "Surprised, yes. But I can't say I'm as shocked as you might expect. My parents were odd ducks. So much older than me. And they never seemed to get along with one another all that well, so... I guess I'm not too blown away that my mother had an affair." It suddenly occurred to her that Suzanne and Sterling were only half-siblings to her, and that felt right and good. Actually, prior to this moment, she wouldn't have been surprised to find she'd been adopted or stolen from another family as a baby. She never had fit into the family constellation very well, and now she understood why. What a burden her mother had to have carried.

"Do you have any questions?"

"Did my dad — the dad I grew up with — ever find out about this?"

"My understanding from your aunt was that he wasn't aware you weren't his biological child."

"And they kept that a secret all those years. Wow."

He set down his tea and picked up a folder. "Just so you know, your aunt gave leave for me to answer any and all of your questions, so I want you to know I'm not betraying her confidences.

I have a release here—"

"That's quite all right," Kennie said. "I trust you. If my aunt had faith in you, then I do, too."

"Thank you. If you continue to retain me as your lawyer after the estate is settled, you need to know that confidentiality is of utmost importance to me."

"Good. I appreciate that."

"Your aunt was a very private woman, Kennie."

"Yes, she was."

"We had three appointments before she came to the decision to inform you of your heritage. She didn't take it lightly."

"She was never one to do anything without a great deal of thought. She was very careful about everything."

"Yes, quite risk-averse. Which is why she didn't suffer many losses when the economy went south. She'd been very sensible with her holdings."

"What holdings are you talking about?"

"She owned a great deal of rental property."

"You're kidding? That wasn't in the will."

"The extent of her holdings isn't specifically detailed in the will, but there are a lot of commercial properties which were purchased and maintained by your unc—I mean, your birth father—until his death, at which point your aunt engaged my father's services. He managed her legal affairs, set her up with a financial adviser, and secured a company to maintain and improve the properties."

"What properties—and where are they?"

"They're all apartment houses, and they're located here in Watertown."

Kennie vaguely remembered hearing talk of Uncle Harold's work at his "properties" and that Aunt Clara had done accounting work from home. She'd thought he was an employee for a company and never knew he actually owned anything other than the house they lived in. "How many?"

"Sixteen."

"Sixteen units?"

"Sixteen apartment complexes."

"Whoa—and the hits just keep on coming."

George grinned. "I think that's the last of the surprises. You would have never known it, but your aunt was an extremely rich woman. By your inheritance, you will now assume a great many assets and be a wealthy woman yourself."

Kennie didn't bother to tell him she was already richer than she'd ever planned—or hoped—to be. Instead, she imagined Aunt Clara, holed up in the small, two-story house, behaving as if her entire life revolved around the TV, take-out foods, and her monthly Social Security check.

THAT NIGHT KENNIE lay in the twin bed in her old bedroom at Aunt Clara's. The room had been regularly dusted, and the coverlet must have been laundered often as well, because it smelled like Downy fabric softener. Otherwise, the room was the same as she remembered it—except for feeling strangely smaller. Her high school summer softball trophies sat upon a shelf above the pedestal desk. When she'd opened desk drawers, they were still stuffed full of her childhood drawings, high school papers, and various aging office supplies.

At one point, she'd been nuts about collecting horse figurines, and there were more than a dozen quarter horses, paint ponies, Clydesdales, Spanish Mustangs, Rhinelanders, Appaloosas, and others on the windowsill and dresser. Once upon a time, she was so carefree that all she cared about was imagining herself riding fast on the back of a wild horse, her hair blowing in the wind, and some other girl riding next to her, face full of admiration. She'd spent hours fantasizing about living in the wilderness with her best friend and their horses. Where had all that innocence gone? She was pretty sure she hadn't thought of her horse collection in twenty years, and now she wondered what she should do with it.

She'd taken most of her clothes with her when she moved, but a couple of winter coats hung in the closet next to a dress she'd once worn to a dance in tenth grade. That was going to the Goodwill for sure.

There was only one new thing in the room. Near the door, several feet from a couple of Madonna and Michael Jackson posters, hung a professionally framed piece of calligraphy. It was matted in a rich royal blue and gold, and the frame was ebony black. The lettering on the parchment paper was sure and stylish:

Grief moves us like love.
Grief is love, I suppose.
Love as a backwards glance.

~Helen Humphreys

Kennie had no clue why the piece of art was in her room rather than somewhere else in the house. Was it some sort of message from her aunt? She could only assume so. But what was she supposed to glean from that bit of wisdom?

She had never thought about the fact that she loved her aunt, but she saw now it was love as a backwards glance, more in death than she had ever loved her in life. They'd had nothing in common, but what her aunt had provided, she'd given freely with no hesitation. Too bad the one thing she never had shared was her depth of grief. Her sadness overwhelmed every aspect of love in such a way that she rarely expressed any emotions at all. The Black Velvet whiskey served only to shroud her real feelings in a fog much more effective than real velvet.

The thought of Aunt Clara's forty-plus years of unhappiness and unrelenting misery made Kennie feel queasy. Was she doing that to herself on a smaller scale about Janeen? Had she been so busy looking backwards that her life was on track to mimic her aunt's?

The idea made her shudder.

How could she help but feel that way though? Her one foray into looking forward had ended badly, a colossal mistake. No way did she want to feel that kind of pain again.

With the exception of when Janeen died, Kennie was certain she hadn't felt this out of sorts in all her life. Even when her parents died, she'd managed to let the pain in only a little at a time, squelching most of her grief until she could deal with it gradually. But lately, everything came crashing down on her like an avalanche, and she hadn't figured out how to make things right.

The horses on her dresser seemed to look her way sympathetically. She turned off the light next to the bed to blot out the vision of relics from a childhood full of lies.

IN THE NIGHT Kennie was awakened by the muffled ringing of her cell phone. A frantic search finally unearthed it in the pocket of the shirt she'd hung from the doorknob. She flipped it open too late to catch the call and had to hit redial.

"Kennie?"

"Yeah, yeah." She yawned and shuffled back to the bed.

"I'm real sorry it's so late, but—"

"Oh, it's you, Max. Everything okay?" She shook her head to clear out the cobwebs, sat on the bed, and turned on the bedside light. The clock read 1:17.

"Miss Quist is dead."

"What?"

"Miss Quist in 6A."

"I know where she lives. What happened to her?"

"We found her dead in her apartment."

"Holy shit. What happened? Oh, my God. You need to call the police."

"I already did that. They came and said it looked natural, and some funeral home guys came to take her away."

"Oh, wow. I'm glad you were there to take care of it. Sounds like you handled it perfectly."

"But what do I do now?"

"Lock up, go to the office in my apartment, and I'll tell you how to find her file with the next-of-kin info."

"No, that's not what I mean. What do I do about the cats? And the couch?"

Kennie fell back onto the bed. "Why don't I shut up so you can start at the beginning and tell me everything, then I'll answer your questions?"

"Evelyn hadn't seen her for two days and was worried. So we went up and knocked on her door. She didn't answer even when we pounded, so I unlocked it and went in. She was lying on a little couch—Evelyn called it a sectional—and she was dead, and it smelled pretty bad in there. The cats were going crazy."

Kennie sat up, suddenly having horror movie visions of the death scene. "What cats? And what did they do?"

"They didn't do anything bad. They were agitated and jumping all around and seemed to know something was wrong with Miss Quist. I was surprised about them because I thought you don't allow pets."

"I don't. It's always been a pet-free building."

"What do I do with them? And what about the couch?"

Kennie was starting to feel like she was in a very bad communication loop. "How many cats are there?"

"Four."

"Shit."

"Yeah, kind of a lot. Me and Renae fed 'em and filled the water bowls. It looks like they spent most of their time in the back area of the apartment, in this really big sitting room. That apartment is humongous."

Kennie had never made it past the parlor inside the front door. Miss Quist had always been very peculiar about letting anyone in. She even insisted on changing the smoke detector batteries herself. Now Kennie knew why.

"Go downstairs to my office and look in the top drawer of the filing cabinet. Miss Quist's nephew or cousin or someone like that is her contact. Hand the cats off to him, if you can. If you can't, go see Adam Vendrick in 2C. Remember he has a pet store?"

"Oh, yeah, that's right."

"He can probably check the cats, make sure they're healthy, and maybe he can find homes for them. I'll touch base with you soon when I'm more awake."

"But wait. What about the couch?"

"The couch?"

"The one where she, uh, died. It's smelling up her whole apartment. It's hot in there with no air conditioner, and you can smell it in the hall."

"Oh." Kennie hated that she felt so out of it, but after a moment, she dredged up some further instructions. "First thing in the morning, call a waste management service and get some guys up there to take it away. Ask for an invoice. I'll pay the bill when I get home. Or if they want money up front, pay them from the petty cash envelope in the front of the file cabinet. Just get a receipt."

"Okay. We can do that."

"Then get Simms to help you take an air conditioner up— actually there are two. If you can get them in and cool down the apartment, that might help. If you can't get them in, just open all the windows. Take the fans from my apartment and point them out the windows to suck out the bad air."

Kennie heard muffled conversation in the background, something about asking how things were going.

Hesitantly Max asked, "Is everything okay? Are you coming back soon?"

In all the confusion of the last three days, Kennie had never called Max. She hadn't called the guys in security either. She felt like a dunce, but the whole situation felt like something out of a Kafka novel. "I have a funeral to attend tomorrow, and I'll be heading home the next day. Can you keep covering for me until then?"

"I can do that for you. Um, so your aunt died?"

"Yeah."

"I'm sorry, Kennie. Real sorry. Renae wants to know if you're okay. Me, too, I mean."

"Yeah, thanks. I just have a lot of arrangements to make. Thank you for holding down the fort while I've been gone."

"No prob."

"Okay, good job. I'll make it worth your while when I return. Just take care of things the best you can, and I'll handle whatever's left later."

After they hung up, Kennie turned out the light and lay in bed for a long time thinking about Miss Quist, the strange little lady who had been so private. No wonder, if she'd been hiding a raft of cats all those years. Too bad she hadn't spoken to Kennie when she announced her ownership of the building. Surely Miss Quist didn't believe Kennie would throw her out after all those years? People, she thought. So puzzling and strange.

Her thoughts turned to what she had left to do before she could fly out of Watertown. She couldn't wait to get away.

Chapter Seventeen

KENNIE LEFT THE airport, well aware she was dragging both her ass and her suitcase. She couldn't be happier to have fled Watertown and touched down in Portland, but she was bone-weary. The funeral service and burial for her aunt had been exhausting. Sterling, Suzanne, and one neighbor were the extent of the actual mourners. The rest were professionals—accountants, building managers, maintenance contractors, the owner of a janitorial service—all of whom attempted to charm her into retaining their services. Little did they know about Kennie's desire to stay completely out of handling any of those decisions. She determined that the best thing was for George Zimmerman and his highly capable partner to assume responsibility for the overall management of her aunt's properties and the arrangements with various contractors and management firms. Time enough in the future to figure out how to dispose of the properties if that was what she decided to do.

Because of the often disingenuous vendor comments ("she was such a delightful woman") and the eulogy by a minister who had no clue about her life ("she was loved by all who knew her"), the service was flat. But what really angered Kennie was Suzanne and Sterling feeling the need to rise and add to the spectacle by reminiscing about Aunt Clara as if she was the nearest, dearest, closest relative they could ever hope to love. Between the two of them staring daggers at her and all the rest of the people insistently trying to square up deals, Kennie had the headache from hell. She couldn't get out of there fast enough, pack, and be ready for the return trip the next day.

Rather than calling Max when she arrived in Portland, she took a taxi from the airport and arrived at the Allen Arms a few minutes after six p.m. She expected someone at the security desk, but the lobby was empty.

As she rolled her suitcase toward her apartment, someone keyed the back door lock and Simms came bustling in, followed by Max.

"Where are they?" Simms said, his voice strained but excited. He caught sight of her and grinned as he hurried by toward the security desk. "Hi-Kennie-welcome-back-gotta-go!"

Kennie looked to Max for an explanation. "The baby's coming. He's got to get to the hospital."

"Found them." Simms held up a key ring, slammed the desk

drawer shut, and hustled toward them. He stopped to fling his arms around Kennie and practically knocked the wind out of her. "I'll let you know as soon as the baby's born."

He let go and raced to the back door, nearly tripping on the way.

Max let out a hoot. "God, I hope he makes it safely and doesn't get in a wreck. I thought he was going to fall down the stairs when we went outside." She paused to examine Kennie's face. "So you're back. I'm glad. You look tired."

"I am."

"Renae brought home a ton of vegetable soup from work. I'll bring some over."

"You don't have to do that."

"When's the last time you ate something?"

Kennie had eaten breakfast at her aunt's before clearing out the refrigerator of perishables, and she'd had coffee and a bagel after her first flight landed in Chicago, but nothing since then.

Max said, "You look wasted. Just go chill, and let me bring you some food."

Before Kennie could answer, Max hurried off, and Kennie didn't have the energy to call her back. She went to her apartment door and let herself in.

In her bedroom, she parked the suitcase and noticed that instead of being greeted with a dusty place with a closed-up-too-long odor, her apartment smelled fresh. She backtracked to the kitchen and, along the way, saw the carpet looked cleaner than before she left. Someone had vacuumed and dusted.

A bouquet of pink roses sprouted from a vase on the center island in the kitchen. The flowers gave off a faint scent that permeated the air and reminded her of a time Janeen had shown up for an anniversary carting a big bouquet of red roses and a gigantic heart-shaped box of Valentine's Day chocolates marked fifty percent off. Kennie had taken one look at the gaudy candy box and quipped, "Were the roses half-price, too?"

Janeen, standing in the doorway with her red-brown hair askew, said, "I didn't really buy them for you. My other girlfriend is so much more appreciative."

They both burst into hysterical laughter, and Kennie had gone to her and kissed her hard. It had been their second anniversary, now that Kennie thought about it. They'd never gotten past the living room. They'd fumbled their way to the sofa where they made love with a passion, flowers forgotten, candy shunted aside. As they lay in one another's arms a bit later, Janeen said, "I hope this never ends, never ever. I'll never find anyone like you again."

Reaching for the candy box on the coffee table, Kennie said,

"That's a no-brainer. Who else would ravish you one hundred percent, then eat fifty-percent-marked-down chocolates and love every bite?" She removed the bow from the box and promptly dumped most of the candies all over them.

"This," Janeen said, "gives new meaning to the phrase 'a roll in the hay.'"

Over the last three years, remembering that moment with Janeen lying against her, both of them laughing and happy, was one of those snapshots in time that made Kennie feel happier—and sadder—than she could bear.

But this time the memory didn't hurt quite so much.

There was a knock at the door, and someone called out her name. "We're coming in."

Hands encased in oven mitts, Renae held a clear glass bowl of steaming soup. Max followed her into the kitchen, carrying a plate of thick-sliced breads.

"This is nice of you two."

"No problem," Renae said. "Slow day for soup today. Must've been the high temps outside. The cook at Signature doesn't usually have a gallon of this good soup left, and he let me have it. It's really yummy."

Kennie started to get down three bowls, but Max said, "We already ate."

"You want something to drink?"

Renae took the bowl from her. "You just sit down and relax, Kennie." She laid out a place setting, took three glasses from the cupboard, and got their requested drinks.

"Hey, thanks to you two for tidying up my place. You vacuumed. And dusted."

"We were doing the efficiency anyway," Renae said, "so I just kept on running the vacuum in here."

Once they were all settled on stools with Renae and Max across from her, Kennie sampled the soup and commented on how thick and tasty it was, just the way she liked it. Renae beamed.

"So," Kennie said, "I'm sorry things have been crazy here. What's the report on the events of the last few days?"

Max put her elbows on the counter and head in her hands. "I've never seen a dead person before—not like that. I mean, I've seen someone dead in a casket at a funeral, but not in their own house."

"Don't go all hyper again." Renae patted Max's hand and wrapped an arm around her shoulders. "She's still kind of freaked out."

"It was just icky," Max said. "She didn't look like herself at all."

"I'm sorry I wasn't here. You kids shouldn't have had to deal with that."

Max bristled and looked up with a frown. "We managed though."

"I know, I know, it's just that I dumped a lot of responsibility in your lap without much warning." She let out a sigh. "It shouldn't have been that way."

Max gazed at her, the frown replaced by a perplexed expression. "How would it have been any different if you'd been here?"

"You wouldn't have had to be traumatized by Miss Quist's death."

"Well, sure I would have. I would've been helping you."

From the tone of Max's voice, Kennie sensed she was in deep water, but she wasn't quite sure why, so she didn't answer.

"You don't get it, Kennie. I've had a lot of time to think about this while you've been gone. I know we've only known each other a short while, but it feels like forever to me."

"To us," Renae said.

"You saved my life," Max said with fervor. "You don't even see what you've done."

Kennie set down her spoon. "All I did was stop your bro—"

"It has nothing to do with my brother, don't you see? I'm not talking about that incident. You gave me respect, a place to stay, somewhere to work. You trusted me, and you did it when I was so low, I thought I'd die." Her voice was thick, as she fought to keep tears at bay. "I'm not sure what exactly I wanted. I think I wanted Derek to just kick me until the misery was over. I didn't see any possibilities. Because of you, I got away from the hell of my life. I couldn't bear the thought of living without at least *someone* who loved me, without my mom. And there was no one. Nowhere to go. And then things changed, and it's all because of you that I could meet someone like Renae and find a friend like Evelyn. But you act like it's nothing, like it's some kind of...of happy accident that has nothing to do with you."

Something clicked for Kennie, and she felt a strange recognition flood through her. At this very moment, under these circumstances, she was Aunt Clara making a place for a traumatized teenager. Aunt Clara providing—but not confiding. Aunt Clara refusing to go all out into a relationship with another person. And now Kennie had the choice to sit around for the next forty years nursing the equivalent of a couple thousand bottles of Black Velvet...or she could actually have a true connection with this blunt, scarred, but resilient kid. Two of them, in fact.

She considered their nervous faces. What had she needed from

Aunt Clara? The woman had given her all the necessary material things and the approval to take matters into her own hands and do whatever she thought best. But she never gave Kennie any real attention. She didn't share any feelings. They never connected.

In a bolt of insight, she decided she didn't want to carry on Aunt Clara's stand-offish legacy.

"I'm glad I could help you, Max." She chose her words carefully. "I didn't do it because you were special, though I've since discovered that you are. One thing led to another, without any sort of a plan, and everything unfolded in ways I never expected. Now here we are, trying to figure out what the next thing should be. Kind of like my whole life, I guess. You need to understand that I truly have no plan. I'm just trying to do the right thing every day...and not always feeling like I have a damn clue what that should be."

Max nodded as if that made sense. "I have to tell you...every day I wonder when all this good stuff is going to end, when I'll get tossed out onto the street."

Kennie felt the urge to hug Max, but something held her back. She reached over and tapped her fist against the kid's shoulder. "I won't do that to you, Max. I promise. I know it may be hard for you to believe, but I've been right where you are. When my parents died, I was a teenager. Tough times. Really, I understand."

"What happened?" Max asked.

Kennie shook her head. "Honestly, I don't even know where to start."

Max's hunched shoulders relaxed. "That's okay. You can tell us another time. You could start by finishing that soup. I'm not kidding that you look like crap, like you haven't eaten or slept for days."

Kennie chuckled. "Well, thank you. Nice to hear an honest assessment."

"You should have some bread, too," Renae said. "Max is right. You look gaunt."

Max's cell phone trilled. She fished it out of her pocket, looked at the screen, then let out a shout. "It's a girl! Seven pounds one ounce — and healthy!"

THE DAYS AHEAD were difficult. Nearly every morning, George Zimmerman called and Kennie spent more time than she ever wanted talking with him about the properties. He asked her twice what she wanted to do about Aunt Clara's house, and she wasn't sure. She finally told him to put it on the back burner, that she'd come to a conclusion eventually.

Each time she received a call, she went to the desk in her apartment and tried to keep track of the information the lawyer relayed. She also wanted her privacy. But each time she rose from one of those long calls, she felt drained. She wondered if she needed to hire a manager to manage the lawyer in managing the various managers. That thought made her laugh.

Out in the lobby, Max sat behind the security desk looking bored. Kennie was impressed with how the kid took care of her uniform, always carefully pressing the pants and shirt. As she came down the hall, Max heard her and spun in the office chair.

"Hey, Kennie, what's happening? Anything interesting?"

"Nope, but I thought maybe you could help me hang the painting here next to the elevator." She stood eyeing the space under the stairs.

"Lily's painting?" Max asked, excitement in her voice.

"The very one."

"Have you heard from her?"

Kennie turned. "Now why would I hear from her?"

Max rose and drew closer, which Kennie appreciated so her voice didn't carry. Quietly Max said, "Come on, you think I'm blind? You two have a thing for each other."

"Had, kiddo. Past tense."

Max crossed her arms and smirked. "Would you care to lay some money on what I think'll happen when she gets back from Barcelona?"

"Not really. I don't think you can afford to lose your ass."

"Oh, oh, oh, a challenge." Max pulled her wallet from her back pocket. "I've got a hundred bucks right here, and I'll gladly lay it on the line."

"Put your money away. You need that for college."

The door to the efficiency opened, and Renae stepped out, wearing a royal blue blouse, tan Capri pants, and tennis shoes. "I'm off to work, hon. Hi, Kennie."

Max put an arm around Renae and said, "I need a witness. I just bet Kennie a hundred bucks about you-know-what and Lily."

Kennie let out an irritated gasp. "You two have a shorthand about my personal life?"

"Oh, yeah," Max said. She and Renae smiled at each other and turned to grin at Kennie.

Renae gave Max a kiss and scampered out the front door, leaving Kennie standing with arms crossed. "You two are cracked."

"Uh-huh. So where's the painting? Let's get it up here."

Kennie brought the painting, a hammer, nails, and a level from her apartment. They spent the next few minutes measuring, lining it up, and re-measuring. Finally the painting was up on the wall.

"Looks really good, doesn't it?" Max leaned in close to whisper, "No woman paints something like this for somebody she doesn't care about. Look at how lovingly she drew you."

"You are so reading into it something that isn't there."

Max pulled the hundred-dollar bill out of her front pocket and waggled her eyebrows. "Lay your money down, or I'll have to report that you're all talk."

"So if we're going to have this bet, I guess you better flesh it out a bit. What are the terms?"

"You two — the horizontal mambo — before, let's say, the end of summer."

"Good grief. Mambo? You are way too young to know that term. It was old when I was your age."

Max grinned wolfishly. "I like it. Heard it on an old TV show. Would you like me to come up with some other sexier description for —"

"No! I get the picture. But you can't even know when she'll return. So do I win by default if she isn't back by then? It'd be a tough way to blow that much money. And even if she does return, well, she'll be occupied with the lieutenant."

"Oh, yeah, you go on thinking that. You blind? You whacked out? She broke up with the lieutenant."

"What?"

"Come on. That shit PJ did to you... Lily isn't the kind of woman who puts up with that. She threw her out."

Kennie knew she probably had the stupidest, dazed look on her face, and she felt a little embarrassed by that, but it seemed more important to try to process this bit of information. After a moment, she said, "How do you know that?"

Max let out an exasperated sigh. "How the heck did you ever manage to get as old as you are and not pick up any clues along the way?"

"Now you're being offensive, young lady." Kennie reached out to cuff her, and Max ducked out of the way, laughing, and took off. Kennie darted across the lobby, grabbed the back of Max's collar, and jerked her to a stop. With a shriek of laughter, Max tried to escape, but Kennie got her bent over in a headlock. Giggling, the two of them did an awkward little dance, and Max kept trying to slip out, but Kennie's grip was too tight. It wasn't until Kennie heard the front door open that she let go. She caught sight of someone entering the lobby. The woman stopped, one hand still on the door, looking amused, and Kennie nearly fainted.

Max straightened her jacket and tie, a wide smile on her face. "Hi, Lily. Welcome home."

Chapter Eighteen

KENNIE MEANT TO go running early in the day before it got hot, but the workmen in Miss Quist's apartment kept calling her for direction and approvals. She finally spent most of the morning in the apartment with them as they tore out various fixtures.

The week before, she and Max had attempted to pull up the shag carpeting in the living room at the rear of the luxury apartment. After fifteen minutes of heavy work punctuated with blasts of cat dander, dust, and curses, Kennie decided to bag it. With so much unemployment in Portland, she had no trouble getting workers in to do the carpet tear-out, and one of the guys ran an interior demolition business, so she hired him to do further work. They came with a tube that went out the window down into a dumpster. Kennie was thrilled that the dirt and dander could go out the window rather than down the stairs where it would make a mess for all the tenants.

As far as she could tell, 6A had never been updated in any way. The fixtures had to be from the Forties, the carpet in the four bedrooms, parlor, living room, and dining room was forty-plus years old, and the kitchen looked like something out of *Gone With The Wind*. She was going to spend a chunk of change to update the unit, that was for sure.

Early in the afternoon, she left the work guys alone and returned to her apartment for a meal. By midafternoon, feeling antsy, she dressed in running shoes, shorts, and shirt and headed for the back door. A blast of hot air greeted her, and she didn't have the energy to brave what felt like a ninety-degree temperature. She reversed tracks and went to the basement, giving herself a big pat on the back for being smart enough to put in a workout area.

After a warm-up on the elliptical machine, she got on the treadmill and set it for a thirty-minute workout. About halfway through, she determined she'd forgotten a major item in her basement project. She should have put a TV in—or at least some sort of music system. She could go upstairs and get an MP3 player and headphones, but she didn't want to interrupt the workout. She'd have to rectify that. And while she was at it, she decided to get a recumbent-style exercise bike, too. Some of the older tenants said they'd like to use one.

Sweating freely and feeling a good strain in her legs, she had the machine up to a six-mile-per-hour pace when she heard footsteps on the stairs. Lily bounced into the room with a smile and greeted her.

For the briefest of moments, Kennie thought her legs were going to refuse to hold her up. She grabbed the handrail to recover from the slight wobble and said, "Hi, what are you doing here?" As usual, she regretted her words immediately. Lily wore a pair of baggy gray shorts and a t-shirt that said *Cabo San Lucas* with a bunch of tropical fish on it. Her running shoes looked brand new. Of course she was in the workout room to work out.

"Thought I'd get a bit of exercise, and it's too damn hot out." Lily crossed to the elliptical machine.

Kennie looked down at herself. Her shirt was damp, her legs dripping with sweat, and suddenly the basement didn't feel very cool at all. Where was her towel? Oh, right, she hadn't brought it. She'd just have to keep dripping. A look at the console showed she only had four minutes left, so that was some consolation.

Lily pushed the pedals slowly, obviously acquainting herself with the machine. "I haven't done this before."

"Would you rather have the treadmill?" Kennie said breathlessly.

Lily smiled across the space, and for the first time, Kennie cursed herself for placing the two machines so their users would face one another. Dumb, dumb, dumb. When she mounted a TV in the corner of the room, she resolved to put the two cardio machines next to one another.

But for now, she had to face Lily. While the other woman concentrated on adjusting the machine settings, Kennie studied her. For someone who'd only recently returned from Barcelona, she certainly hadn't gotten any sun. Her legs, arms, and face were downright pale. She'd pulled her hair back in a ponytail, and she wore no makeup. Kennie didn't think she needed any makeup, but she had noticed Lily often applied blush and mascara.

Lily finished fiddling with the buttons, glanced up, and caught Kennie watching. Kennie knew her face was flushed from the workout—could it get any redder? From the additional heat, she thought it had.

Lily said, "I think I have this set up right."

Breathing hard, she managed to grit out, "Are the numbers for strides...and distance and all that...progressing?"

"Looks like it."

"Then just kick back...and enjoy."

Lily laughed, which made her look a lot less tired. "I'm not sure 'enjoy' is the proper term here. I'm so out of shape I'll probably fall off this thing before I even get my heart rate up."

Kennie couldn't stop herself from imagining a scenario where she launched off the treadmill just in time to catch her, like a knight-errant saving a damsel from falling off a horse. The brief image was so ridiculous that she smiled, and Lily smiled back. Oh, boy. She couldn't continue to look into Lily's shining blue eyes, so she focused to the right, on the Universal gym.

Two minutes left—plus some cool-down time—and her anxiety rose. She gradually reduced the treadmill speed, all the while trying not to look at Lily. The cool-down period kicked in, and after less than a minute of walking, she slowed the machine to a gradual stop and stepped off.

She was grateful to drop down to the mat in the yoga/stretching area. Somehow being off to the side, planted on terra firma, gave her courage. "So, Lily, how was Barcelona?"

Lily glanced to the side. She leaned forward significantly on the elliptical machine, and Kennie didn't think she looked any too steady. Abruptly Lily came to a stop and stepped off the machine. "I think I had better call that good for the day." She went across the room to the treadmill.

Great, Kennie thought. Now she's facing me again. She lay back to do some abdominal work and looked at the ceiling. After a count of ten, she rested, then did another set. The hum of the treadmill was steady when she sat up and positioned her legs for butterfly stretches. This gave her a good vantage point to watch Lily who was now flushed and sweating. Some of her hair had come out of the ponytail, and she wasn't walking any too fast a pace. Lily looked up, but Kennie leaned down, focusing on the inner thigh stretch. When she shifted around on the mat to kneel, Lily was watching her.

"I've always hated stretching. You seem like you have a whole set you do."

Kennie said, "I ran track in high school, so I did a regular routine, and I guess I've always stuck with it."

"You'll have to show me. I took just enough ballet in college to learn the moves, but never enough to get a system down. All I know is that doing the splits was never going to be one of my goals."

Kennie blushed. She couldn't stop a flood of images that illustrated quite sensuously how perfectly agile and flexible Lily was in bed. She didn't need any help there. She leaned back from her kneeling position and stretched her quads, then stood up, making a note that she needed to bring a stock of hand-towels with her next time. She wished she could wipe her face and had to settle for the sleeve of her t-shirt.

"Well, that's it for me. See you around, Lily."

"Bye."

As nonchalantly as she could, Kennie strolled to the doorway, but once she got around the corner, she pounded up the steps as fast as she could. She was in the shower before it occurred to her that Lily had artfully dodged her question about Barcelona.

LATER IN THE afternoon, Kennie stopped in the lobby to talk to Simms. He was still an exultant father and ready to show around photos of his darling baby girl.

"What did you settle on for a name?" she asked.

"We duked it out to the end," he said, "but I had to let the wife win. Amanda Louise Simms. After her mom and my grandmother."

"The wife? *The* wife? Doesn't she kick your ass for that?"

Simms leaned in conspiratorially. "You don't think I'd ever call her that anywhere she could actually overhear, do you?"

"Whew, glad to hear you're not as dumb as you look."

She could see the war in his face. Now that she was his employer, the old camaraderie they'd had wasn't quite comfortable for him. He didn't know where they stood. "Geez, Simms. Just say it. Quit second-guessing yourself just because I own the building." Then she laughed. "You know you're a perfectly acceptable employee, even if you are late occasionally."

"I can't lose this job, Kennie."

"Why would you? Look, it's probably time for me to give you an employee evaluation. I never have. And it's time for you to get a raise. Let's meet tomorrow after your shift. Can you do that, or does *The Wife* have something planned?"

He snickered. "The wife always has something planned, but don't worry, I'll stay late."

"We'll count it as on the clock. Tell her it's overtime."

"Will do, boss."

"Cut out the 'boss' crap. I mean it." She gave him a mock stern look, then relented. She took a breath to make another teasing quip, but the front door opened and when she saw who was darkening her doorway, she couldn't speak.

"Aren't you going to say hi and help us with our bags?"

Her sister Suzanne swished inside dressed in culottes and a splashy pink and yellow blouse decorated with shiny spangles that caught the light every time she moved. White go-go boots topped off an outfit that would have looked better on someone forty years younger — perhaps Renae.

Behind her, Sterling dragged two suitcases up and over the threshold and stopped to pull a handkerchief out of the breast pocket of his lightweight tan summer suit. He wore a white shirt under the jacket and a pair of beige and white wingtips.

"What are you two doing here?"

"Just thought we'd visit," Suzanne said.

Simms came around the desk. "Are there more bags you need me to get, sir?"

"Yes, we have—"

"Wait a minute," Kennie said. "Where are you two staying?"

"Well, why not right here?" Suzanne said.

"Because this isn't a hotel. It's an apartment house. I don't have rooms I can check you in and out of."

"What about your apartment?"

"Which one of you wants the couch and which the floor?"

Suzanne had the grace to merely say, "Oh."

Sterling put away his handkerchief. "I told you we ought to grab rooms down near the convention center, but oh no, you insisted."

"Hush, Sterling." She gave Kennie a patently false smile and looked Simms up and down. "Hello, handsome. You can help us get our bags back out to the taxi, then. Kennie, would you like to have dinner with Sterling and me?"

She'd have preferred swimming in an alligator-infested swamp, but said the only thing she could think of: "Sure."

SIMMS WAS LONG gone when Kennie returned from a most trying evening. Not only had her siblings been boring and querulous company, they both ordered expensive seafood platters and pounded down glass after glass of Glenlivet, the most expensive Scotch whisky on the menu. Each chose a fancy dessert and ate only a few bites. The check came, and they both ignored it. When Kennie suggested the evening draw to a close, Sterling excused himself to go to the men's room.

With a sigh, Kennie reached for the check while Suzanne busied herself with a compact mirror to reapply eyelid liner that needed no improvement.

Never in her life had Kennie paid over four hundred dollars for a dinner. Her grocery budget for the month had never exceeded that amount. Once she and Janeen had treated an entire softball team to beer and Mexican food at Chi-Chi's, and it hadn't come anywhere near the bill she held in her hand now.

The money didn't bother her. She knew that. It was the callous disregard—the expectation that she should pony up because Aunt Clara had left her an inheritance. She handed the waiter her credit card and leaned back in her chair.

"So, Suzanne, what exactly do you want?"

Suzanne snapped her compact closed and tucked it into her

purse. "Whatever do you mean?"

"Nobody takes three flights from Watertown to Portland, Oregon, in the heat of summer for no reason."

"We were interested in some sightseeing, and we'd never seen this part of the country, so we thought it an excellent way to kill two birds with one stone."

Killing birds sounded like exactly the kind of thing her sister wanted to do—and her eye was on the goose that laid the golden eggs. Kennie had no doubt that Suzanne and Sterling were after money. She wondered how much it would cost her? Could a sister—a half-sister—divorce her siblings?

Sterling returned to the table behind the waiter. Kennie gritted her teeth when she added a hefty tip and signed the credit receipt.

"You picked up the check, little sis?" Sterling asked ever so innocently. "That was nice of you. Thanks."

She didn't bother to respond to that, just tucked her receipt into her wallet. Her brother was one of the most passive and humorless men she'd ever known. He'd been henpecked by Suzanne and by all three of the wives he'd married, then lost. She'd always wondered how he'd managed to avoid siring children. Then again, if she remembered correctly, all of his wives had been older than he was, the last by ten years, and probably couldn't have or didn't want children. How long would it be before he found a new virago to replace the previous trio?

Suzanne rose, haughty and smiling. "Sterling and I thought we'd visit the downtown area tomorrow and do some further exploring the next day."

Sterling's head swiveled toward her with an expression of disbelief. Kennie could tell Suzanne was making up shit as she went.

"Let's get together again for dinner the day after tomorrow."

"Sure," Kennie said. "I'll be happy to prepare it. How about you come over around seven?" She didn't offer to pick them up. They could damn well take a taxi.

Sterling hemmed and hawed, but Suzanne grabbed his arm. "That'll be fine."

Kennie led the way out to the parking lot at such a fast pace that Suzanne soon lagged behind. She knew both of them were aware she was angry, and she didn't care. The only consolation she felt was they had absolutely no idea of the extent of their aunt's holdings, and she didn't plan to ever tell them.

Chapter Nineteen

KENNIE STILL FELT steamed the next day about the visit from her brother and sister, and she couldn't stop thinking about how underhanded they could be, especially Suzanne. She ran into Max and Simms in the lobby after lunch and gave them the rundown on what had happened.

Max said, "Shit, Kennie, I thought I was the only one with assholes in the family."

Simms shook his head and said, "There are definitely some benefits to being an only child."

Kennie and Max gave him a bad time about that for a while, and then Kennie couldn't stand her nerves anymore. She dressed in workout clothes, grabbed some hand-towels and headed for the basement. She was only five minutes into her warm-up when Lily came down the stairs. Her face fell when she saw Kennie on the treadmill.

"Hey," Kennie said, "give me a few more minutes and I'm switching to the elliptical."

"You sure?"

"Yeah."

"I'll just stretch a little then."

Kennie noticed that Lily lowered herself to the mat as though her legs hurt. Her observation was confirmed when Lily, groaning, attempted to lean forward and touch her toes without success.

The treadmill dinged and slowed. "Lily, why don't you warm up a bit on the treadmill. It'll make stretching a lot easier later." She hopped off the machine and, without a thought, went to the mat and held out a hand to hoist Lily up.

"Oh, thanks. I feel pretty stiff."

"Get your muscles warmed up. Then when you stretch you won't risk pulling anything."

While Lily got set up on the treadmill, Kennie started her elliptical workout, marveling that she had just taken Lily's hand as though it were the most natural thing in the world. Maybe she was making progress.

"So how's the painting going?"

Lily made a noncommittal humming noise. "How's Miss Quist's apartment coming together?"

"Not too bad. I'm glad I hired guys to do a lot of it. The plumbing fixtures alone would have been a huge headache for me.

They had to retrofit some piping and lay some other pipes. I don't understand why that apartment never got any updating done."

"Did you look and see how long she lived there?"

"I know it was long. I think she was the oldest tenant in the building."

"It's my understanding that her parents rented that apartment in the 1940s, and when they died, she stayed on."

"But that's over fifty years ago."

"More like sixty-five or so," Lily said, grinning. "I see your math skills have been compromised by all that exercise you're doing over there."

Kennie felt complimented by Lily's observation, but she wasn't actually trekking too hard on the elliptical at all. She increased her pace a little. Lily was still strolling along slowly.

Lily said, "I could be Miss Quist in a few years, you know. Once her parents were gone, she was alone. She had no siblings — just that bumbling great-nephew."

"He didn't seem too sad about her death."

"No, he didn't. I still think he ought to have had a memorial or some kind of service. I would have attended. So would most of the people in this apartment house. She got no recognition in death, just like in life."

"Have you got any brothers and sisters?"

Lily said, "I had a brother a year younger than me, but he died of a drug overdose when he was twenty."

"That's terrible."

"Yeah, it sure was. I heard you had relatives visit recently."

"My half-sister and half-brother." Kennie said that with a feeling of satisfaction. Quite a bit of anxiety had leeched away after she found out Sterling and Suzanne were only her half-sibs.

"Are you close?" Lily asked.

"Not at all." Who could be close to those money-grubbing fools, Kennie thought.

"How about your parents?"

"Dad had a heart attack about ten years ago. My mom died four years ago. In fact, that's how I met PJ."

"Oh?" Just hearing the name roll off Lily's lips irritated Kennie. She sped up.

"My mother was out shopping and collapsed. PJ was a sergeant back then. She and her partner were the first officers on the scene. They resuscitated her and kept her breathing until the medics got there."

Her voice was so wistful that Kennie could tell Lily had loved her mother deeply.

Lily went on. "She lived a few hours more. Never woke up, but they stabilized her long enough for me to arrive and say my goodbyes, hold her hand, you know, just spend some final time with her. When I came out of the hospital room after she died, PJ was waiting in the hallway. She was a sergeant then. She'd come by after her shift to check on my mother. I was completely torn up, and she was so kind."

Kennie found it hard to believe that the cold, competitive PJ Jarrell could ever have been kind enough to attract a woman like Lily, but then again, maybe Lily brought out the best in people. "Were you forty yet when you met her?"

Lily gave her a perplexed look. "How did you know my age?"

"Um, you mentioned it that night—you know." She closed her eyes, horrified at her comment. "Trust me, you told me."

"I was thirty-nine when Mom died and turned forty just a couple of weeks later."

Kennie wanted so badly to ask if she'd celebrated it with PJ, but she couldn't bring herself to be so catty. She herself had had the best night of her life when she turned forty, and she didn't want to hear Lily say the same.

"I've been meaning to say I'm very sorry your aunt died, Kennie."

"How'd you hear that?"

"The grapevine around here is quite efficient. Were you close to her?"

Kennie explained a little about her parents' death and how she'd lived with her aunt. "But I can't say we were particularly close. She was a troubled woman."

"I see."

They continued to talk about family circumstances, and Kennie answered a number of questions about her high school and college years. In no time at all, thirty minutes had passed. After a brief cool-down, Kennie stepped off the elliptical machine, grabbed a towel, and wiped her face and neck. She plopped down on the mat.

"Oh, good idea." Lily turned off the treadmill. "Why don't you stretch, and I'll follow along?"

With a strange sense of comfort, Kennie talked her through the entire routine, and when they were done, she gave Lily a hand up.

"This is good for me," Lily said. "I'm so incredibly out of shape."

Kennie had to restrain herself from commenting on Lily's delectable, completely gorgeous shape, that it looked good in clothes and even better out of clothes...

Snap out of it, Kennie thought, her heart beating wildly again. She couldn't let herself go there so she simply said, "You look fine."

"It's got to all be diet. I sure as hell don't do enough exercise."

"You'll get it all back soon. Just keep on moving, and you'll be surprised how fast you'll feel fit again."

Marveling at the ease of their communication, Kennie followed Lily up the stairs. She tried very hard not to watch the sexy hips and trim legs ahead of her. But she failed.

THE DREADED DAY of Suzanne and Sterling's visit arrived overcast and cool. Kennie hoped for a torrential downpour—a lightning storm, a monsoon—anything that might keep them from showing up. She didn't figure the weather would save her though.

She navigated the back steps of the Allen Arms, lost in thought. She had so many errands to do she wasn't sure which to take on first. Glancing at her list, she caught a movement out of the corner of her eye. Before she could turn, something plowed into her. She flew sideways, unable to stay on her feet.

She fell with a shout. "What the hell!" Silhouetted in the sun, someone stood above her.

"Where is she?" a man's voice demanded.

Kennie shot to her feet only to be smacked down again. This time she rolled in midair slightly. She cracked her elbow and knee on the pavement but pushed herself up and launched away from her attacker.

She got two fast strides in before he hit her in the back. They both went down. He straddled her back, hands clutching the collar of her shirt. She scrambled to crawl away, but for such a small man, he was surprisingly heavy.

He screamed, "Where is she?"

She leaned to the left and brought her elbow up and back, hard. Nailed him in the head. He yowled, but instead of letting go, his fingers encircled her neck.

"Get off me, get—" she screamed before her air supply was cut off. Oh, shit, she thought. I'm in so much trouble.

With all her strength, she bucked and twisted. He fell to the side. Gasping and choking for air, she scooted away on her butt. On his knees, he sprang at her like a rabid animal. He grabbed her shirt collar. His fists slammed her collarbones and accentuated his words. "How many times I gotta ask? Where is she? Where are the rings?"

With all the strength she could muster, she punched him in the face. He didn't let go, but he did lose his balance. No matter how she twisted or jerked, he hung on with a hand, like a leech she couldn't remove. He got an arm under one of her legs. For a minute she thought he was trying to pick her up. She kicked his feet out from under him and got in another couple of shots before he clocked her on the forehead, near her brow.

She gasped in pain.

Something warm and sticky ran down her face, flooding her eye, stinging, burning. She couldn't see clearly.

Through the blur, another figure, tall as a tree, appeared over her.

"Oh, fuck, there're two of you?" Kennie mumbled. She thought she was done for and let loose a flurry of wild blows that didn't connect well because of the angle at which she sat. Her attacker loosened his hold and was suddenly gone.

"Hold up, Kennie. Stop flailing." The voice was low, but female.

Kennie heard a buzz-crackle and a strangled yodeling sound.

"You want more?" the woman asked. *Buzz-crackle.*

With her sleeve, Kennie wiped blood out of her eye. Lily's lieutenant stood over Max's brother, a taser in one hand. Derek lay groaning on the ground, both arms twitching.

"What are you doing here?" Kennie asked.

"Apparently being your bodyguard. I called for backup."

As if to affirm her words, a faint, thready siren sounded in the distance, steadily getting louder.

PJ held out a hand and helped Kennie up. The guy on the ground tried to roll onto his side. PJ kicked him hard enough to flatten him on his back again. "Stay down, asshole, or I'll taser you again." The words came out hard, almost growling, and Kennie shivered with fear. PJ's voice would be enough to make her do anything she was told.

PJ stepped back so Kennie and Derek were both in her sights and said, "I don't have any cuffs on me so let's just keep a close eye until a squad gets here. Here, take this."

Kennie accepted a handkerchief and pressed it to her eyebrow to stop the blood flow. The cloth smelled clean, like fabric softener. She looked down to see her polo shirt was spattered with blood. Her knee was scraped and bleeding. Both of her forearms were gashed as well. Her butt felt bruised. "God, I'm a mess."

In contrast, PJ was dressed in khaki shorts and a bright blue polo shirt that looked as if it had been ironed. Her long legs were muscled and deeply tanned. Her hair was perfectly coiffed. No wonder Lily was attracted to her. Kennie had to admit the woman was a knockout.

Kennie mustered as much dignity as she could, limped over to the back stairs, and sat. "If only I'd seen him coming."

The siren was loud out front, then stopped in mid-squeal. Seconds later, a male cop inched around the side of the building, gun drawn.

"Chambers, Vega," PJ called out. "Suspect's down."

The officer holstered his gun. He gave Kennie a hard glance as he strode past. She rose and saw another officer had come around the other side of the building. He, too, holstered his weapon.

Derek groaned as one of the cops cuffed him and jerked him to his feet.

"His name's Derek Wallington," Kennie said. "He jumped me."

"Boyfriend?" the Latino officer asked.

"Hell, no. I wouldn't fuck this bitch if you paid me."

"You can shut up now," the other officer said. "I'd advise it."

Derek leaned forward, scowling first at one cop, then the other. His eyes were wild, hair mussed. Kennie'd obviously got in a few good punches; the right side of his face looked red and swollen.

"Chambers," PJ said, "put him in the car and take him in." The officer jerked Derek's arm and led him away.

To Vega she said, "We'll sort out the charges at the station. Ms. McClain here owns this apartment building, and she's not at fault. She'll come down and make a statement later. Go catch up to Chambers and make sure there's no funny business by that jackass."

"Yes, ma'am." He took off at a jog.

Kennie shaded her eyes from the sun and examined PJ's face. "That was unexpected. I'm surprised you didn't take his side and throw me down and slap on the cuffs."

PJ closed her eyes tightly and shook her head. "Look, maybe I've been a bitch to you, and I don't really regret it, but you don't deserve having the shit kicked out of you." She opened her eyes. "I may be vindictive, but I'm not murderous. And that guy was really dangerous. Obviously hopped up on drugs. I think you might want to call an ambulance."

"It's not that bad. This is bleeding a lot, but that's how face wounds are."

"You've got something else going on there on the back of your neck." PJ stepped closer. "May I?"

Kennie swiveled to the side.

PJ swept some of Kennie's hair out of the way. "Yeah, it's not deep. Just bleeding like a son of a bitch. Let's go in, and I'll help you bandage it."

Kennie spun, laughing and a little incredulous. "First you sweep in like Batman, and who are you now—Florence Nightingale?"

PJ sighed.

Kennie headed for the back stairs. She touched the back of her neck, and her hand came away covered in blood. "Shit, how did this even happen?"

PJ trailed her up the stairs. "I don't know, but you're going to want to get checked thoroughly. I'd go to Urgent Care if I were you."

"I want to see it all first. I don't think it's that bad."

PJ fished in her pocket and came up with a backdoor key. Stepping past Kennie, she had it in the lock before Kennie realized the significance. "Hey, you don't live here. Why the hell do you have a key? Nobody but tenants should have access through the back."

PJ pocketed it with a smug look on her face. "Lily gave it to me."

Kennie stepped into the building and turned for her apartment. "You can just give it to me now."

"I'll give it to Lily. It's her spare."

"No, I'll take it."

"What's the matter—you don't trust me? I'm a cop, remember?"

"Didn't stop you from making an illegal false report on me."

"Can we just forget the prior shit and bad acts and move on?"

Kennie shook her head. "You know, we could've been friends, or at least somewhat friendly. You had to go and make this all an evil-ass mess."

"I know. Believe me, I know. But come on," she said and glared at Kennie, "you slept with my girl."

Kennie snorted. "She wasn't yours then. You'd broken up months earlier."

"Still..."

Kennie held out a bloody palm. "Turn it over."

"I promise I'll give it to Lily. Today."

Kennie unlocked her door and left it ajar. PJ stood outside looking uncomfortable.

Kennie paused, exasperated. "You may as well haul your dumb ass in here. If you're actually serious about helping me, that is. I can't see the back of my neck."

"Nothing I'd like better than putting some nice rubbing alcohol on it for you." PJ grinned, a rather evil display from the glimpse Kennie got.

In the bathroom, Kennie surveyed her face in the mirror. "Well, shit."

"Yeah, that's got to hurt. You're going to look as bad as that kid did when she first moved in."

"Same attacker, so it's no wonder."

"What? You're kidding. Why wasn't that reported?"

"Long story." Kennie opened a side cabinet and hunted around until she came up with a couple of red washcloths. She moistened one with cold water and pressed it to the cut on her eyebrow. "Owww…" The bleeding had stopped, but the pressure caused it to ooze a little. Didn't look like it would leave a scar. While PJ slouched, arms crossed, against the doorframe, Kennie carefully cleaned the cut and wiped the dirt and blood from her face, chin, and the front of her neck.

With a wetted clean cloth, she started to work on the back of her neck, but PJ stepped forward. "I know you can't see that. Let me fix you up." She dabbed and prodded and wiped it clean. "There. That's good."

Kennie got out a first-aid kit, laid it open on the counter, and selected some antibacterial ointment to hand to PJ. "I'm sure you'd prefer to use iodine or something else that burned the shit out of me."

PJ chuckled. "Remember some of that old-school crap, you know, those sprays our parents used on cuts and burns? I think that shit hurt more than the wound itself."

"Yeah, one time in college I slid into second base and totally shredded my hip. Nothing like having the trainer work on half your ass for everyone to see right there in the dugout. Hurt like hell to have it cleaned out, sprayed, and bandaged, and he was in a big damn hurry because I couldn't come out of the game."

"Put your chin on your chest." PJ squeezed ointment onto the wound. "You played ball in college?"

"Oh, yeah. Pitcher," Kennie said, then winced. "For cripesake, ever heard of being gentle?"

"As you can probably suspect, it's not my strong suit."

Kennie stole a glance in the mirror. PJ's face was slightly red, but she didn't elaborate. Kennie thought that a strange admission, but she didn't follow up.

"Okay," PJ said, "now rip open one of those gauze pads."

Kennie had to laugh. "No wonder those cops were bowing and scraping before you. You always so imperious?" She handed a pad over her shoulder and watched PJ blush a darker shade of red as she pressed the gauze pad against her neck.

"Tape now."

Kennie handed her a strip.

PJ said, "Command voice is pretty important."

"I'll bet it is…when you're on the job. Not so important in personal relationships though. Ouch! You made it start bleeding again, didn't you?"

"No," she said with a huff, sounding offended.

"Lucky you didn't become a nurse."

"I thought about medical school." PJ accepted a second strip and stuck it to Kennie's neck. "I'd have been a doctor though."

"Yeah, great bedside manner, too, I bet. Law enforcement was the better choice. Seems like you're pretty good at it, especially if you're a lieutenant."

"Yeah, I'm good—real good at paperwork. I miss being out on the street. I actually enjoyed the little altercation with your druggie pal."

"He's no pal of mine."

"So, tell me, have you got any more red washcloths to bleed on?"

"What? Why?"

"Have you checked out your knee? Or your elbows?"

FIFTEEN MINUTES AND a lot of gauze pads, Band-Aids, and antiseptic later, Kennie was patched up and feeling strangely grateful to PJ.

She offered her a soda, and PJ accepted. They stood in the kitchen, and PJ looked around as she sipped a diet Coke. "Nice place."

"Thanks. What do I have to do next about Max's brother?"

PJ explained the process and ended by saying, "We can hold him for a ton of time, especially because you have me for a witness, but it would be best if you visited the station sometime today to make your statement and sign the paperwork. If he's a druggie, he's going to have a fun time in jail coming down off his happy little high."

Kennie couldn't stop herself from wishing he'd suffer big time. But she wondered also if he might be a halfway decent person, like Max, if he weren't on drugs. "I'll go to the police station first and do my errands after. By the way, how come you happened to be in the parking lot when all this went down?"

"Supposed to meet Lily—oh, shit." She looked at her watch. "I'm really late. I better get up there." She set the half-full glass on the counter. "Thanks for the drink."

"Least I could do. Thanks for saving my ass."

PJ headed toward the front door, then stopped and whirled around. "Oh, so now you admit I saved your ass. I thought you said you had it handled."

"I was making progress." Kennie opened the door, and PJ stepped through. Kennie followed her out and meant to say something, but before she could get the words out, someone gasped.

Lily stood in the hallway, her face aghast. "Oh, my God, what did you do to her? PJ, you've gone too far this time."

PJ's mouth opened and she stammered, but no intelligible words came out.

"Wait, wait, wait," Kennie said, but Lily advanced and shook a finger at her ex. "You couldn't keep your hands to yourself? What's wrong with you?"

Kennie watched, amused to see PJ backing away, hands up and palms out. "I—"

"Don't lie to me. Not again."

"But you don't under—"

"How could you?"

Kennie couldn't stand it anymore. Though it was amusing to see six-foot-tall PJ backed up against the wall looking like a whipped dog, she thought she'd better intercede. She put a hand on Lily's shoulder and gently turned her. "Lily. Lily, calm down. I'm okay. Listen to me."

Lily paused with her tirade. When she looked up at Kennie, her eyes were moist, and Kennie felt a familiar lurch in her stomach that turned hot and liquidy and meandered south. She took a deep breath. "PJ had nothing to do with this. She saved my bacon."

Lily's hand came up, as if she were going to cradle Kennie's face, but she must have thought better and pulled back. Again, Kennie felt that shot of white-hot lightning go through her.

Now Lily's face went red. She looked back and forth between Kennie and PJ as though she didn't believe them.

PJ finally found her tongue. "Max's brother attacked Kennie."

"What?"

Before anyone could go on, Kennie said, "Hold on. No need to discuss this out in the hall. Come on, let's go inside. Lily, you want a soda?"

She freshened up PJ's Coke and brought it out to the living room along with glasses for Lily and herself. The other two women sat at opposite ends of the sofa, and the level of chilliness emanating from Lily amused Kennie. PJ, on the other hand, looked so contrite, so lost, that for a moment Kennie felt sorry for her. The feeling passed when PJ turned toward Kennie, sporting such a sullen expression it was all Kennie could do to keep from bursting out laughing.

"Are you all right?" Lily asked.

Kennie sat in a wingback chair. She started to cross her legs, then winced. "Ouch. Well, it probably looks worse than it is. The little creep jumped me, and if it weren't for PJ coming along when she did, I don't know what would've happened."

Lily took a sip of her drink. "PJ, I apologize for assuming... I didn't... I just..."

"It's okay. I don't blame you." PJ ran a hand through her dark hair. "Just another symptom of how our trust level eroded away to nothing."

Uh-oh, Kennie thought. These two weren't going to rehash their relationship issues, were they? And here she was in the inconvenient therapist's seat. During the awkward pause, everything seemed so surreal that she felt like running around shrieking like a crazy person. Deep inside, a kernel of something hopeful and happy was uncurling. She couldn't quite explain it, but she felt like a tingling lightning rod with no wire to ground it. To break the silence, she said, "PJ's going to help me at the police station, Lily."

"She ought to."

"I will." PJ rose and put her glass on the coffee table. She pulled the apartment key out of her pocket and set it next to the drink.

Kennie leaped out of her chair. "Thanks for helping me."

"Yeah," PJ said grudgingly as she stalked toward the door. "If you ever need first aid again, I expect you can find someone a lot more gentle than me."

"You did fine. I just hope no one ever trusts you with chest compressions."

PJ opened the door and looked at her blankly, then the meaning dawned on her. "Only if they want a few broken ribs." She grinned and reached out a hand. "Truce?"

"Of course." It wasn't lost on Kennie that PJ damn near crushed her hand, but she didn't comment. The woman had already taken a few shots to her pride, so she gave her a free pass. "I'll head down to the station before too long."

PJ pulled out her wallet and handed her a business card. "Call me if you need help. I'll be in and out of there all day."

Kennie pocketed the card and shut the door behind PJ. Heart beating fast, she swung around and met Lily's gaze. The woman looked more than miserable. Hunched over on the couch, she held her glass in a death grip.

"That was awful," Lily whispered. "Damned awful."

Kennie returned to her seat not able to think of one comforting thing to say. "She came over to return the key?"

"She said she wanted to talk to me. For old time's sake, she said. I don't know what that meant. I didn't want to see her, but she talked me into it, one last time. I've been dreading it all day."

"If it makes you feel any better, she was a complete gentleman." Kennie smiled to see the tiniest grin on Lily's face. She wasn't out of her misery yet, but she was trying to get there.

"Are you sure you're okay?"

"I've got more bruises and scrapes than what you see, and actually, half of them are starting to throb." She almost laughed aloud. Her wounds weren't the only thing throbbing. She stifled the thought. "I better take some ibuprofen and get a good book. I'm sure it'll take hours down at the station."

Lily hopped up from the couch. "You want me to drive you?"

"Oh, no. I'm fine." She accepted Lily's glass and limped into the kitchen.

Lily followed, carrying PJ's glass. "I like your apartment."

"You've been in here before."

"Yeah, but I didn't really look at it then. It's comfortable."

"Thanks. I'm happy with it for now. When I move out, Max and Renae want it."

"You're not moving anytime soon, are you?"

Kennie dumped the ice in the sink and took the third glass from Lily. "I don't know what I'm going to do. I'm in a holding pattern."

Lily leaned a hip against the counter and crossed her arms as though protecting herself. "Are you thinking of moving back to New York."

"Nuh-uh, not ever."

A glimmer of a smile played around Lily's mouth. "At least you're certain about that."

"Yes, I am. You never told me how you liked Barcelona."

"It was incredible. Beautiful. But lonely."

"Did you paint?"

Lily pursed her lips, a bleak expression on her face. She took so long to answer that Kennie thought she was going to ignore the question. Finally she said, "I'm not in the zone right now for my work." She stepped back. "I guess I've taken up enough of your time."

Following Lily to the door, Kennie was at a loss for what to say. All she really wanted was for Lily to sit down on the couch and pour out her heart, tell her where she'd been, why it had been lonely, what she needed in order to paint with abandon again. She wanted to touch her, to comfort her. But not a word came to her lips. She struggled to think of something, anything, and felt a pounding in her head instead.

"See you later, Kennie."

With a mute nod, she watched Lily hasten down the hall.

Chapter Twenty

PJ HADN'T LIED. When Kennie got to the police station, she was given VIP treatment. She never even got a chance to crack her book. The detectives took pictures of her injuries, interviewed her, and had her statement typed up faster than she could believe. She was out of there in just a little over an hour.

As the day wore on, her body got stiffer and she developed a headache. When she put on sunglasses in the car, she inadvertently bumped her eyebrow and the cut opened again and started bleeding. She found PJ's handkerchief still in her shorts pocket so she used that to try to stanch the bleeding, making a mental note that she owed the cop a hanky.

But the cut wouldn't stop bleeding.

"That tears it, dammit." She drove to Urgent Care. There she did get a chance to crack open her book, for over an hour. Finally she saw a doctor with deft hands who put in eight teeny-tiny stitches. She also checked Kennie's other scrapes and bruises, offered her ibuprofen, and told her to go home and employ multiple ice bags.

But first Kennie had to buy groceries for the evening's dinner. She dragged her wounded body around the store, finally deciding to take the easy route. She went to the deli and bought a baked chicken and a couple kinds of cold salads. With a container of Rocky Road ice cream and an eight-dollar bottle of red wine, she completed her purchases and took them home. She couldn't wait to serve up the cheap wine. There'd be no Glenlivet served at her place tonight.

She heard Suzanne and Sterling long before they arrived at her door, and she hauled herself and her ice bag up off the couch. She wasn't sure what Suzanne was complaining about, but her voice, when raised, had the quality of a buzz saw.

Kennie opened the door before they could knock, and the shock on her sister's face made her smile.

"What in the hell happened to you?"

Kennie reached up to finger the thread in her eyebrow. "Had a little altercation today."

"Little?" Suzanne said. "You look like you got used as a punching bag."

"It's not that bad, is it, Sterling?" Kennie stood back and they shuffled in.

Sterling wore the expression of a man frightened that someone was going to ask him to step up and do something brave. "Looks painful to me."

Suzanne had moved on. She surveyed the apartment. "What is this, a two-bedroom?"

"Yes." Kennie shut the door and readied herself for an onslaught of questions.

"The security guy told us there's a penthouse. Why aren't you living up there?"

"Besides the fact that it's already inhabited, why would I need a penthouse? I'm only one person, and that place is huge."

Suzanne made for the easy chair, and Sterling took the couch where he sat looking wistfully at the TV.

"Yo, bro," Kennie said, "you want to watch the news or something?"

"Golf? If you two wouldn't mind?"

Before Suzanne could wind up with her typical criticism, Kennie said, "Sure, and me and Suze will go get dinner rounded up." She clicked on the TV and handed him the cable remote.

One down, she thought, one to go.

She'd already put the macaroni and potato salads in bowls in the fridge and sliced up the chicken to heat in the microwave at the last minute. She left Suzanne cutting up tomatoes for a green salad and went to the bathroom to look in the mirror. What she saw shocked her. No wonder Thomason had given her the eye earlier when she came home. Her brow now sported a purpling bruise, one eye was going black, and bruises were coming up along the right side of her jaw. The skin that wasn't bruised was reddened from the ice pack she'd been applying. Her sibs weren't overreacting to be so startled. She laughed, and that sent a shot of pain through her jaw and cheek.

She rinsed her hands and was drying them when she heard a faint shriek and then a deep voice saying, "Who the hell are you?"

Kennie whipped open the bathroom door and hastened down the hall to find Sterling pointing the TV remote as though it were a Star Trek phaser. A compact, black-haired kid with more silver piercings in her brows, nose, and ears than Kennie had seen lately, stood in the hallway near the connecting door. Max was behind her, not quite as tall, but resembling her in every way except for the piercings. Renae was half in the connecting door and looked like she was ready to bolt.

"Whoa, whoa," Max was saying, a note of fear in her voice. "Where's Kennie?"

"Hey, everyone, calm down," Kennie said. "Sterling, these are my neighbors. They're good friends of mine."

"Oh." With the threat past, he lost interest and returned to the couch to watch golf.

Max gave Kennie a look that she ignored. "My brother and sister are here, kiddo. That was Sterling. Suzanne is in the kitchen."

"No, I'm not. I'm right here. Who are your little friends?" She held a knife in one hand and fluttered blood-red fingernails as if she were saying goodbye.

"Max and Renae live next door, and if I'm not mistaken, this is Max's sister, Olivia." She stuck her hand out. Olivia looked down at it and hesitantly reached out to shake it.

"Hi," the kid said shyly. "Max has told me a lot about you." She let go of Kennie's hand and studied the floor, but not before Kennie got a look at brown eyes very much like Max's. She wore a black long-sleeved shirt, heavy-duty black jeans, and black shoes. Goth look without the makeup.

Renae pushed forward. "What the heck happened to you, Kennie. Your face—"

"Yeah, I know. I'm okay, but I want to tell you about that later. Can we meet up later tonight?"

Max shot a glance across the room at Suzanne and turned back and said, "We were going to ask if we could take you out to dinner."

"Can't since I have company. Bring me back some dessert?"

Max nodded. "We'll come by later." The three went swiftly through the door.

Before it was even closed, Suzanne said, "Is that safe? You've got a bunch of punk rockers next door, and you're just letting them come and go as they please?"

Kennie strode across the room. "Max works for me."

"The metal-faced one?"

Kennie let out an exasperated huff and didn't dignify the comment with a response. She squeezed past Suzanne into the kitchen, stuck the chicken into the microwave, and slammed the rest of the stuff around.

"What?" Suzanne twirled the knife in her fingers.

"You know what."

"I'm only interested in your safety and welfare."

Kennie laughed mirthlessly at that.

"I'm serious."

"Why don't you cut to the chase, Suzanne?"

Her sister took on a hurt expression, the same one Kennie remembered her using whenever she got caught teasing Kennie when she was little. What kind of twenty-year-old sister hid a pre-schooler's toy horses and trucks and laughed when the child cried?

Suzanne had been born with a cruel streak—and a selfish one.

Before their parents were killed in the car accident, Kennie had been so anxious to please her older sister. She did all she could to win her approval, but nothing she did helped. The summer her parents died, Kennie had given up. When the accident happened, Suzanne's insane histrionics at the funeral and in its aftermath further cemented the separation. Nearly twenty-five years had passed, and though Kennie had changed and grown in so many ways, her sister existed in a time warp where all that mattered was her getting her way.

Suzanne tossed the knife into the sink with a little more force than needed. "You've never respected my point of view. Never. Even as a child you were willful and obstinate."

"You're one to talk."

Suzanne let out a tiny shriek. "You are the most maddening person I've ever met."

Meal preparation forgotten, Kennie crossed her arms and leaned back against the kitchen counter. "How can you even say that? You've spent more time with me in Portland this week than in the last twenty years."

"Which is why it may be time for you to move back home."

"To Watertown?"

"Why, yes—that's your hometown."

"You couldn't pay me enough."

"Because you're so attached to this monstrosity of an apartment building?" She raised her arms in a pose that reminded Kennie of worshipers asking for manna to be rained down upon them. "The whole place looks like a money trap."

"What do you care? It's my money."

"And is some of that from Aunt Clara? Are you selling her house to finance living here?"

"I haven't decided what to do."

"Why not use her house? Pack up and move back there. We could be a family again, you, me, and Sterling."

Kennie couldn't figure out where the catch was. There had to be one. Even if her sister had been struck by an overnight conversion from her previous self to a new and improved, lovable one, Kennie wasn't going anywhere. "No, that won't work for me."

With a petulant exhalation of breath, Suzanne said, "But that makes no sense. Why would you want to stay here, far from family, far from decades of your past? You can't even visit our parents' graves."

If Suzanne knew the truth of Kennie's parentage, would she be fighting about this matter? Upon reflection, Kennie thought she would. Money was involved. Aunt Clara's house was an issue. As long as that was the case, Suzanne would pester her.

"I can say with a fair amount of certainty I don't plan to ever move back to Watertown."

"But why?" Suzanne fumed and went so far as to stomp one high-heeled foot. "It's a wonderful and historic place, full of amazing people."

"There's nothing particularly historic about Watertown."

Defensively, Suzanne said, "We had the first Five and Dime. Where do you think Woolworth's came from?"

"Oh, right, Woolworth's? They went out of business fifteen years ago."

"We have famous inventors."

"Yeah, yeah, I learned all about that in school. Some Watertown guy invented the safety pin. Big woo. What about that other guy? The Genesee River serial killer?"

"You would bring him up. An aberration who's dead now. Jesus, it's not like you've moved to a thriving metropolis. I suppose you're impressed with the fact that this little city has a lot of gay people living here."

"How the hell do you know that?"

"They're everywhere," Suzanne said with a dramatic gesture. "Dykes and fags everywhere we went. Your little neighbor friends and fifty zillion others just like them."

"That's it. Get out."

Suzanne looked at her blankly.

"I mean it, Suzanne. I'm done with your attitude and your bigotry and your unwillingness to accept me. Get out."

"But—"

Kennie advanced toward her, arm outstretched and pointing to the living room. "Take your horseshit attitude and get out of my house." She knew she was desperately close to losing control, and it took all the strength she had to rein in a lifetime of memories where Suzanne manipulated, mocked, and took what she wanted. The helplessness and fury welled up like a geyser of bitter acid. The pain in her jaw and eyebrow didn't help matters either.

In the face of her insistence, Suzanne backed up. She whirled and stalked through the living room. "Sterling. Sterling! Get your head out of your ass. We're leaving."

The expression of confusion on his face was laughable, but Kennie was too angry to do anything but stand in the kitchen doorway and try to control her breathing.

At the doorway, Suzanne turned back, her eyes glittering with hate. "You can expect to receive legal papers about Aunt Clara's estate."

"Yeah, yeah, yeah, I knew all along it'd come to that."

Sterling looked back and forth between the two of them.

"What's going on here?"

Kennie ignored him. "Before you go, tell me this. If I'd given you the house outright, would you have left me alone?"

Suzanne stuck her nose in the air and opened the front door. "We all know you're too damn selfish to do the right thing."

After the door slammed shut, Kennie leaned against the doorjamb and waited for the shakes to pass. As the anger drained out of her, she anticipated feelings of contrition to flow in their place...but no such thing happened. Instead, a gradually increasing sense of lightness filled her.

She felt free, an emotion so unexpected that she laughed out loud. She bent at the waist, laughing with a glee she hadn't felt in ages. She heard a light tapping at the connecting door, but before she could cross the room, the door smacked open.

"Kennie? Are you all right?" Max barreled into the room followed by Renae. Olivia hovered in the background looking strangely vulnerable despite her Goth get-up. "We saw them leaving in a big hurry. We thought—"

"Oh, my God," Renae said. "They hurt you."

"No, no, I'm fine," Kennie said.

Max said, "You're beat to shit. What do you mean 'fine'?"

Kennie brought a hand to her chin and willed herself to stop laughing. "They didn't—"

"She had a knife!" Max shouted.

"Ha. She'd need a lot more than that to put me down. They didn't touch me, really. I got in a dust-up with someone else. I'll tell you about it later. Don't worry about my brother and sister. They're snakes, but they're harmless snakes."

Max looked skeptical. "That guy was your brother? I thought he was going to throw the TV remote at me."

"Don't worry, my brother's a bad shot, and besides, his phaser is always on stun."

"What?"

"Not a *Star Trek* fan?"

"Haven't seen any of the movies yet."

Kennie laughed. Sometimes she forgot how young Max was. "Thought you guys were going to dinner."

Renae and Max glanced at one another and spoke at the same time: "We were worried."

Kennie's legs felt weak. The adrenaline shot must have finally run out. She sat heavily on the couch. "How would you three like to stay for dinner? I've got plenty."

"You look all done in," Renae said. "I'll fix something."

"It's pretty much ready."

"Great, I'll go pull it together. How about we eat at your

dining room table?"

"Whatever," Kennie said, suddenly so tired she didn't think she could drag herself to the table.

Max sat in the easy chair across from her. Olivia stood uncertainly next to Max.

"I'm glad to finally meet you, Olivia. It must be a relief not to have supervised meetings anymore."

Olivia's face flushed, and she looked to Max.

"That's one of the things we wanted to talk to you about," Max said. "Liv has sort of, you know, skipped out."

"Skipped out? On what—her foster parents?"

Max nodded.

"Shit. When? Just today?"

Olivia nodded. She and her sister looked like matching bobble-heads.

"Have you at least called your foster parents to let them know you're all right?"

"No."

"Will you please do that?"

"They'll order me home."

"Which is as it should be. They're responsible for you."

Max leaned forward in the chair, her elbows on her knees. "But she doesn't like them, Kennie. They're overly strict."

"In what way?"

"She has to come straight home after school and never gets to go anywhere. They won't let her have a cell phone. Plus, they rag on her all the time about her clothes and piercings. And they don't seem to like me, so it's like they really don't want us visiting anyway. I'm on a twice-a-month schedule, but we have to go to the county building and there's shit for privacy."

Kennie didn't want to be judgmental, but if she were a foster parent, she might require all the same things. She turned to Olivia. "How old are you now?"

"Sixteen. Just turned."

Old enough to be dangerous but too young to have the kind of discernment adults could trust. Kennie knew Max wasn't ready for the responsibility of caring for a headstrong, troubled, grieving younger sister.

Renae called out, "Let's eat, people."

Kennie eased off the couch, every muscle in her body hurting. Someone knocked at her door. Shuffling slowly, she figured it would be just like Suzanne to return and press her points exactly when Kennie was at the lowest level of energy. She whipped open the door, which hurt her upper back, and drew a breath to speak, but stopped.

Lily stood in the doorway, dressed in baggy shorts and a Blazers t-shirt, a surprisingly sloppy outfit considering the makeup she wore and the lustrous golden hair cascading around her shoulders. She was a goddess in Kennie's eyes, no matter how she dressed.

Her blue eyes, full of sympathy, met Kennie's. "I was worried about you. I thought I'd come by and check to see if you're all right."

"Come in. Join the crowd. Have you eaten?"

"I don't want to intrude."

"Oh, please. We're having some stuff from the deli—nothing special."

When she turned to face the three teenagers sitting at the dining room table, Kennie felt like she was moving in slow motion, but not so slow that she missed Max elbowing Renae with a smirk on her face.

"Max, Renae. Oh, and who is this?" Lily said.

Max made introductions while Kennie limped along behind Lily. She didn't have it in her to be a proper hostess, but Renae, who got up to put down a fifth place setting, had laid out the placemats, silver, and paper napkins and arranged the food.

"Thanks, Renae. I defer completely to you," Kennie said as she sat across from Renae and Max. "You're in charge of all things kitchen-related tonight."

"Like every night," Max said in a teasing voice.

"Yeah," Olivia said, "we know who wears the pants there."

Olivia sat at the end of the table, near the wall, and Lily took the chair at the head, on Kennie's left.

Kennie let out a sigh. "This chicken isn't going to be anywhere near as good as that stuff you fed me on my birthday, Lily. I just got it at the Fred Meyer deli."

Lily blushed. "I'm sure it'll be fine." She dug into the potato salad and passed the bowl to Kennie.

"I only hope I'm still able to chew," Kennie said.

Lily passed her the macaroni salad. "Here, suck on this."

Now it was Kennie's turn to blush, but she accepted the bowl and dished out a spoonful. "Olivia was just telling us she's on the lam. Her foster parents don't know where she's at."

"Uh-oh," Lily said and looked at Olivia. "What are you all going to do?" She paused, holding the platter of sliced chicken.

Kennie liked how Lily passed no judgments, made no assumptions. She calmly threw the issue back at the kids.

Olivia shrugged, but Max piped up right away. "You're going to have to go back, at least for a while, I think."

The expression on Olivia's face turned peevish. "I figured. I knew it was too good to be true."

"What's too good to be true?" Lily asked.

"I don't know. I don't know at all." Olivia set down her fork and slumped against the chair back looking as defeated as Max had when she'd first shown up at the Allen Arms.

Kennie knew she should say something, try to make things all better, but her brain was moving too slowly. Luckily, Lily took over.

"What are your options? Go ahead and brainstorm."

Olivia didn't speak, but Max and Renae threw out a number of ideas: run away permanently to another state; quit school, get a job, and hole up somewhere nearby; request a new foster family; lie about her age and join the army; sleep in the basement on the weight bench.

The last was added by Max with a twinkle in her eye.

Olivia closed her eyes, but tears leaked out. "You guys aren't taking this very seriously."

With a sigh, Max said, "It's not like we're throwing you to the homeless shelter, Liv."

"I may as well go live at Dignity Village."

Kennie frowned and looked to Lily who said, "You haven't heard of Dignity Village?"

"I don't think so."

"It started out as a tent city established by a lot of the homeless and has turned into quite a development."

"Where is this?"

"Right here in Portland. Near downtown on some public land that squatters claimed."

Max said, "It's become a lifesaver for some people. I went down there with some friends and visited, got some free food back when I was homeless."

Kennie swallowed a bite of potato salad. "How long were you homeless?"

"Kind of like from before our mom died to when you found me."

"November to April? Six months? You were out on the streets for six months?"

"Well, kind of. I kept going back to the house and staying there off and on, but Derek had a lot of creepy friends coming and going. This one asshole woke me up one night, trying to undress me, and I got the hell out. That was around Valentine's Day. Lucky he was high 'cause he was a lot bigger than me, and he could've raped me easy."

"Oh, Max," Lily said, "that's just awful."

"But I'm one of the lucky ones. I met a lot of other kids who weren't so lucky. We used to sit in Siggy Starshine's and try to figure out the best ways to beg for cash so we didn't have to steal. The cook at Siggy's was cool. He was always good for letting us score day-old stuff. Some of the kids bussed the tables and ate leftovers." She looked down for a moment before going on. "Actually, I did that a few times when I was dead broke. And then along came Renae, and she started looking after me." They shared an affectionate look, and for a minute Kennie thought they might lean in and kiss one another, but Olivia interrupted.

"You had to beg?" The shock on her young face was almost comical.

"Yeah, I did. Sometimes."

"Oh, my God. I could never do that."

"See, that's the thing," Max said. "You do what you have to do. Derek took over everything Mom left us, and I didn't have many choices. But Livvy, you have some choices here. Not a lot, but you have a couple."

Kennie stole a look at Lily. She was purposely focusing on her dinner plate, and Kennie did the same.

Renae said, "What's the worst thing about the Bertrams?"

Olivia sneered. "They're control freaks."

"But they have no real control over you," Max said, "don't you know that? They're probably freakin' completely right now, and they can't do anything about it. *You're* in control 'cause you can walk out anytime you want. The county can put you in another home, and you can do the same thing there if you want. So stop feeling helpless. You're not. 'Specially since you've got me and Renae, whether they like it or not."

"But they'll be mad."

"So?"

Olivia couldn't respond. She sat with a quizzical expression, looking back and forth between Renae and her sister.

"What do you want from these people?" Renae asked.

"Nothing," Olivia said.

"But are they nice?"

Grudgingly, Olivia said, "They try to be."

Renae pushed her plate away. "Seems to me they're just trying to do the job they've been assigned by those bureaucrats at the county."

Max nodded. "I think we ought to go over after dinner and make a deal with these Bertrams."

Olivia sat forward, her thin face a little hopeful. "A deal?"

"Yeah, you hand them back the control they need to have, and we get them to chill out about you and me spending time together. Let's get these social services people out of the mix, and at least take back that little bit of control."

"That'd be good," Olivia said.

"Kennie," Max asked, "could I please borrow your Jeep tonight?"

"Sure. Just take the spare keys and put them on your ring, why don't you. You may as well keep hold of them since you actually need to drive more often than I do. I think we should set you up with insurance and get you some wheels of your own."

"Can't really afford that right now."

Kennie said, "Let's talk about that later. What's the plan for dealing with the Bertrams?"

"They need to meet Renae, and I need to talk with them so they can see I'm not a gangsta. It'll be three against two. If they're not reasonable, and if they're not gay-friendly, then Liv, you just take all the control and keep leaving. They can't lock you up, right?"

"I guess not."

Max let out a snort. "Quit being so chicken-shit and man up."

Olivia glared at her. "You can shut up now, Max."

Kennie was glad to see the flash of anger Olivia displayed. The kid was no pushover, even if she did seem scared and out of her element.

"Okay, okay," Max said. "But eat something, will ya? I'm not stopping on the way over to buy you a bunch of crappy fast food."

Kennie peered sidelong at Lily, and they shared an amused look. Kennie wanted so badly to comment on how remarkably Max had handled Olivia's situation, but she didn't dare say that in front of the little sister. She had a hunch, though, that she'd be seeing a lot more of Olivia in coming days.

Renae said, "This whole conversation brings me back to Dignity Village and the homeless in Portland. Last I heard, our city had the biggest bunch of homeless people of anywhere in the U.S."

Lily said, "I've read that in the newspaper. Per capita anyway."

"The owner and all of us at Siggy's do a benefit with a Silent Auction every year at the end of the summer. I wasn't here for last year's, but they've started planning the next one. The big problem is the café is so dinky, we have limited space for it. We could bring in a lot more donations if we had more space."

Lily said, "Last year I donated a painting to a homeless outreach program that they auctioned off to help pay for a job-training program."

"That's an excellent idea," Renae said. "You want to do that again?"

"Hmmm. Wouldn't the space in my penthouse serve as a better place for the Silent Auction?"

Renae's mouth dropped open. "Would you actually consider that?"

Lily turned to Kennie. "I would, but it's really Kennie's call. It's her building that people would be traipsing through."

Kennie's brain wasn't working too quickly, but she did think to say, "I'd just have to hire extra security. That wouldn't be too hard. We could also use the party room, if we needed it for storage or whatever."

Renae clapped her hands softly, then held them together as though she were praying. "Can I run this by people at the café?"

"Sure," Kennie said.

"And yes, I could donate a painting again this year," Lily said. "That is, if I ever start painting again."

"What?" Max said. "How come you're not painting?"

"Long story."

"We have time," Max said. "You can tell us, and then Kennie can give us the scoop on what happened to her face."

Renae put a hand on Max's arm. "No, we actually don't have time. Eat quick, and I'll help clean up. We need to take Olivia back home now—I mean to her foster parents' home—if we're going to drive a bargain that gets her out of the doghouse."

Lily said, "You're hereby relieved of kitchen duties. I'll clean up."

"That's okay," Kennie said. "I can do it."

Lily rolled her eyes. "Ignore her, kids. Her brain was rattled earlier."

"What the heck happened to you?" Max asked. "You run into a post up in 6A or what?"

Lily stood. "Kennie can share that with you later. Get a move on. It'll be dark soon, and it's always better to deal with something like this while it's still light out. Go be the Three Musketeers."

"Hey," Max said with a big grin, "I like that."

They filed out through the connecting door, talking all at once. Kennie rose and staggered over to the couch. Lily sank down at the other end and said, "I hope we haven't got ourselves in over our heads."

"We? All I agreed to was security."

"Come on," Lily chided. "You've always wanted to be a philanthropist, haven't you?"

Kennie didn't avert her eyes when Lily gave her a challenging look, but for the first time since early morning, the jolt of sexual longing she received gave her unexpected energy. She had never thought about being a philanthropist, but she was pretty sure it beat the hell out of planting a tree.

KENNIE HAD NO idea when she fell asleep. One minute she was hearing Lily bustling around in the kitchen, and the next, the living room was shrouded in darkness and she felt a warm hand on her forehead.

"Hmmm? What?" She roused, confused and headachy.

"You're feverish, Kennie." Lily stood at the end of the couch, silhouetted in the glow of the streetlamp coming in through the side window.

"This couch is like a heater." Kennie swung her legs around to the floor and sat rubbing her eyes. "What time is it?"

"Three a.m."

"What! I can't believe I slept that long and kept you up."

"I fell asleep, too. Don't worry about it."

Lily headed into the kitchen and turned on the light. "You need to take some ibuprofen, I think." She returned with a glass of water and some pills. "Take these. They'll help with the swelling. She perched on the coffee table in front of Kennie and handed over the glass. "Your poor face. You look so...so damaged."

The expression on her face appeared more anguished than Kennie's actual pain level, so Kennie joked, "It's my inner Freddy Krueger coming out."

"Don't say that. It's so not true." She rose, waited for Kennie to hand over the glass, and took it into the kitchen.

Kennie wondered why Lily seemed so peeved. When she came back to the kitchen doorway, she leaned against the jamb, arms crossed.

Kennie said, "I'm okay, Lily. Sorry to zonk out like that. You didn't have to stay. What an inconvenience for you."

"Forget about it." A few moments passed before Lily said, "If Renae's boss decides to hold the event here, we ought to follow it with a dance, get a DJ and everything. We could invite everyone in the building as well as all the people who attend the Silent Auction. In all the years I've lived in the penthouse, the ballroom has never been used for dancing, just for occasional receptions and art crawls."

"What do we want to do for entertainment—for a distraction during the auction? People aren't going to just want to stand around waiting for the last minute."

Lily sat in the easy chair to Kennie's left. "Good question. We should probably do wine and cheese and some kind of hors d'oeuvres to keep people snacking. I know several comedians. What if we did a handful of fifteen- or twenty-minute spots from, say, eight to ten p.m.?"

"I think that would be all right. And we could use the party room for all the financial stuff once people win their bids."

"Good idea. That'd help clear things out. We'll just send the winners downstairs." Lily gazed up at the ceiling thoughtfully. "The ballroom looks so enormous, but once we put in a horde of table rounds and chairs, not to mention the auction items all around the room, it's going to be jam-packed."

"You've also got that big hallway down the middle of the apartment. Lots of room there."

"True."

"I hate to say it, but we're going to need a lot of oversight to make sure nobody swipes anything. And we have to ensure that no one goes toward the back bedrooms or down the hall to the other wing."

"I'm pretty sure the kids will show up and help, and I have another idea. But you might not like it."

"Try me." Kennie shifted back on the couch, and winced as she tucked her stocking feet under her. She was very sore, but no way did she want this conversation to end, even if it was about the mechanics of an event that might not happen.

"PJ owes me big time. I think I could probably get an entire entourage of uniformed, off-duty cops for security. In fact, it's possible we might be able to get the Portland PD to co-sponsor this event. PJ's captain has a lot of connections. I should be writing all this down."

"Let's just meet in the morning and over the coming days and make a whole plan. A punch list kind of thing."

"Punch list?"

"Yeah, you know—a big action plan with all the details like construction guys put together. That's what I do for every apartment that needs work done so I can prioritize and make sure I cover all the basics. If we organize this once, and it works, we'd have a plan for the future."

"It seems simple, you know? But even if Siggy's does the catering and most all of the serving, we still have the setup, security, customer service, and cleanup. Oh, and possibly entertainment. It's a lot."

"Yes, and of course there's one other important thing."

"And that would be?"

"A certain painter just promised a piece of art." Even in the low light from the kitchen, Kennie saw Lily blanch and look away. "Why aren't you painting, Lily?"

"It doesn't matter."

"Yes, it does. What's wrong?"

Lily rose. "Don't worry about it. I'll get back on track soon enough. And if I don't create something new, nobody will care so long as I haul something suitable out of storage."

"You have canvases in storage?"

Lily gave her an inscrutable look. "What do you think I use all those extra bedrooms in the penthouse for?"

Chapter Twenty-One

WHEN KENNIE WAS eight years old, she'd ridden her bike off the sidewalk into a usually calm side street. Unfortunately, she didn't see or hear a four-door Camry motoring along quietly. She hit the front edge of the grill, at the right quarter-panel, and the force of the impact knocked her back ten feet. She escaped with bruises and scrapes. If her parents could have spanked her for her carelessness they would have, but she'd suffered so many cuts and abrasions that her mom's anger had passed long before the time they could have safely paddled her. As it was, her mother just kept reminding her that she deserved the injuries for being so stupid.

Getting out of bed the day after the brawl with Derek reminded her of the morning after her childhood altercation with the car. Every muscle hurt, and the scabbed-over places on her elbows, knees and calves felt tight, like they might burst open and start bleeding any minute. Looking in the full-length mirror in the bathroom was scarily reminiscent of her eight-year-old assessment, without the little-kid fascination and novelty. The bruises looked awfully similar, though.

Feeling like an old woman, she showered slowly and dried off with care, but still she managed to break open the cut on her right elbow. After smearing Neosporin on all the scrapes and scratches, she re-bandaged her knees and elbows and applied lotion to every part of her body she could reach, hoping that would minimize more bleeding. She dressed in shorts, flip-flops, and a loose t-shirt. The less pressure against her wounds, the better.

Her morning tea tasted like mud. So did the cereal. Nothing tasted good because her entire body was off. Everything ached — even her taste buds. She couldn't believe it was already ten a.m. either.

She hobbled out to the front lobby to check on things. Simms glanced up from a paperback book and did a double-take. He popped up out of his chair. "What in the world happened to you?"

"Max's brother came back."

"When? Where?"

"Yesterday morning. Back lot. He jumped me."

"How did I miss all that? I would have helped you."

"Simms, it happened so fast, there was no way you could have known or done anything." She told him the details and finished by saying she had gone straight into her apartment.

"That son of a bitch!" He smacked his fist into his palm. "I'd like to kill him. I hope you gave him twice the beating he gave you."

"Not sure about that. I'm just glad the police have him locked up."

"What was the point of attacking you?"

"He's a drug addict, and he's obviously a little crazy. But he's in forced rehab now." She laughed mirthlessly. "Enough about that. When are you bringing little Amanda in for me to meet?"

Before he could answer, the door to the efficiency opened. Renae came out dressed in a light blue blouse, navy Capri pants, and sandals and carrying a shoulder bag. "Hey, Kennie. How are you this morning?" Her eyes narrowed as she surveyed Kennie's face. "Those bruises sure have blossomed. You should try out for Ultimate Fighting."

"Smart ass," Kennie said, holding back her grin because it hurt to smile.

Renae said, "Seriously, are you in pain?"

"Nope, not too bad. Nothing a little ibuprofen can't cure."

Renae went to the front window and looked out. "Here they come. Max went over and picked up Olivia. They're dropping me at work and going to the movies together."

"So everything went okay with the Bertrams?"

"Yes, and just between you and me" — she sped up talking to get the words in before the front door opened — "those people are really cool. Olivia will be fine there."

Max and her sister came in. Max shook her head in mock solemnity. "No offense, Kennie, but you look like hell."

"That's what Renae just said." She lifted her arm to lean against the security counter, but thought the better of it when a shot of pain zinged up through her elbow.

"So what's the scoop?"

"Just like you've always said, your brother came back."

Blood drained from Max's face. She looked like she was going to faint.

Olivia let out a gasp and put a hand to her mouth. "Oh, my God, is Max going to have to move?"

Kennie frowned. "Because of Derek?"

Olivia looked totally confused, and Renae said, "I think she's worried that someone in their family beat you up, so she and Max must be guilty, too." Renae set her bag on the lobby bench, went to Olivia, and put an arm around her. "We told you — Kennie's not like that, Liv."

Max had both hands on her head, pulling at her own hair. "I can't believe he did that, Kennie. I'm so, so, so sorry."

Olivia shook Renae off. "I don't even want him as a brother. He's a crazy-ass goon."

"Luckily," Kennie said, "he's one goon who's going to stay in jail for a while. Maybe he'll get off the dope and turn his life around."

Simms stepped around the counter and went to open the front door. "Good morning," he said to a messenger, his voice perky and extra helpful. She was long and lean and wore a helmet, skimpy hot pink top, and tight black bike shorts that showed off a seriously shapely butt. She greeted everyone, but her gaze lingered on Kennie. She set a manila envelope on the counter and handed a clipboard to Simms for a signature. While he signed, she leaned on the counter and addressed Kennie. "So how's your day going?"

"Had better, but also had worse, so I won't complain."

Simms handed back the clipboard, and the messenger said, "See you around. I hope." She sashayed out the door.

Renae let out a hoot. "She liked what she saw, Kennie, even with all the whuppin' marks. Bet you could follow her out and get her phone number."

Kennie couldn't control the heat that wafted up into her face. "Get outta here. She was just being nice."

Renae said, "For a hoochie mama."

Max fumbled in her pants pocket, pulled out a bill, and waved the money in front of Kennie. "This Benjamin says she only has eyes for one woman, Renae." She took both ends of the bill and snapped it so that Kennie saw it was a hundred-dollar bill.

"Jeez, Max. You're carrying that much money around with you?"

"Why? Aren't you? You should be, because any day now, you're going to be paying me the loot. Better start saving your dead presidents, 'cause I'll be collecting soon. Very soon."

Embarrassed, Kennie peered over at Simms, hoping he didn't know what they were talking about. He looked just confused enough to relieve Kennie of that worry. She asked, "Don't you all have someplace to be now?"

Renae looked at her watch. All business, she said, "Pack it up, girls. I don't want to be late." She grabbed her bag from the bench. "I'll be talking to Phil today about our Silent Auction idea. Is that still okay?"

"Go for it, and let me know as soon as you can."

Olivia couldn't meet Kennie's eyes, but she sidled over. "I'm real sorry 'bout what my low-life fidiot brother did to you?"

"Fidiot?"

Max mouthed "Fucking idiot."

"Ahh, good word. I'll have to remember that."

Simms said, "This is yours, Kennie," and handed her the manila envelope the bike messenger had brought. With the attorney's name on the return address label, she suspected it didn't bode well.

EVERY DAY KENNIE watched the bruises on her face, neck, and body fade. She was surprised at how fast the gash in her eyebrow knitted back together — much faster than her elbows healed. Despite the lingering aches and discomfort, she bore it all cheerily with spirits buoyed by daily contact with Lily. Every morning, one of them called the other with progress reports for the event, and most days they ran into one another in the lobby or met in the gym to discuss their plans.

Siggy, whose name was actually Phil, came to the Allen Arms to tour the penthouse and pronounced it marvelous. He accepted the offer of space and began to collaborate with excitement. After his visit, Kennie drove Lily over to the café twice. Both times they were treated to soup and sandwiches and completely pampered by Renae.

The end of summer was fast approaching, and Kennie hadn't felt very productive ever since the incident with Max's brother. She knew she had babied herself, but soon she needed to devote herself to work in three different apartments. The tear-out in Miss Quist's place had long been done, and she still had painting to do before new carpet and tile was laid. One thing at a time, she told herself. Everything would get done eventually.

Kennie drank tea and sat at her desk in the office looking out on the neighborhood. The morning had dawned sunny and cool with the promise of temperatures in the high nineties later in the day. The cell phone rang, and with a pleasure she felt somewhere in the vicinity of her heart, she answered.

Lily said, "You sound chipper. Did you sleep well?"

"I did."

"And are you still looking like a zombie from *Dawn of the Dead?*"

"Not so much."

"Excellent."

They got down to business and were talking about whether they ought to hire Adam Vendrick to do cake and decorations when Kennie's house phone rang. "I have to get this other line," she told Lily.

"I'll bring down the agreement from Captain Hendricks in a bit."

"Okay."

Kennie clicked off her cell and picked up the cordless phone, knowing exactly who was calling. She recognized George Zimmerman's voice even before he identified himself, and with a feeling of increasing dismay, she listened to his report. All the positive emotions she'd been feeling moments before poured out of her like precious nectar through a sieve.

"So you're saying they're asking for discovery? Like you're supposed to give up all the data about everything personal Aunt Clara entrusted you with?"

"Yes."

"Can they make you do that?"

"Maybe. Their attorney's sniffing around, trying to decide whether he dares to allege fraud on your part."

"Fraud? I didn't do a thing. I knew nothing about what Aunt—"

"I know, Kennie, I know. You and I know that. Your sister just won't let go of any of this. I needed to understand her motivation, so I put a PI on the case."

"For what?"

"I didn't feel I had a choice. I needed to get information about your sister and brother, and now that I have it, you need to know it."

"Oh, great." Maybe she'd find out they were adopted. Or aliens. Or Bonnie and Clyde on the run.

"Actually, this may be good for you. Your brother's alimony payments are killing him. His CPA business isn't doing well, mostly because of the downturn in the economy. So he's having financial difficulties. But your sister, well—did she mention her finances to you?"

"Not a thing. If she's having troubles she'd be way too proud to tell me."

"She's not just having troubles—she's on the verge of bankruptcy."

"What? Why?"

"Housing market has completely tanked here, and her lifestyle is high maintenance. She's leveraged up to God. Her house is marked for repossession."

"Why the hell didn't she tell me that?"

"You just said it. She's far too proud."

"Okay, what do you think I should do—give them money? Split the properties among us?"

"Neither. What they don't understand is that your claim to the inheritance, as the stepdaughter of Mrs. McClain, supersedes theirs. They are merely a niece and nephew. Much of the holdings were your birth father's, and your aunt's desires were very clear. We would win in court in a New York minute."

"What do I do?"

"You can blow them out of the water with the information of your paternity."

"Oh, no, George. I can't do that to them."

He sighed. "Kennie, you're a good person, so I really don't want to share this affidavit with you then. Trust me when I say that the rantings and complaints to which your sister swears would be enough to sour you completely."

"I don't think so. I don't care enough about her opinion anymore, and I don't need the money enough to warrant this campaign by my greedy-ass sister. What else can I do?"

"Short of divulging parentage?"

"Yes."

"I could offer them your aunt's house and a chunk of money and see where that gets you. At this point, that's the only real property they're aware of, and you can shift some funds from this year's rental profits to pay them off."

"How much do you think it'll take?"

"Hard to say. Why don't you authorize me up to a certain level, and I'll try to negotiate."

"Okay. Fifty thou."

"Total for both?"

She hesitated. "No, go ahead and cap it at fifty thousand each. It'll be worth it."

"You got it."

When she hung up the phone, Kennie felt tired and defeated. She didn't want to keep Aunt Clara's house forever, but at the same time, it had always been a safe place in her early childhood, and when she lived there, it became familiar. Comfortable. Loved. She had known all along she wouldn't hang onto it, but the longer she had been able to put off the inevitable, the less time she'd spent feeling regret.

She was on the way to the kitchen when she heard light tapping. With a sigh, she answered the door, hoping she didn't look as awful as she felt.

"What's the matter?" Lily said right off the bat.

Kennie closed her eyes as she backed up to let her in, feeling wrung out and hopeless. "Family stuff."

"Anything you want to share?"

"All I've got left are my brother and sister, and they're snakes. Would you like a glass of wine?"

Lily smiled. "It's only ten a.m. but sure, let's get drunk and cry our eyes out."

Kennie led her to the kitchen. Lily slid onto a stool and tossed a folder down. She put her elbows on the center island and her chin in her hands. Kennie opened a cupboard, spotted a package of shortbread cookies, and reconsidered. "Instead of wine, would you prefer some tea?" She set the cookies on the table.

"Actually yes, that'd be perfect."

Kennie put two mugs of water in the microwave, feeling like she should be providing entertaining conversation, but all she could think about was how betrayed she felt by Suzanne and Sterling. She leaned back against the counter, crossed her arms, and closed her eyes, while fatigue washed over her.

The microwave dinged, and she carried the hot mugs to the island. She grabbed a couple of spoons from the drawer and slid a sugar bowl and a wire basket of tea bags across to Lily. "No milk, a little sugar, no honey."

"How'd you know that?"

"Tsk, tsk, tsk, how quickly they forget. I've made you tea before."

"Oh, that's right. Thank you for remembering."

They busied themselves with tea bags and sugar. Kennie plucked a shortbread cookie from the container, dunked it in her tea, and nibbled on it.

"So," Lily said, "do you want to tell me what's got you upset about your family?"

"Not really."

Lily gave her an exasperated look.

"Okay, I'll make you a deal. I'll tell you anything you want to know about that if you explain to me why you're not painting."

Lily swallowed, but she nodded. "All right. You go first."

"Figures you'd say that. Let's see, do you recall me telling you about how Janeen's death left me well fixed?"

Lily nodded.

"Now my Aunt Clara has left me all her money and worldly possessions, and my dear sweet sister and brother are trying to get the will overturned." She hesitated. For a moment she meant to leave it at that, but something prompted her to pour out the whole story — her parentage, details about her parents' deaths, what it was like living with her aunt, and her extreme disappointment in what little family she had left, Suzanne especially.

Through it all, Lily listened intently, nodding occasionally, but not interrupting.

Stirring her cooling tea, Kennie ended by saying, "I've never had a family, not a normal one, not one that stuck by you through thick and thin like families are supposed to. Today's news from the lawyer was like the final straw, and I just feel too damn sad." Her eyes filled with tears again.

"You do realize you've created a family here in the building, right?"

Kennie stared at her, not understanding.

"Most of the people here at the Allen Arms would do a lot for you and help you in any way they could. You've been good to all of us. You earned our respect, and people began to trust and like you. You do what you say you will, and you don't complain. You're kind to everyone, and those security guards worship the ground you walk on."

Kennie was finding it hard to take in Lily's comments, and she had no idea how to respond.

"And then there's Max. Mrs. Faulkner thinks you're the greatest person who ever lived for doing what you've done with Max. You've given her a chance. Renae and Olivia, too. This Silent Auction we're doing, did you know that every tenant in the building except Lee Nguyen is coming and they've all pledged to bid?"

"Why not Lee?"

"He'll be out of the country visiting family in Indonesia. The rest want to do anything they can to help. I reached Adam by phone before I came down here, and he promised to do the cake and decorations at cost. The Halliwells said they'd handle the cash box. Since they're a lawyer and CPA, they're both bonded. No doubt the rest of the tenants will do whatever they're capable of to help us."

"You've really gotten around and talked to people."

"I've had some free time on my hands, so I've talked to everyone. You know, they say blood is thicker than water, but I don't really believe it has to be true. My point is, blood isn't the only way people are connected, and if you let yourself relax and enjoy these folks, they *will* be your family."

Kennie sat pondering that. She and Janeen hadn't been able to marry, and yet, while she'd been alive, they had both felt like the other was all the family they needed. Having one person love her unconditionally for all those years had been more than enough to replace any number of Suzannes or Sterlings. "I see your point. I'll have to keep thinking about that now. I never looked at it that way before."

Lily looked at Kennie so warmly it was like the sun shone brighter through the kitchen window.

Moving her tea mug to the side, Lily said, "We've got a lot of details to discuss, and I brought the agreement from Captain Hendricks."

"Oh, no, you're not changing the subject now, Lily Gordon. You made a deal. I over-shared, and now it's your turn."

"What do you want to know?"

"What's happened to you and your painting?"

Lily let out a deep sigh.

"That bad, huh?"

"This happens every once in a while. It's like the well goes dry, and I can't even face a canvas."

"How long has it been?"

Lily turned red from her neck all the way to the roots of her hair. To give her a moment, Kennie got up, slung her half-empty mug into the microwave and heated it for thirty seconds. When she took it out and turned back, Lily had regained her composure. "You want a warm up?" she asked.

Lily shook her head. "I'm good." She stared into her tea for so long Kennie didn't think she was going to say anything more, but she finally lifted her eyes to meet Kennie's gaze. "I wish I were like all those artists—Van Gogh, Pollock, Rothko, Picasso—who painted like demons when they were in the middle of a crisis. But I'm not. If I don't feel grounded and my life isn't at least somewhat normal, whatever that looks like at the time, I can't muster up the energy or the inspiration to paint. I can stand there for hours until all the paint on my palette dries up and...nothing."

"What do you usually do to get back your mojo?"

"I don't know. I just have to wait it out, that's all." She pasted on a bright, perky smile. "In the meantime, I'm happy to plan this charity event, and I've done a lot of promotions for my past work. I updated the greeting card line and granted licenses to a variety of people who want to use my art for one reason or another. So that's been good."

"But it's not painting."

"No. It's not."

Kennie had never been a creative person in the way Lily was, so she wasn't sure what it would be like not to be able to work on a beloved art. From what she'd seen of Lily when she was working, she got into a zone so intent that the only comparison Kennie could make had to do with having sex. Her creative process, the way she poured out vitality with paint and brush, seemed almost as though Lily was making love to the canvas. How sad and awful not to be able to express that energy, to have it all bottled up inside—or, even worse, to have it dissipate, never to return.

"I don't have any wisdom to share, Lily. I'm sorry."

Lily's smile was sweet, but sad, too. "I didn't expect you to. Thanks for understanding—and for not shaming me. I had a teacher once who insisted that if I just got off my dead, lazy butt and stood there long enough, the inspiration would come."

"I assume you considered him full of shit?"

Lily's laugh answered that question.

"Why don't you show me the paperwork from the cop shop."

"Come around here and look over my shoulder, then."

Kennie slid onto a stool next to Lily. "Lay it on me. Although if you went over it, I don't know why I need to."

"You never know. I might have missed something."

Chapter Twenty-Two

THE DAY OF the Sixth Annual Siggy Starshine Silent Auction for Charity arrived, and Kennie awoke nervous as hell. So much seemed to be riding on the success of the event, and so many people were involved, she couldn't begin to keep track of everything.

After a fast meal, she scurried up to the penthouse. Lily's front door was open. Kennie called out and, getting no answer, strolled through the foyer, down the hallway, and to the first doorway for the ballroom. Inside, men in light-grey uniforms were assembling narrow tables and locking them together around the perimeter of the room. Another man stood talking to Lily whose back was to Kennie. Lily held a clipboard in her left hand, almost as if it were a palette. In her right hand she had a pen, and she gestured with it as though it were a paintbrush. A painter through and through, Kennie thought. She hoped that whatever was blocking her creative output would disappear soon.

Lily wore white sandals and a butter yellow-colored blouse tucked into a pair of white shorts. How many women looked that good in stark white shorts? Kennie couldn't think of many. Lily laughed and backed away from the man, then whirled and seemed amused to catch Kennie checking her out. The only thing worse than being caught looking at Lily's shapely behind was the effect of looking at the front of her. Kennie's mouth went dry, and she couldn't stop the way her face flamed. Did she look like Rudolph the Red-Nosed Reindeer yet again? Lately, it seemed all she did was turn crimson around Lily.

Lily's hair was tousled and damp, as if she'd just showered, and her face was aglow with excitement. "This is really happening, and it's all coming together perfectly," she said as she tucked the pen in her pocket. She reached Kennie and took her arm to lead her down the hallway toward the back of the apartment. She was moving so fast Kennie felt like she was on a tow rope.

"I figure we'll cordon off all the parts of the apartment that people shouldn't get into. The security guards agreed to man the two hallways. However, check this out."

She ducked to the left and opened a double door to the roof terrace, which Kennie had only ever seen in passing.

Kennie stopped in the doorway, her mouth open. "Wow, I feel like I've just walked out of Auntie Em's broken-down farmhouse and into Oz."

"I know. Isn't it wonderful?"

Adam Vendrick barked directions at two guys holding an enormous white trellis. They worked under a tent that was at least twenty feet high at the middle and fifteen feet or more along the edges. The three walled sides of the terrace afforded a view of the city.

"The food will go out here. Adam thought of it. This solves the problem of people dumping snacks all over the ballroom. They can come out here to eat and get fresh air."

Adam saw them and hastened over, smoothing his unruly blond swoop. "The tent was a bear to set up, but now — isn't it marvelous?" He made a flourish, one arm high. Kennie half expected him to bow before them like an old-time courtier before his queen.

"Everything will be gold and silver and shiny purple, with a gorgeous outpouring of summer flowers, just as you requested, Lily. We'll have gloriously sexy lighting, and I've got an electrical man who can wire us up. Is that okay? We'll need plenty of outlets to power the chafing dishes, lighting, and music."

Kennie looked at Lily, then back at Adam. "The circuit boxes are updated, so installing extra lighting should be all right, but isn't this a little more than we budgeted for?"

"Don't even fret one single moment," Adam said. "I have this completely under control. Lily and I decided this would be my little gift to the event, didn't we?" He put an arm around Lily and squeezed. "It's going to be astounding. Mark my words. And it's all good for my business. New clients will be begging for us to cater for them." He checked his watch. "Duty beckons! Come back later and see how it looks."

He skipped away, remarkably like Peter Pan. Kennie muttered, "Why do I get the idea he was the lead in every musical at his high school?"

"Because you're an insightful woman who knows people?" Lily asked, a playful smile on her face.

Kennie stood for a moment, watching the men affix a second trellis on the apartment wall. Another man opened a dark green plastic bag set in a five-gallon bucket and pulled out an armful of red roses.

"Are those real?" she whispered to Lily.

"I hope so. This is going to be the most amazing party ever set up in the penthouse since I've lived here. I can't even believe how well it's all coming together."

"I'm glad you think so. Should I be feeling this nervous? Everything seems to have spun out of control. Our simple little charity event has turned into a hugely complicated affair."

Lily threaded her arm around Kennie's waist and turned them to go back inside. "You have nothing to worry about." She held up the clipboard. "I've got everything completely under control."

You do, do you? Kennie said to herself as she enjoyed the feel of Lily's warm touch on her waist. Too bad she couldn't say that about her own heart rate. There weren't enough clipboards in the world to control that.

KENNIE OWNED NO fancy formal wear, so she'd made an appointment several days earlier at a shop called Well Suited over on Broadway. To her surprise, she discovered she looked good in a tuxedo. The tailor there had completed alterations, and she left late in the afternoon for a final fitting.

She was glad to get away. Everything at the Allen Arms was completely nuts. Tenants wandered the halls, excited and jabbering. Workmen and delivery personnel continued to come and go. The entire staff of Siggy's went up and down the elevator with crates and carts and boxes. The building pulsed with frenetic intensity, and Kennie felt like a giant sponge, taking in more of that strange zeal than she could manage. She couldn't even retire to the basement and run off her nerves on the treadmill. Too many boxes and supplies had been stacked all over down there.

The event was scheduled to begin at six p.m. sharp, but Phil and his crew had cautioned her and Lily not to expect much of a crowd until later in the evening. So when she arrived home at 6:45 dressed in a black tuxedo, black tie, and wingtip shoes, she was surprised to be unable to find a parking place. A delivery van was parked in her designated spot in the back, but before she could work up a fury, it backed up and she slid the Jeep into its slot.

Kennie sat for a while gathering courage to get out of the vehicle and enter the mobbed building. Before she could make a move, her cell phone rang. She didn't recognize the number, so she answered it.

"Kennie?"

All the wind went out of her. "Yeah," she said wearily.

"You're really letting go of Auntie Clara's house?"

"Why? Don't you want it?"

"Oh, my God, yes, I want it," Suzanne said. "Thank you. You've saved my ass."

Kennie didn't know what to say. Was this her older sister, actually babbling excitedly about how she planned to move right into the small home? When she could get a word in, she asked, "What about your current house?"

"That monstrosity? The ex and I never should have bought it. I can't even begin to afford the heat bills, much less the upkeep on the grounds. That's going on the market ASAP."

"I see. So then what's the deal? Are you saying you're not suing me?"

"Oh, that," Suzanne said dismissively. "Lawyers – they're always so over-eager. When George Zimmerman called today to finalize the details of my part of the inheritance, I fired that attorney like a thieving maid. I talked to Sterling, and he's relieved to get the funds that we're each getting. I'll take out a loan to pay Sterling for his half of the value of Aunt Clara's house, and we each get twenty thousand. I'm just so happy!"

"I'm glad, Suzanne." As she said it, Kennie realized that she *was* glad. And relieved as well. "I'm on my way to an event, and I have to go now."

"All right. I'll call you next week and let you know how the move-in goes. I can't wait to get started."

Kennie closed the cell phone and exited the Jeep. Maybe her sister was capable of sharing good news, and maybe things would improve between the two of them. Who knew? Kennie didn't count on it, but stranger things had happened.

She walked around the side of the building. Out front, the street was like a parking lot. Cars stopped, and people emerged clad in outfits every bit as fancy as those worn to the Academy Awards. She was happy to see two of Portland's Finest directing traffic, and there was an officer up on the front porch as well. In the brief time she stood watching, she saw the chief of police, a mayoral candidate, and a local reporter interviewing people on camera as they strolled the walkway.

Kennie ducked away. No way did she want to be on camera. She felt so nervous and out of sorts that she'd count herself lucky if she didn't barf all over the tuxedo.

Sneaking in the back and making it to her apartment unseen turned out to be harder than she expected. The lobby was cram-packed with gabby people waiting for the elevator, and she couldn't get her key in the lock fast enough. Someone called her name, and she went cold. Then she saw it was Renae, coming down the hall dressed in soft tan leather boots, a matching leather beret, and a multicolored peasant-style smock belted over dark-green leotards. All she needed was a bow and quiver, and Kennie would have to start calling her Maid Marian. The effect was intensified by the young man ambling along beside her in a brown shirt and tan jeans. He was so hulking and broad-shouldered, and his white-blond hair so sparse, that Kennie wanted to call him Friar Tuck. Olivia and Max followed, dressed in dark jeans, black-leather jackets, and motorcycle boots.

Kennie whipped open her door and ushered the kids in. "Have you been upstairs yet?" Her words came out rushed, and to her own ears, she sounded frantic.

"Chill, Kennie," Renae said. "It's all cool. You look sa-weeet."

"Yeah," Max said. "You clean up pretty good."

Before Kennie had the chance to get more embarrassed, Olivia said, "You haven't met Doogie yet."

Friar Tuck stuck out a meaty hand to shake. "Pleased to meet you, ma'am."

He was so earnest it brought a smile to her face. "Doogie?" she asked.

"My parents watched some doctor show with a Doogie on it, and the nickname stuck. Real name's David, but I don't answer to it."

"How do you know these three musketeers?"

"Olivia and I went to the same school last year. We've kept in touch, and now I've become their D'Artagnan."

"How delightful you can be that for them. Every threesome needs a D'Artagnan to round things out. How in the world do you even know about D'Artagnan?"

"Saw the movie when I was a kid. And they're doing a new version of *The Three Musketeers* this fall, didn't you know?"

"Nah, haven't been to the movies in a real long time. I'm glad you four are keeping up the cultural literacy even if I'm not."

"That's right," he said with a smile. "Birds of a feather rock together."

"O...kay. Glad to have you."

Max said, "We can use him as a bouncer if things get rough. He can benchpress twice his weight."

"Impressive." Kennie looked him over and winked. "Shall we go check out the proceedings?"

"It's too crowded out front to use the elevator," Max said, "but if we take the back stairs to the second floor, we can grab it there."

QUITE A CROWD stood in the entryway when Kennie and the kids got off the elevator. They made their way through the chattering socialites into the ballroom, and Kennie stepped to the side, transfixed.

Despite the outside light, the room was dim and cozy. The wood floors shone, the walls looked velvety red, and upon nearly every bit of wall space, paintings and other art were displayed. Strings of spotlights illuminated the narrow tables circling the room where all the auction items were exhibited. She wondered where the spotlights had come from. They hadn't been there before.

Doogie stood next to Kennie, shaking his head slowly. "Whoa," he said. "This is truly the bee's pajamas."

Kennie stared up at him. "You mean the bee's knees? Or the cat's pajamas?"

"I like using the bee's pajamas. It kills two clichés with one stone. I want to think outside the trapezoid."

"Huh. Okay, then. I guess I have to agree with you."

Down the middle of the ballroom ran a wide table, covered from one end to the other with more items. In the corner near the first ballroom door, a bartender worked hard behind the counter of his drink cart. At the opposite end of the room, in the far corner, "Raffle Central" had been set up. One of the ways they hoped to keep bidders on hand was by pulling prizes from the raffle barrel every half an hour. The kids were assigned to help with that, and with a wave, Max summoned her crew to head in that direction.

Kennie wove between clots of people standing together laughing and talking and made it to the center table. She saw a package offering gourmet dinner for eight, a barbecue bash for forty, weekend getaways to the beach, Mount Hood, and various places around the region too numerous to count. Dozens of single and season tickets to various college and professional sports teams were offered. She marveled at the number of baskets of books, food, wooden dolls, toy cars, perfume, massage oils, candles, handmade cards, and passes for fun places like water parks, movie theaters, concerts, golf, indoor shooting ranges, and NASCAR. It was dizzying to see the array of necklaces, earrings, bracelets, picnic baskets with wine, finely crafted furniture, and service packages from gardeners, home improvement experts, and closet organizers. There was even a brushed silver chandelier.

And that was only half of the long table!

Kennie had been pleased that she managed to get a selection of twelve bottles of wine from Hip Chicks Do Wine and a gift certificate from a home security expert who would assess and outfit one home for free. But her two small contributions paled in comparison to the zillions of other items. How had Phil and his people managed this?

She heard a commotion at the rear door of the ballroom and a trill of laughter. Someone said, "The woman of the hour!" Kennie searched the crowd until she spotted her. Lily walked the gauntlet, shaking hands and greeting people with the grace of an aristocrat. Her blonde hair was up in a French twist, accentuating the elegant sweep of her neck. She wore a white pantsuit with the two-button jacket fastened and nothing underneath. No blouse, no shirt, no bra. A diamond pendant necklace above her cleavage caught and reflected light almost as effectively as Lily's bright blue eyes, which, Kennie suddenly discovered, were trained on her.

Lily sauntered her way confidently, stopping twice to shake people's hands, and then she was near enough to say, "Oh, my God, Kennie, you look smashing."

"I could say the same about you."

Lily smiled wide and came close. For a brief moment, Kennie thought she was going to hug or kiss her, but Lily reached up and adjusted her tie. "You're just a little crooked here."

Kennie's blood beat so hard in her body she wasn't sure there was enough room for all of it. Lily stood so close that Kennie could see a vein throbbing in her neck. It took all her resolve not to lean down and kiss that pulse. Lily patted her lapels and stepped back, and Kennie choked out a thank-you.

"Have you seen Adam's crowning achievement on the terrace?" Lily asked.

"No."

"He actually set up a tiny waterfall. Before the evening's over, make sure you get a look at it. I hope someone gets a picture. I can't imagine how he made the thing work." She took Kennie's forearm in both hands and squeezed. "I've got such a good feeling about tonight. We're going to make a lot of money."

And then she was gone, pulled away by a man and woman asking about a particular painting.

Kennie couldn't take her eyes off her.

THE FIRST RAFFLE prize went to Dan Rothschild of Rothschild's Motors, and his winning an 18-speed bicycle provided much laughter. Kennie meandered through the crowd to ask Renae and Doogie how the raffle tickets were selling.

"Great," Doogie said. "This is more fun than twenty yards of bubble wrap."

To Renae, Kennie said, "Is he always like this?"

Renae nodded. "Never boring either. He must spend six hours a day thinking up new sayings."

Doogie gave Renae a radiant smile, then accepted tickets from a tiny woman and leaned down to listen to her question.

"Where are Max and Olivia?" Kennie asked.

"They're off getting something to eat. Did you see the spread? Phil outdid himself."

"I'm so glad, Renae. I haven't managed to leave the ballroom yet, but I'll check it out."

The next couple of hours passed quickly. Somehow, people figured out Kennie owned the building, and she started getting all manner of questions. At one point, an elderly couple asked about leasing an apartment, and after much discussion, she took them down to 6A to show it to them. Although the unit wasn't finished, she thought they might want it.

When she finally made her way out to the terrace, she was ravenous. She chose some meat rolls, deviled eggs, a vegetable quiche cup, and a grilled chicken kebab while avoiding everything with a sauce. So far she'd managed not to get her white shirt dirty, and she wanted to keep it that way.

Every chair available was taken, and other people stood talking and eating at tall pub tables. Kennie ate swiftly, just enough to quell her hunger, and returned to the ballroom. Wherever she went, she kept an eye out for Lily who was here, there, and everywhere. No way could Kennie have kept up with her.

Twenty minutes before the ten p.m. deadline, a rush of bidders came clamoring for last looks at all the goodies. The paintings were, by far, accumulating the highest bids. Kennie took time to search the names of the artists, and when she couldn't find a piece of art with Lily's name on it, she sought her out.

"I'm not finding one of your creations."

Lily shook her head sadly. "I decided to make a monetary donation rather than hang a painting I wasn't happy with."

"But I thought you had a whole room full?"

"Of rejects. Not one of them was good enough." She brightened. "But I did get the work of thirteen other painters and sculptors, and they're selling well. If it makes you feel any better, a businessman from Salem offered a sizable amount for the painting in the lobby next to the elevator."

Tensing up, Kennie asked, "What'd you tell him?"

"It's not mine to sell. That's yours."

Kennie took a deep breath, and relief coursed through her. "That's good to know."

"You can't seriously think anybody would sell that out from under you?"

Kennie shrugged. "For all I know, someone could swipe it right off the wall."

"Not tonight." Lily chuckled. "We have an amazing number of police here tonight, and some of them aren't in uniform."

"Good to know."

"Are you staying for the dance?"

"I guess," Kennie said.

"If you're still around when this gets over at midnight, come down to the party room to find out the haul we made, all right?"

"I wouldn't miss that for the world."

AT LONG LAST, the bidding closed, and the process began of announcing winners and herding people to the party room to pay for their purchases. For half an hour, Kennie stayed out of the way, behind the raffle display, talking to the kids. After the auction items were removed, a group of four men and two women went through the ballroom and broke down the tables and moved them out. Pretty soon the raffle table and display were gone, and Kennie stood in the corner with Max's crew and Pete Ackerman. Pete had been delighted to win a raffle prize of a dinner for four at Jake's in downtown Portland. Renae was trying to convince him of all the reasons he should take her and Max with him.

Kennie's feet hurt, and she was only half-listening to the banter. She didn't pay close attention when Max said, "Can someone tell me why this place is called the Allen Arms? There aren't any arms here."

"Yeah," Olivia said, "did this used to be a place where people stockpiled weapons?"

"That'd be an armory, dumbass." Doogie said it mockingly but with enough affection that Olivia blushed with pleasure rather than hurt.

"Oooh, cruel," Max said, laughing. "Want me to hit him for you?"

"No, we'll let him live for now," Olivia retorted, "but he'll pay later."

Max turned to Kennie. "What's the story? Did you name the building?"

"Huh — what?"

"The Allen Arms — did you name it?"

"No. It was called that when I bought it, and I wasn't about to tear down the concrete and brick edifice out front with the name carved in it."

"What's the deal with arms, then?" Max asked.

Pete Ackerman said, "I might be able to explain. During previous historical eras, inns and pubs often displayed a well-known shield or coat of arms, usually representative of the family who owned the establishment."

"But why *arms?*" Max repeated.

"You've seen a coat of arms, right? With a name like Wallington, you probably have one that has a crest and animals or crowns and wreaths — some sort of combination of symbols that represent your family. A coat of arms was a heraldic device often worn over a soldier's armor so fighters on the same side could identify each other. You fought for the king — you usually wore his coat of arms. Of course the rich guys of the time figured if the king had a specific kind of emblem, then everyone who could afford to have one designed and made should have one as well. The nobles had their own made up."

"Ahh," Renae said, "keeping up with the Joneses."

"Exactly. Maybe the king's design was of a roaring lion holding an arrow in one paw and a dead rabbit in the other paw. Add a crest made up of interwoven pikes on the top, a couple of swords on the sides, and some flashy royal blue as a background color, and suddenly it's King Leo's Arms. Max, let's say your family shield was black with four gold fleurs-de-lis representing the 'wall' in your name. When your shield got hung up anywhere as an identifier, they wouldn't call the place Four Gold Stylized Lilies on a Black Field. The place would get referred to as 'Wallington Arms.'"

"Oh," Renae said. "That's very interesting."

Max said, "Even more interesting is how the heck you know all that, Pete."

Pete tapped his forehead. "Got a mind for minutiae. Besides, I loved studying English history in college. And then there's the business angle. Over time, schools, churches, guilds, even corporations created emblems and designs to reflect their origins or histories. Nowadays, some of those are considered trademarks, which is something I help companies protect as part of my legal practice."

"Hmmm," Max said, "so who was Allen?"

"Can't help you with that." Pete grinned. "The only historical Allen I can think of off the top of my head was Thomas Allen, a sixteenth-century mathematician famous for his knowledge of antiquity, philosophy, and astrology. He was rumored to be a magician. Speaking of magicians..."

Lily had sidled up to the group, and Max and Renae shifted to let her in.

"You guys are talking magic?" Lily asked.

THE CROWD WAS nearly wall to wall, and the ballroom floor shivered with writhing bodies, but Kennie had eyes for only one. Standing along the edge, a drink in hand, she watched Lily dance first with a woman, then a tall man in a gray suit, and in a small group. Even PJ Jarrell had shown up for the dance. She was moving and shaking quite capably with a stunning flame-haired woman in a black dress who she'd introduced to Kennie as Special Agent Sarah Cordell. An FBI agent? Kennie was almost certain PJ had met her match. She hoped Agent Cordell kicked her ass.

With every song the DJ played, the pulsing music pounded louder, and someone kept turning the lights down until it was quite dark. Only faint light from the ceiling lamps and a lot of strobing from a disco ball hanging in the center of the room provided illumination.

A fast-paced Flamenco song had everyone moving fast, twisting, twirling, laughing. She saw some sort of dance routine that involved clapping and shifting right, patting a rhythm on thighs, then sashaying left with another round of clapping. Lily was a terrific dancer, moving effortlessly, with the kind of grace someone involved in ballet always possessed. Kennie wondered if Lily had taken dance lessons. She seemed to know all the steps, all the moves, whether the music called for a two-step, a waltz, a mambo, or something more modern. Or maybe Lily was just one of those lucky people with innate rhythm, even if she couldn't figure out the elliptical machine. Kennie smiled and closed her eyes. For a moment, she was overcome with lightheadedness and the music pulsed through her, in her, right to the core of her groin.

The DJ overlapped a new song and faded out the Flamenco. This, too, was a Latin melody, but sinuous, sensual with a bass line Kennie felt in her bones. With one gulp, she tossed back her Seven & Seven and set the tumbler on a tray. Heart beating wildly, she stepped onto the dance floor and came up behind Lily. She encircled the slim waist with her right arm and found Lily's left hand and held it out in a much more demure pose than she intended.

"I'm lonely for you," she said in Lily's ear.

At that, the smaller woman melted into her arms. The song called for little more than a rhythmic swaying and an occasional slide, and it took no time before they had found a flow. Lily turned her head slightly, and as if Kennie had no control at all, she leaned down and placed her lips on Lily's neck.

Lily trembled in Kennie's arms. Without warning, Kennie felt weak in the knees. She tightened her grip around Lily's waist and rested her chin on her shoulder, shifting enough to move her knee between Lily's legs. Now with every movement forward, every movement back, she pressed in. All around, other dancers whirled and glided by, no one seeming to notice their very intimate foreplay in four-four time.

Lily put her hand over the top of Kennie's and moved it slightly upward, just below her breast. They still held left hands out, attempting to maintain proper decorum, but with her palm so near Lily's heart, Kennie shivered with desire. She brought her left arm in and laced her fingers around Lily's middle. With a shudder, Lily reached up to return Kennie's lips to her neck.

Kennie closed her eyes and danced to the music. Had there been an explosion of light? Kennie felt, rather than saw, lights flashing at the same tempo as her breathing. She opened her eyes and saw nothing but slivers of light from the disco ball overhead. Lily's hand, stroking her neck, was sweet torment. Kennie breathed into her ear. She couldn't stop whispering, "Beautiful. You are...so...beautiful." She wasn't able to see Lily's face, but she felt the body she held responding, melding to her own, rubbing against her, taunting her for wearing clothing that was in the way of the skin-on-skin contact she craved.

Some part of her attempted to access logic and rationality, to remind herself they were in public. A kernel of caution blossomed, warning her this could only lead to embarrassment, perhaps even pain. But the sweet agony of desire she felt was much more powerful than anything words could say. She could barely stop herself from lifting Lily up and carrying her off to a lair, like a caveman. She silently laughed at that image. If only she had a lair closer than six floors down.

The few minutes of total abandon and joy came to an end when the DJ abruptly cranked up a Madonna tune that overrode the Latin song until the sexy beat was gone.

The tempo changed; the rhythm was lost. Lily extricated herself and looked back with such pain in her eyes that Kennie was struck speechless. Before Kennie could recover, Lily fled. Weaving through dancers, ducking past someone in a ballroom gown, she was gone.

Kennie stumbled to one of the cocktail tables and fell into a chair. She took a moment to catch her breath and shivered when other partygoers shifted and a blast of air conditioning hit her.

Someone grabbed her shoulder and leaned in, lips close to Kennie's ear. "Holy shit," Max said, "that was some kind of dirty dancing there. Didn't know you had it in you."

Kennie blushed so much she could feel heat in the roots of her hair. She had no idea how to respond.

"I think you blew her socks off."

Renae materialized beside Max and said, "I think she had a little more than her socks to go change. That was some grind you did. You two practically had sex on the dance floor."

"You're crazy," Kennie managed to say over the music. "It wasn't that bad."

Max and Renae looked at each other and fell into one another's arms, laughing hysterically. When they came up for air, Kennie tried to give them the evil eye, but she couldn't maintain it. "All right. She may like me again. Maybe."

Max pulled something out of her shirt pocket. "She more than likes you. Don't worry about that."

Kennie rolled her eyes when she saw Max waving that damn

hundred-dollar bill. "If you're so smart, maybe you can tell me why she ditched me like that."

Renae said, "You melted her. She was too damn hot. She's probably off taking a cold shower this very minute."

"You two are waaaaay too young to know all this stuff about women and sex."

Renae grinned like she had a special secret. "My generation has a lot more fun than yours does."

Max said, "Go find her." She smacked Kennie on the shoulder. "Get yo' ass up, and go find your girl."

Without a word, Kennie rose to do just that.

FIRST KENNIE SEARCHED the terrace. The Siggy's crew was still putting out food, and a couple dozen people were enjoying the ambience, but none of them was Lily.

She reversed course and went back to the front of the apartment. She ran into Simms near the foyer, guarding the hallway that led to the kitchen, dining room, and other rooms in that wing, most of which Kennie had never seen.

"How's your evening, boss?" Simms asked.

"Good, thanks. This has gone well. Have you seen Lily?"

He pointed a thumb over his shoulder. "She went that way, but she seemed upset."

"I'll check on her."

He stepped aside to let her through. She didn't know where she was going. Every door down the hallway was open but one, and she figured that'd be the one she needed. She tapped on it. She heard some muffled sounds but couldn't make out whether it was a call to come in or not, so she turned the knob and stepped half in.

"Lily?"

She sat on a divan for two, almost unnoticeable because the upholstery was exactly the same white as her suit. One wall of the room was filled floor to ceiling with books. The window side of the room looked out on the terrace, but the blinds were half-closed. Kennie couldn't make out anything more than the lighting and some people milling about. On either side of the windows, she saw a stereo, racks of compact disks, and a TV with surround sound. Across from the divan, three easy chairs looked inviting. Only one table lamp was on, and it didn't throw much light.

"Lily?" Kennie repeated. "What's the matter?"

Lily wouldn't look at her.

Kennie had never been one for the dramatic, but she felt the situation called for it. She moved to the divan and dropped to her knees in front of Lily. "Please. Tell me." She put one hand on each of Lily's knees.

Lily sat with her eyes closed for so long that all of Kennie's hopes sank. She hunkered back on her heels and lowered her head, thinking this might be the last time she got to touch Lily like this.

Then Lily spoke in a soft, faraway voice. "It's not supposed to be like this. I'm not supposed to feel this way."

Kennie jerked her head up. "What way?"

"I don't deserve you. You shouldn't want anything to do with me at all."

"But I do."

A spark flashed in Lily's eyes, and she met Kennie's gaze. "What for? You like damaged goods?"

"If you think you're damaged goods, you're crazy."

"I'm a mess. I leave a mess in my wake, too. I already hurt you terribly. It was unconscionable. I can never make up for that."

Lily didn't seem to know what to do with her hands. She kept opening and closing them as though they hurt. Kennie touched them and found them ice cold. She gripped them softly, and after a moment, Lily squeezed back.

"Lily, I don't blame you. If I'd been in your shoes—"

"But you weren't in my shoes. If you had been, you never would have done to me what I did to you."

"Look at it this way. If Janeen came back to life and presented herself to me, I would have to go with her, just like you did with PJ."

"That is *so* not the same."

"You weren't done with PJ. And I never got to finish with Janeen. That's a lot of grief and hope and uncertainty to deal with. It doesn't have to be that way this time."

"What's different this time?" Lily said bitterly. "Don't you worry PJ will come back again?"

Kennie chuckled. "Not after tonight, I don't."

"What? What's different about tonight?"

"Apparently you didn't see her grand entrance earlier this evening with her new squeeze."

"What?"

"Miss PJ got herself a ball-of-fire FBI agent. She's a spitfire redhead, about thirty going on hell-raiser, and PJ is completely enthralled."

"What a slut. We just broke up not that long ago." The half-smile she wore belied her tone.

"She's in for it this time," Kennie said. "This new woman is nothing like you. I can only hope she gives PJ a run for her money. But PJ doesn't matter at all. Only you do. Only you and what you think and feel matters to me. Please don't shut me out. I couldn't bear it if you shut me out."

"Because I'm doing such a great job at that?"

Kennie gave her a pointed look.

"What you did to me on the dance floor...that was cruel. You're heartless, Kennie McClain. Absolutely heartless."

"No," Kennie whispered, as she straightened up off her heels, back to her knees, and pulled Lily to her, "I have a heart, and it's beating hard for you. For a long time it was broken, but now it's not."

Lily's hands, still cool, cradled Kennie's face. Kennie leaned in and pressed her lips to Lily's. She tasted sweet, like strawberries. Behind closed eyes, Kennie saw starbursts. Every nerve and synapse in her body lit up. She felt like she was going to burst into flames and broke off the kiss. She tucked her face into the side of Lily's neck. It was silky and smelled of a perfume that aroused her further.

"Oh, God," Kennie said with a groan. She was hot and wet and panting far harder than any single kiss had ever caused before. "Lucky I'm on my knees. Otherwise, I probably would have fallen over after that kiss."

"You're such an exaggerator," Lily said breathlessly as she stroked the side of Kennie's face.

"I'm not, really. I'm not." Kennie couldn't take her eyes off the two buttons holding Lily's suit closed. She unbuttoned the first with one hand and met Lily's gaze to silently ask permission. Lily seemed to be holding her breath, and she didn't stop her. Kennie unbuttoned the second, opened up the jacket, and touched the softest, warmest skin. She took a breast in each hand and stroked the nipples with her thumbs.

Lily moaned.

Kennie whispered, "You like that, huh?"

"It wouldn't be an exaggeration...to say I'm in...heaven."

Kennie leaned in and tongued one nipple. With a sharp intake of breath, Lily tightened her grip on Kennie's neck. "Oh, God," Lily said. "You could do that to me all night."

"Good point," Kennie said. She pulled back. "I definitely want to do that to you all night. I want to love you until you're speechless and completely senseless." She pulled the lapels of Lily's jacket together and fingered the top button.

"Wait a minute. You're not going to stop now. Don't give me that evil smirk."

As she buttoned her up, Kennie said, "We can't get carried away now. You're the hostess. We have to go back out there."

"I doubt they've missed me."

The pleading in her voice made Kennie laugh. "Don't tempt

fate." She leaned back and rose, pulling Lily up with her. "Whoa. Could I take a quick trip to Cold Showerville?"

Lily put her arms around her. Her head fit perfectly under Kennie's chin. "If I have to deal with these side effects, then so do you."

KENNIE STOOD NEAR Lily in the apartment foyer, thanking people for attending. It was after midnight, and she couldn't wait to get rid of all the partygoers. She'd sent Lily back to Phil and his workers to tell them to stop serving food, and she'd had Max tell the DJ to play a couple of slow songs and wind down the dancing.

At one a.m., the last guests and most of the workers finally left. The Halliwells came upstairs to announce that the Silent Auction had, so far, yielded almost $87,000—and there were still some outstanding payments. It would likely be more in a few days. Max, Renae, the DJ, and Phil's people cheered and did various celebratory dances. Lily used that excuse to hug Kennie, and Kennie left her arm around her.

It took another twenty minutes for people to clear out with promises to come back the next day for cleanup. When Lily shut the front door, she threw her arms around Kennie and leaned her head against her chest.

Kennie felt a contentment unlike anything she'd ever known. Teasing, she said, "Hey, you'll mess up my tie. It's been a chick magnet all night. Everybody wants to straighten it—even some of the butches."

Lily peered up at her. "Did you open up their clothing and fondle them?"

"Oh, yeah. At every opportunity."

Lily smacked her. "Can we go to bed?"

"Are you tired?"

"Exhausted. But I could be revived with the proper ministrations."

Kennie laughed. "I'll try my best to figure out which ministrations those are." She pointed toward the back of the apartment. "Your place?"

"Could we go to yours? First thing tomorrow, Simms and Max are going to be letting people in to clear away the mess, and I don't want to be up here then. Don't you want to sleep in?"

"Good idea."

"Let me change clothes and get some things. I'll be down in a few minutes."

"I'll leave the door unlocked."

Kennie took the elevator downstairs, and as she descended, a funny feeling in her stomach increased. For a moment she thought it was the elevator's free fall, but once on the first floor, she realized that she had butterflies of a completely different kind. Oh, my God, she thought in wonderment, this is really happening.

She didn't know how much time she had. She burst into the apartment, checked her bedroom to see it was as tidy as she'd left it, and went to the linen closet to grab several candles. After setting them around her room, she stripped out of her clothes, took a quick shower, and donned sleep shorts and a t-shirt.

She was lighting the candles when she heard the front door open and close. She peeked out of the bedroom and saw Lily shoot the lock. Out of her white suit but with her hair still up in the French twist, she was dressed in gray sweat bottoms, a loose t-shirt, and flip-flops, and she carried a small duffel bag. As she crossed the living room to the bedroom hallway, Kennie said, "Somehow I was expecting the chance to unbutton that lovely jacket again."

"And I was looking forward to taking your tie off" – she grinned wickedly – "and other items of clothing."

Kennie shrugged. "Guess we get the real us, not the fancified versions."

Lily dropped the bag and walked into her arms. Kennie held her tight, feeling an elation she hadn't experienced in a very long time. She brought a hand up to stroke Lily's neck, which was damp. "Hey, you took a shower?"

"Seems like I'm not the only one who's damp."

Kennie snickered. "You have no idea."

Lily smacked her on the arm. "Very funny."

"Don't mind me. I'm a little punch-drunk now."

Lily leaned around her to survey the room. "You've been busy, I see. Nice ambience."

"Thanks."

Lily shooed her backwards, toward the bed, and when the back of Kennie's knees hit the edge, Lily pushed her onto the soft surface, settled on top of her, and nuzzled her neck.

"Hey, don't you want to bring your little bag of tricks with you?"

"What?" Lily asked.

"The duffel you brought."

"That's some clothes for the morning." Lily went very still and studied Kennie's face for long enough that Kennie knew she was blushing yet again. "I don't need anything tonight but you, Kennie. Your hands, your mouth, your skin—just you. I don't want anything to come between us. No props, no toys, nothing. I hope that's okay."

Kennie closed her eyes and let out a groan. "You are so hot.

You make me feel weak. I don't need anything but you either."

Lily lowered her mouth and gave her a searing kiss, leaving Kennie panting with desire. When they came up for air, Kennie whispered, "Let me undress you."

Lily slid off the bed and Kennie sat up. Lily stepped out of the sweat bottoms and eased into the V of Kennie's legs. Her arms on Kennie's shoulders afforded Kennie a perfect angle to remove Lily's t-shirt and press her face to the soft flesh of Lily's breasts.

"Ohhh," Lily said with a moan, "thank God this time you don't have to stop."

She cradled Kennie's head in her arms, and Kennie heard the powerful beat of Lily's heart, in time with the insistent throbbing between her own thighs. She drew one hardened nipple into her mouth, and Lily sagged against her.

"Uh-oh," Kennie said.

"Sorry, I don't know why—"

"Shhh, it's okay. Let's get comfortable." Keeping hold of one of Lily's hands, she scooted up to the head of the bed and tossed the covers back, then pulled Lily, shaking and breathing hard, to her.

"What about you?" Lily gasped out. "First I don't get to take off your tuxedo, and now you're still dressed."

Kennie smiled. As Lily settled on her back, Kennie went up on her knees, took off her t-shirt, and slipped the sleep shorts down. She lowered herself onto her side, on one elbow, and Lily sat up to slide the shorts off and toss them away. In the process, Lily's hand found the overheated spot between Kennie's legs, and there was nothing cold about her hand now. Her fingers burned, and the sparks of bliss Kennie felt stunned her momentarily. She couldn't catch her breath. Lily rolled onto her, her tongue a weapon of pleasure on Kennie's neck.

Kennie spread her legs to accommodate Lily's questing fingers. She was desperate to move, to lift her hips, to satisfy the intense throbbing. Lily's fingers found her wetness and slid inside, slowly, and Kennie lay frozen, not daring to move for fear the exquisite delight would end. Lily paused, and Kennie begged, "More, more, please..."

Lily straddled one of Kennie's thighs. Hovering above, she began a rhythm that sent waves of feeling to the depths of Kennie's soul. She stroked Lily's sides, and the soft skin beneath her hands felt as sleek as the finest velvet. Lily was definitely in control. She had Kennie frozen in place just by the touch of her hand, and Kennie lost the ability to do anything but beg for more.

How is this happening? Kennie thought. She realized she'd spoken the words aloud because Lily laughed and said, "Because I love you." Her body relaxed against Kennie's chest. The heat and friction of Lily's body against her torso, her fingers inside, her hand against Kennie's clit built a tempo that beat in Kennie's ears like a drum.

She was unprepared when Lily's mouth covered one breast and sucked hard. A shot of liquid electricity caromed back and forth between her breast and clit. She felt Lily's heart pounding, her hot breath against her breast. Lily's free hand lightly caressed her other breast, and the sensation on her skin and nipple was so unbearably delicious that a low moan escaped from deep inside and rose in volume. Kennie had never been a noisy lover, but the thrust of Lily's hand loosened something inside her. She was a pool of aching need, all her intensity focused on the relentless hand that she kept begging not to stop. She cried out, moving against Lily, their breaths mingling.

Lily spoke softly, words of love, words of encouragement, urging Kennie on. "Come," she said. "Come for me. Come on..."

Kennie bucked against her. Pleasure radiated through every muscle, every nerve, and when she reached the pinnacle of bliss, the intense explosion left her gasping, with her soul ripped open. She slid down that pinnacle, pulsing, shuddering, crying out Lily's name. As the trembling gradually slowed, she had tears in her eyes.

One escaped and ran down her cheek. Lily wiped it away. "Are you all right?" she asked.

"Yes," Kennie said. Fingers still inside, Lily's hand was like a hot iron between Kennie's legs. "That was so—indescribably amazing. I can't begin to even explain what happened, but I can still feel it." She didn't understand how something she'd done before hundreds, maybe thousands of times, could feel so new and fresh and intense, even more so than the first time she'd made love with Lily. Had Lily really said she loved her? That wasn't a dream, was it? She couldn't find words to express all the feelings that raced through her mind and soul.

Lily whispered, "That might have been almost as much fun for me."

"Oh, no, you ain't felt nothing yet, lady."

"I'm counting on it," Lily said. Gently, she slid her fingers out and shifted until Kennie held her to her side, her head resting under Kennie's chin.

Kennie ran her fingers through Lily's hair, some of which had come loose from the French twist. Around the back, she gingerly fingered metal pins. "You haven't been endangering our lives with these hairpins, have you?"

"They're just bobby pins and some special clips." She pushed up onto her knees, still straddling Kennie's leg, and raised both hands to let down her hair.

Kennie reached for Lily's breasts and stroked them. In the candlelight, she watched the golden tresses tumbling down onto Lily's shoulders.

Lily let out a sigh and sat back on her heels, eyes closed and hands on her thighs. In the low light, her skin appeared golden, as if she were a priceless treasure. Gently, her arms came up, and she stroked Kennie's forearms. She grasped Kennie's wrist and pulled her hand down. "Touch me. I want you so bad."

Kennie palmed Lily's abdomen, caressing the soft skin there while still stroking one breast, then slid her hand between Lily's thighs, which were quivering.

"Ah, babe, you are so wet."

Lily trembled. Her breath came hard and fast, and she looked at Kennie mutely, an inexplicable expression on her face.

"What do you want?" Kennie asked.

"I want...you. Please, touch me. Make me come."

Kennie sat up, put an arm around Lily, and lowered her to the side, allowing Lily to move her legs out from underneath. Now she lay sideways across the bed, her torso in Kennie's lap with Kennie's left arm cradling her shoulders and her right hand pressed against her clit.

Kennie leaned down and tongued a breast, found the nipple, suckled it, bit it gently. With her fingers, she explored Lily's wetness, which felt plush and hot, like a flower opened to accept the heat of the sun.

Lily whimpered, still breathing hard.

Kennie kissed her, all the while continuing the relentless stroking on Lily's clit. The kiss went deep, her tongue exploring, tentatively at first, then insistently. She pressed her lips to Lily's neck, tickled with her tongue, and blazed a trail up to Lily's ear. She whispered, "You feel fantastic—so soft, so silky." Lily opened her legs farther, and Kennie found her way inside her. Her thumb kept up a circular motion as she thrust her fingers inside the slick canal.

Lily gasped, then writhed with the rhythm of Kennie's hand. Moaning, she choked out, "Oh, God, oh, oh, oh..."

Kennie clasped Lily's upper body and held tight as her hips thrashed. Concentrating on the motion of her right hand, Kennie felt a familiar tingling and pulsing of her own and grinned to think how much Lily turned her on. Holding her, Lily's hair soft against her shoulder, she felt as complete as she ever had.

Lily's breath came shorter now, and without warning, her body stiffened and her legs pressed tight against Kennie's hand. "There. There. There," Lily said, "don't stop, don't..."

Kennie felt a shudder all the way up her arm. Lily let out a heaving breath and went tense, but Kennie continued to alternately circle and press upon her clit. Lily's eyes opened, but didn't seem to focus.

"Stay with it. Just breathe," Kennie whispered. "I can do this all night. I'll make you come twenty times, a hundred, whatever you need."

Lily trembled in her arms again, closed her eyes, and moaned. Kennie could feel her coming, over, and over, and over again. She lost count of how many times and eventually ducked her head against Lily's chest and clutched her tight, trying to ignore the increased shaking in her left arm.

With a final gasp, Lily sagged against her, panting as if she'd run a quarter-mile at top speed. She opened her eyes and gazed up, her vision clear, and a smile playing at the corners of her mouth as she tried to catch her breath. "Pretty good hands there, McClain."

"You ain't seen nothing yet. Wait'll you feel my mouth on you."

"Could I be allowed to recover for a while first? I don't think I can feel my legs."

Kennie laughed. "Feel free to feel mine."

KENNIE DIDN'T LOOK at the clock until Lily drifted off to sleep. She lay nestled into Kennie's side, her golden hair fanned back on the pillow. Relaxed, the planes of her face were smooth and unworried, and she looked like a madonna in repose. It was now nearly five a.m. Kennie hoped like hell nobody disturbed them until at least noon, maybe longer.

They'd made love for hours, and Kennie's legs were pleasantly sore. She moved her left arm and decided she was going to have a very sore biceps, too, but it was so worth it. Just thinking of holding Lily, touching her, loving her, made her feel all liquidy and warm deep inside her abdomen. The scent of her was intoxicating, even now while she slept.

She couldn't get over the profound sense of rightness she felt. Lily's words of love echoed in her mind, and Kennie felt blessed, as if God had gazed down upon her and realized she'd had a long hard time and now deserved a giant helping of grace. Making love with Lily felt holy, like a sacrament all their own.

She hadn't been allowing herself to think about a future, but now she desperately wanted one with Lily. She wanted to go to bed each night and hold her in her arms, to love and kiss her and make her feel all the wonders that sex could bring, and to wake up and share their days together. Was that too much to ask? Was it possible?

With a deep breath, she snuggled closer to Lily and closed her eyes.

EIGHT HOURS SEEMED to have passed when Kennie woke up. She felt rested and ready for her day, but the bedside clock read only 9:05. She glanced down at Lily, who lay in basically the same position as when they'd fallen asleep, and was surprised to find her awake.

"Good morning, you party animal," Kennie said. She raised a hand and cupped Lily's face, softly stroking her cheek. "Are you exhausted or what?"

Lily yawned. "I feel very relaxed. I could get up...but I don't want to. Do you know you're the perfect temperature? Not too cold, not too overly warm."

"You certainly made me overly warm last night."

Lily smiled and tightened her grip on Kennie's waist. "Seems like it's taken far too long to get back to this place, which is where we should have been all along. I feel like that's my fault."

"I don't blame it on you—I don't have to. Not when PJ has such broad shoulders."

Lily frowned.

"Hey, I'm kidding. I can joke about it now. I'm past it."

"I'll try to get there, too. I have to admit that, in retrospect, PJ and I weren't very compatible. She wanted to possess me, and I wasn't strong enough to deal with that. Within a few months, I knew it would never work, but I kept trying. We didn't like enough of the same things. Even worse, she was jealous of my painting."

"Of your talent."

"No, she was possessive of that, too, as if it had something to do with her, but what she was jealous of was the time and energy it took."

"But why?"

Lily smoothed a lock of hair away from Kennie's brow. "See, that you would ask that question makes all the difference in the world. Art is a jealous lover. I've never had a partner who could accept that."

"It seems to me it's like a job that's filled with a lot more passion and satisfaction than most jobs are."

"It's erratic. I get obsessed. I go away in my head at times. This has never been acceptable to anyone."

"I suppose if the house is on fire, it might not be acceptable to me either, but on a day-to-day basis?" She snuggled closer to Lily, tightening her grip. "You're miserable if you're not being creative. Any fidiot can see that."

"Fidiot?"

Kennie laughed. "I'm picking up the lingo from the kids. Any fucking idiot could see you're not whole when you're not painting. I've been watching you for weeks—since you came back from Barcelona. You haven't been yourself."

"I haven't been able to paint since your birthday."

Kennie lay silent for a long while before she finally said, "You seemed like you were painting."

"I tried. I put on the clothes. I mixed the paint. I even slopped some on a couple of canvases. I couldn't make it happen. It was like hearing discordant music in my head—and loud, way too loud. I couldn't take it."

"I guess I don't understand. I thought you went to Barcelona to paint."

"I went to get away from you and from PJ and from everything. I knew I wouldn't paint. I needed time to think. All I could think about, obsessively, was what if I could never paint again? What would I do? And after what happened with you, a part of me believed I deserved that. I'd never gone a whole summer without painting. In fact, I can't remember when I ever had problems in summer. It's such a beautiful time of year and so inspiring. My problem was more than that, deeper than that. A broken heart cracked me open, actually, and in the process of mending, something that had long been penned up got released. I thought my talent and inspiration and desire went with it."

"No. That won't happen. You'll get it back, Lily."

"I know that now. I want to paint so much right now my body is literally singing."

"You're funny. I feel those same things right now. It's just all those good hormones blasting through our bloodstreams."

"It's more than that. It's you. I've been in love before—the thing with all the hormones—and yes, I feel that now, but there's more this time. I like you. We're compatible."

"There's so much we don't know about each other, though. We haven't talked music or movies or—"

Lily waved a hand and cut her off. "None of that matters. It's the way you listen to people, and to me. It's the quiet kindnesses you do. It's the way you understand about sadness and grief and desperation. I can't quite explain it. You're different from any woman I've ever been with. They always chose me, and I went along, flattered by their attention, and none of them ever worked out. They wanted to change me, to remake me into their own image."

"Very God-like of them."

"Right. But you're not like that, Kennie. And hey, I chose you."

"You were braver than I was. That's nothing for me to be proud of."

"I didn't have to spend more than that one dinner to know you were different. I already had a hunch from seeing you around the apartment house, and on your birthday, I knew in less than two hours. That's why I could've kicked myself for what happened with PJ."

"What did happen?"

"Are you asking if we had sex?"

"Actually, no. I don't care about that. How did she go about convincing you to try again?"

"I was an idiot—a fidiot." She grinned. "It took me a long time to really grasp this, but what happened with you was so amazing that at some level, I didn't think I could trust it. And PJ came waltzing in, making promises and apologizing and being charming. And I was stupid enough to believe she'd changed. But it didn't take more than a few days for her to return to true form. She's bossy and rough and demanding. She can't change. She won't change. I got hit with the proverbial two-by-four and knew I'd made the biggest mistake of my life, and one I had no way of undoing. You couldn't even look at me. The level of betrayal...it was too much. I haven't stopped feeling awful about it."

Kennie rolled onto her side and stroked Lily's abdomen, then leaned down to kiss her. "It's okay," she said when she came up for air. "Things have a way of working out. That was then, and this is now. I think you may want to put a limit on me for the number of clichés I can use at any given time."

Lily gave her a wicked grin. "We'll chop that tomato when the salsa runs out."

Kennie froze. "Oh, Lord, you've caught the virus that Doogie kid has."

Lily let out a shriek of laughter and sat up. "When he said that to me last night, I about fell on the floor laughing. He was so serious about it, too."

"Those kids are characters, that's for sure."

Lily tucked her hair behind her ear and pushed Kennie onto her back. She rose on her knees and straddled Kennie's stomach. "You got any energy left?"

"For you? Always. Besides, hadn't I better live it up now since any minute I'm going to be eclipsed by your other mistress?"

Above her, Lily gazed at her with a shocked expression on her face.

"Your painting, hon. I'm talking about your passion."

"Oh." Lily lowered herself so that her torso lay atop Kennie, knees and lower legs still on either side, and her arms cradling her head. "You're my passion. The painting is an outlet for all the energy you give me." She kissed her and shivered when Kennie caressed her sides.

"Shift upwards, and..." Lily crawled forward, and Kennie buried her face between her breasts, her hands kneading them. "Mmm hmmm," Lily said with a sigh, "exactly what I had in mind."

LATER, THEY LAY in one another's arms, quiet for a long while. Kennie liked that she didn't feel the need — or an expectation from Lily — to be talking all the time. She'd never been with a woman comfortable with silence. Even Janeen was high maintenance and couldn't sit still for long. Kennie needed to luxuriate, to relax, and with Lily, she could.

After a time, though, she asked Lily what she was thinking about.

"There are a lot of nooks and crannies in this building. It'd be fun to make love in all of them."

Kennie burst out laughing. "That is so not what I thought you'd say. How very risqué of you."

"Thank you. Just saying."

"I could probably accommodate," Kennie said with a wink.

"Just don't expect me to relish you jumping my bones anywhere near that damn treadmill."

"What? It's a nice flat surface. If we ran it for a bit, it'd even be warm."

"Ha! That miserable thing just about killed me."

"But you kept coming back."

"Of course. Because you were down there. I had to have some excuse."

Kennie laughed again, delight coursing through her. "You're kidding, right?"

"Nope. I know it's pathetic, but all I did half the day was take the elevator down to the second floor, hit the back stairs, and check the basement for sounds of the machines."

"Why not take the elevator all the way down?"

"Right. The first time I did that, it opened on the main lobby, then went to the basement, and you weren't in the gym. An hour later I checked once more, and the damn elevator opened up in full view of Simms. Again. He looked at me real funny. Between him and Max, I had to figure out a way to sneak around."

Kennie marveled at the extent of Lily's efforts to connect — and all the while she hadn't had a clue. She'd been lost in that maelstrom of sadness and pain. Maybe she'd been a dummy about

Lily, but things had eventually worked out. When she'd first met Lily and watched her come and go from the Allen Arms, she thought she was unattainable. But over time, she came to see that Lily, though talented and extraordinary, was also a normal person with the same kinds of problems and faults she herself possessed. They were both human, and they'd both make mistakes. Surely they'd hurt each other at times, but there was something more between them.

Without further thought, Kennie said, "I love you, Lily."

Lily blushed with pleasure. "I love you, too."

"I love you different from anyone I've ever known."

"Me, too."

"It feels somehow stronger, more powerful, but realistic."

Lily kissed her and squeezed her tight. Her legs entwined with Kennie's, and they shared a breathless moment before Kennie said, "Remind me to make double-damn sure I see Max later today."

"Why?"

"I owe her a hundred bucks."

The End

Other Yellow Rose Titles You Might Enjoy:

The Other Mrs. Champion
by Brenda Adcock

Sarah Champion, 55, of Massachusetts, was leading the perfect life with Kelley, her partner and wife of twenty-five years. That is, until Kelley was struck down by an unexpected stroke away from home. But Sarah discovers she hadn't known her partner and lover as well as she thought.

Accompanied by Kelley's long-time friend and attorney, Sarah and her children rush to Vancouver, British Columbia to say their goodbyes, only to discover another woman, Pauline, keeping a vigil over Kelley in the hospital. Confronted by the fact that her wife also has a Canadian wife, Sarah struggles to find answers to resolve her emotional and personal turmoil.

Alone and lonely, Sarah turns to the only other person who knew Kelley as well as she did-Pauline Champion. Will the two women be able to forge a friendship despite their simmering animosity? Will their growing attraction eventually become Kelley's final gift to the women she loved?

ISBN 978-1-935053-46-0

Love Another Day
by Regina A. Hanel

Plagued by nightmares and sleepless nights after a tragic loss, Park Ranger Samantha Takoda Tyler longs for a calm day at Grand Teton National Park in Wyoming. But when she's summoned to the chief ranger's office and introduced to Halie Walker, a photojournalist working for The Wild International, her day is anything but calm. When she's assigned to look after Halie, their meeting transforms into a quarrelsome exchange. Over time, the initial chill between the women warms. They grow closer as they spend time together and gain appreciation for each other's work.

But Sam's fear of loss coupled with rising jealousy over an old lover's interest in Halie grinds their budding relationship to a halt. Halie finds that anywhere near Sam is too painful a place to be, and Sam is unable to find the key to open the door to a past that she's purposely kept locked away.

With fires raging out West and in the Targhee National Forest, Sam works overtime, helping fill the staffing shortage. She misses Halie and wants to take a chance with her. Before she gets the opportunity to explain herself, Sam learns the helicopter Halie is on has crashed. Ahead of an oncoming storm, Sam races to the rescue. Can she save the woman she loves? Or will the past replay, closing Sam off from love forever?

ISBN 978-1-935053-44-6

More Lori L. Lake titles

Gun Shy

While on patrol, Minnesota police officer Dez Reilly saves two women from a brutal attack. One of them, Jaylynn Savage, is immediately attracted to the taciturn cop—so much so that she joins the St. Paul Police Academy. As fate would have it, Dez is eventually assigned as Jaylynn's Field Training Officer. Having been burned in the past by getting romantically involved with another cop, Dez has a steadfast rule she has abided by for nine years: Cops are off limits. But as Jaylynn and Dez get to know one another, a strong friendship forms. Will Dez break her cardinal rule and take a chance on love with Jaylynn, or will she remain forever gun shy? *Gun Shy* is an exciting glimpse into the day-to-day work world of police officers as Jaylynn learns the ins and outs of the job and Dez learns the ins and outs of her own heart.

ISBN 978-1-932300-56-7

Under the Gun

Under the Gun is the sequel to the bestselling novel, *Gun Shy*, continuing the story of St. Paul Police Officers Dez Reilly and Jaylynn Savage. Picking up just a couple weeks after *Gun Shy* ended, the sequel finds the two officers adjusting to their relationship, but things start to go downhill when they get dispatched to a double homicide—Jaylynn's first murder scene. Dez is supportive and protective toward Jay, and things seem to be going all right until Dez's nemesis reports their personal relationship, and their commanding officer restricts them from riding together on patrol. This sets off a chain of events that result in Jaylynn getting wounded, Dez being suspended, and both of them having to face the possibility of life without the other. They face struggles—separately and together—that they must work through while truly feeling "under the gun."

Second Edition
ISBN 978-1-932300-57-4

Have Gun We'll Travel

Dez Reilly and Jaylynn Savage have settled into a comfortable working and living arrangement. Their house is in good shape, their relationship is wonderful, and their jobs — while busy — are fulfilling. But everyone needs a break once in a while, so when they take off on a camping trip to northern Minnesota with good friends Crystal and Shayna, they expect nothing more than long hikes, romantic wood fires, and plenty of down time. Instead, they find themselves caught in the whirlwind created when two escaped convicts, law enforcement, and desperate Russian mobsters clash north of the privately-run, medium-security Kendall Correctional Center. Set in the woodland area in Minnesota near Superior National Forest, this adventure/suspense novel features Jaylynn taken hostage by the escapees and needing to do all she can to protect herself while Dez figures out how to catch up with and disarm the convicts, short-circuit the Russians, and use the law enforcement resources in such a way that nothing happens to Jaylynn. It's a race to the finish as author Lori L. Lake uproots Dez and Jaylynn from the romance genre to bring them center stage in her first suspense thriller.

ISBN: 1-932300-33-3
(978-1-932300-33-8)

Ricochet In Time

Hatred is ugly and does bad things to good people, even in the land of "Minnesota Nice" where no one wants to believe discrimination exists. Danielle "Dani" Corbett knows firsthand what hatred can cost. After a vicious and intentional attack, Dani's girlfriend, Meg O'Donnell, is dead. Dani is left emotionally scarred, and her injuries prevent her from fleeing on her motorcycle. But as one door has closed for her, another opens when she is befriended by Grace Beaumont, a young woman who works as a physical therapist at the hospital. With Grace's friendship and the help of Grace's aunts, Estelline and Ruth, Dani gets through the ordeal of bringing Meg's killer to justice.

Filled with memorable characters, *Ricochet In Time* is the story of one lonely woman's fight for justice — and her struggle to resolve the troubles of her past and find a place in a world where she belongs.

ISBN: 1-932300-17-1
(978-1-932300-17-8)

Different Dress

Different Dress is the story of three women on a cross-country musical road tour. Jaime Esperanza works production and sound on the music tour. The headliner, Lacey Leigh Jaxon, is a fast-living prima donna with intimacy problems. She's had a brief relationship with Jaime, then dumped her for the new guy (who lasted all of about two weeks). Lacey still comes back to Jaime in between conquests, and Jaime hasn't yet gotten her entirely out of her heart.

After Lacey Leigh steamrolls yet another opening act, a folksinger from Minnesota named Kip Galvin, who wrote one of Lacey's biggest songs, is brought on board for the summer tour. Kip has true talent, she loves people and they respond, and she has a pleasant stage presence. A friendship springs up between Jaime and Kip — but what about Lacey Leigh?

It's a honky-tonk, bluesy, pop, country EXPLOSION of emotion as these three women duke it out. Who will win Jaime's heart and soul?

ISBN: 1-932300-08-2
(978-1-932300-08-6)

Stepping Out: Short Stories

In these fourteen short stories, Lori L. Lake captures how change and loss influence the course of lives: a mother and daughter have an age-old fight; a frightened woman attempts to deal with an abusive lover; a father tries to understand his lesbian daughter's retreat from him; an athlete who misses her chance — or does she?

Lovingly crafted, the collection has been described as a series of mini-novels where themes of alienation and loss, particularly for characters who are gay or lesbian, are woven throughout. Lake is right on about the anguish and confusion of characters caught in the middle of circumstances, usually of someone else's making. Still, each character steps out with hope and determination.

In the words of Jean Stewart: "Beyond the mechanics of good storytelling, a sturdy vulnerability surfaces in every one of these short stories. Lori Lake must possess, simply as part of her inherent nature, a loving heart. It gleams out from these stories, even the sad ones, like a lamp in a lighthouse — maybe far away sometimes, maybe just a passing, slanting flash in the dark — but there to be seen all the same. It makes for a bittersweet journey."

ISBN: 1-932300-16-3
(978-1-932300-16-1)

Shimmer & Other Stories

In these tales of hope and loss, lovers and found family, Lori L. Lake has once more given us an amazing slice of life. A frightened woman stumbles through her daily existence, unsure of her place in the world, until she comes into possession of a magic coat... Tee has a problem with her temper, and now that she's being tested again, will she fail to curb it again? Kaye Brock has recently been released from prison and doesn't have a single friend — until Mrs. Gildecott comes along...

These women and many others, unsettled and adrift and often disillusioned, can't quite understand how they arrived at their present situations. But whether rejected, afraid to commit, or just misunderstood, even the most hard-bitten are not without some hope in the power of love.

Lori L. Lake's talent shines like never before in this collection of glittering tales. Sharply rendered, the tone of these stories reflects their title: silver and gray, shimmery and wintery, yet also filled with the shiny hope of summer. These are stories that bear rereading.

ISBN: 978-1-932300-95-6

The Milk of Human Kindness: Lesbian Authors Write About Mothers and Daughters

Edited by Lori L. Lake, this anthology contains stories, essays, and memoirs by some of the brightest stars in the lesbian writing world:

Cameron Abbott + Georgia Beers + Meghan Brunner + Carrie Carr + Caro Clarke + Katherine V. Forrest + Jennifer Fulton + Gabrielle Goldsby + Ellen Hart + Lois Hart + Karin Kallmaker + Marcia Tyson Kolb + Lori L. Lake + SX Meagher + Radclyffe + J.M. Redmann + Jean Stewart + Cate Swannell + Therese Szymanski + Talaran + Julia Watts + Marie Sheppard Williams + Kelly Zarembski.

Don't miss this unforgettable collection!

ISBN: 1-932300-28-7
(978-1-9232300-28-4)

Snow Moon Rising

Mischka Gallo, a proud Roma woman, knows horses, dancing, and travel. Every day since her birth, she and her extended family have been on the road in their vardo wagons meandering mostly through Poland and Germany. She learned early to ignore the taunts and insults of all those who call her people "Gypsies" and do not understand their close-knit society and way of life.

Pauline "Pippi" Stanek has lived a settled life in a small German town along the eastern border of Poland and Germany. In her mid-teens, she meets Mischka and her family through her brother, Emil Stanek, a World War I soldier who went AWOL and was adopted by Mischka's troupe. Mischka and Pippi become fast friends, and they keep in touch over the years. But then, the Second World War heats up, and all of Europe is in turmoil. Men are conscripted into the Axis or the Allied armies, "undesirables" are turned over to slave labor camps, and with every day that passes, the danger for Mischka, Emil, and their families increases. The Nazi forces will not stop until they've rounded up and destroyed every Gypsy, Jew, dissident, and homosexual.

On the run and separated from her family, Mischka can hardly comprehend the obstacles that face her. When she is captured, she must use all her wits just to stay alive. Can Mischka survive through the hell of the war in Europe and find her family?

In a world beset by war, two women on either side of the conflagration breach the divide-and save one another. *Snow Moon Rising* is a stunning novel of two women's enduring love and friendship across family, clan, and cultural barriers. It's a novel of desperation and honor, hope and fear at a time when the world was split into a million pieces.

ISBN: 978-1-932300-50-5

About the Author

Lori L. Lake is the author of eight novels, two books of short stories, and editor of two anthologies. She is a 2007 recipient of the Alice B. Reader Appreciation Award, a 2005 Lambda Literary Finalist in the anthology category, and winner of the 2007 Ann Bannon Award and a Golden Crown "Goldie" for *Snow Moon Rising*. Lori lived in Minnesota for 26 years, but re-located to Portland, Oregon, in 2009. When she's not writing, she's at the local movie house or curled up in a chair reading. She's finished the first two novels in a new mystery series and is currently working on the next novel in the "Gun" series. For more information, see her website at www.LoriLLake.com.

VISIT US ONLINE AT
www.regalcrest.biz

At the Regal Crest Website You'll Find

- The latest news about forthcoming titles and new releases

- Our complete backlist of romance, mystery, thriller and adventure titles

- Information about your favorite authors

- Current bestsellers

- Media tearsheets to print and take with you when you shop

Regal Crest titles are available from all progressive booksellers including numerous sources online. Our distributors are Bella Distribution and Ingram.

CPSIA information can be obtained at www.ICGtesting.com
Printed in the USA
LVOW08s2142261113

362919LV00002B/347/P